I0675869

StarRacer

Golden Terrace Colony Series Book 2

R.L.S. Hoff

The Pencil Princess Workshop

To Craig, my sweet love and constant support

CHAPTER ONE

One week.

StarRacer would take off in one week.

Anya couldn't quite believe it. She'd always known the fast ship would take off for the planet almost immediately after they announced who had won places on the Golden Terrace Colony team, but somehow it hadn't sunk in.

Now, as she gawked at the schedule scrolling across the screen embedded into her left forearm, she thought there wasn't near enough time for all the team meetings, leadership sessions, and training.

"When are we supposed to sleep?" she asked David Ryerson, the smart, gorgeous materials engineer who'd agreed to be her partner on the colony team. She still couldn't quite believe that either.

Maybe this was all a dream, and she'd wake up, back in her old bunk, frightened of her parents fighting and too scared to speak up for herself.

David didn't feel like a dream when he put an arm around her and bent closer, so he could read her armband screen. "Wow. Your schedule looks even worse than mine. I guess you'll sleep next week—after we leave *Hope*?"

"Very funny." Anya stared morosely at her armband. There was hardly any free time in here at all, except for a few random hours labeled "reserved for goodbyes."

That made sense. *Hope* was the only world they'd ever known, and the big ship wouldn't make it to the planet until about thirty years after *StarRacer* arrived. The colony team was leaving behind everyone and everything they knew.

Most people would need all that reserved time to say goodbye to family and friends, but she didn't have all that many friends, and she probably couldn't talk to her family. She wasn't allowed to visit Grandma Anderson, and her brother-in-law would never let her near her sister, Kristi, or her niece, Tiny.

Even if her parents were willing to talk to her, she wasn't sure she wanted to talk to them. Not after the beating her father had given her when she told him she wanted to try out for the colony team—and the way her mother had stuck up for him instead of for her.

She glanced around Skreetches, the restaurant that belonged to her friend Borsk's family. Most of the other colony team members clustered in small groups around the tables, sipping tea and comparing notes about work assignments and training schedules. It didn't look like anyone else was worrying about filling their "goodbye" time slots.

"So, I have an important question," David said, giving her shoulders a squeeze.

Anya looked up. "Yes?"

"Will you marry me?"

"Um..." Anya thought that's what being partners on the colony team meant—they'd get married and have kids together down on the planet. Had David been expecting something else?

"I mean, this week. Before we take off. My mom would really like to be at the celebration."

"Uh..." Anya's mind blanked out. She had no idea what she thought of this plan. She'd sort of imagined they'd have time to get to know each other before marrying for real.

"You don't have to answer now. Think about it. Maybe talk it over with your family—I mean, your guardians. Obviously, you wouldn't be old enough for a couple of years under ordinary circumstances. But bunks on *StarRacer* are in short supply, and Captain DeLang has recommended couples hook up before rather than after the trip. They've cleared it with the ship legal types."

"They have?"

David smiled, and for a second, Anya couldn't think about anything but the way his dark brown eyes twinkled.

"It's in the legal file under marriage," he said.

"Huh?"

His smile got wider, and he shifted so that he could reach her armband. "Let me show you."

He tapped a bit on her screen until a document came up. Anya frowned as she read through the dense legalese. If she read it right, then *StarRacer* had shifted its rules so that people could get married at any age so long as they had permission from the colony leadership. "They're doing this because of limited bunk space?"

"Sure, but we don't need to worry about that. We'll get two bunks because of Abuela, anyway. That's in the housing specs. If you're not comfortable getting married yet—or bunking with me even if we are married, you can share with her. And even if we're married and bunking together, we won't do anything until you're sure you're ready for it."

Anya's head was swirling. "You're saying that my choices are bunking with you or with your grandma?"

"Whatever you want."

"How does she feel about that?"

"Abuela would bunk in a privy if it got her to the planet."

Uh huh. Anya looked four tables over to where David's grandma was cackling at something little Jimmy Wilcox had told her. The old woman had never smiled that way at Anya. Had she ever smiled at Anya at all?

Marriage was scary, but was it as scary as bunking with Abuela Ryerson for three years? "I'll think about it. I should see what the Lancets—"

David interrupted her with a kiss that made her toes tingle.

Hmm. There'd be definite advantages to being married to David.

It was normal to feel nervous about this kind of thing, right?

How she wished she could talk to Grandma Anderson or Kristi.

୫ ଓ

Borsk hated waiting tables. Even if he weren't apt to drop trays full of breakable dishes and messy foodstuffs, he lacked the patience and charm that his sister Sarka used to turn disgruntled customers into satisfied ones.

Plus, the noise and smells gave him a headache, especially this morning when he'd hardly slept. He was happy for Anya and the rest of the *StarRacer* team, he really was. He just wished they'd take their bubbly conversations and celebratory drinks elsewhere, so he could sneak away to enjoy his newly returned net privileges in private.

Not that there were any other public places where the newly minted Colony team could go. Thomas Cartier had threatened to bankrupt anyone who supported the colony, and the man wasn't known for idle threats.

Borsk almost wished his mom hadn't decided to risk it. Then he looked over at the table where Anya Cartier and David Ryerson were kissing. Anya's face had lit up, and with the lamplight glinting off her straight, chin-length, light brown hair, she looked almost pretty.

They made a good couple, and Borsk couldn't be sad that they were getting their chance to be a part of the colony they both loved.

He was even glad that his family's restaurant had played a part.

Still, this was not the way he'd imagined spending the first morning he had full net access returned. He yawned, and the tray of dirty dishes he was holding tipped.

Sarka grabbed it and righted it before anything could fall. "What's wrong with you today? You didn't even trip on anything that time."

Borsk shrugged, setting the dishes rattling again. "Lack of sleep, maybe?"

Sarka looked uncharacteristically concerned. "Mama did say you were out half the night at some meeting. Maybe you should take a break once you return those dishes to the kitchen. Take a nap or something."

Seriously? Borsk couldn't remember Sarka ever suggesting he take a break before. "Are you feeling OK?" he asked her.

"Of course. Why wouldn't I be?"

"You just suggested I take a break."

"You're usually just faking exhaustion to get more time with your precious machines."

"How do you know I'm not faking it now?" Borsk spat out before realizing he shouldn't argue with good fortune.

"You lost your net privileges. What are you going to do? Write out code on a blank school tablet?"

Sarka didn't know the ship had restored his privileges? Sweet. "Well, whatever your reasoning, I'll take it."

Borsk set the tray down on a nearby empty table for long enough to give Anya a wave goodbye. Then he resumed his clinking walk back to the kitchens.

He'd only lost his access for a few days, but it felt like an eternity.

℘   ℭ

A poke from Abuela Ryerson's cane interrupted Anya's kiss with David before she'd fully explored how it made her feel.

"I take it this means the girl said yes," the old woman said.

"Well, I—"

"Good. Ming will be pleased. If you need to get someone else's permission, best do that now. You have a leadership team meeting in half an hour."

Anya glanced down at her armband screen. Bother. She did have a leadership team meeting soon. And even if she still wasn't sure she was ready to be married, she was very sure she'd rather bunk with David than with his grandma. "I'll go right away."

As she left Skreetches, David and his grandma started up a heated conversation that she wished she could understand. She wondered if she'd need to learn Spanish to get along in her new family.

The walk to her temporary guardians' quarters felt long and gave Anya plenty of time to think about the weirdness of this situation. The Lancets would have been her in-laws if she'd agreed to go through with the marriage her parents had planned for her since birth, and Anya was sure it was no accident that they'd been put in charge of her when she needed temporary custodians after her father beat her up. It would feel exceedingly strange to ask them for permission to marry someone other than their son.

Anya still hadn't figured out what to say when she arrived at the Lancet's quarters. Standing and staring at their blue screen, she realized this wasn't her house, and she didn't know the code. Awkwardly, she pushed the doorbell.

She'd begun to think no one was home when the beads clicked, and she was able to push through. Mr. Lancet was stumbling out of his bunk, pulling on a shirt. "I'm sorry, Stacey. Didn't anybody give you the code?"

Anya shook her head. Now probably wasn't the best time to try to explain that the name he'd been calling her since she was a baby wasn't one she appreciated.

"Well, here. You should definitely have it, though I hear you won't need it long. Congratulations. Colony team. That's quite the accomplishment."

"Apparently, they needed somebody with lots of greenhouse experience…" She trailed off as a code flashed up on her armband screen. She saved it, so she wouldn't forget.

"Well, of course, they do. And you're perfect for that. So, when do you go?"

"We take off in a week. David's family is hoping we can get married before we go, so they can celebrate with us."

Mr. Lancet yawned. "I can see why they'd feel that way, but you're awfully young. Are you sure that's what you want?"

Anya wasn't entirely sure, but she nodded anyway.

"Tell you what. Why don't you have the young man come by for dinner, and we can all talk about it then? Janet and I should probably meet him before signing off on a marriage for you two."

"Oh…um…" That made sense. Anya glanced down at her armband, wondering if David's schedule was as packed as hers. "I'll see if David is free. They haven't left us much time for saying goodbyes."

"It did look like an unreasonably tight schedule, but I'm sure David's family can spare him for at least part of an evening."

Mr. Lancet hadn't seen the way David's family clustered around him after the testing. But maybe David wouldn't mind too terribly. Anya started the first few words of a message to him, erased them, started again, erased again, and finally sent out, "Mr. Lancet wonders if you could come by for dinner tonight to talk about the marriage thing."

A reply popped up almost immediately. "Needs persuading?"

"Yes."

"Fair enough. What time?"

Anya asked Mr. Lancet, and after a back-and-forth about schedules that took way longer than Anya thought reasonable, they worked out the details.

By then, Anya was late enough that she had to run to her first leadership team meeting. She did not want to be the last one in the room. It would be bad enough being the youngest person there.

CHAPTER TWO

*E*very time Borsk started a string of code, a sense of panic washed over him. If he got caught breaking rules, even a little, he could lose his access faster than Uncle Hirsch's dumplings disappeared into hungry mouths.

Part of him wished he could go back to the way things used to be—when he hacked without any thought for the consequences. But he'd been careless. Too often in the past couple of weeks, when he thought he'd covered his tracks, Thomas Cartier had found him. Granted, the man had used mainly illegal means to find him, but that didn't seem to matter. Up until now, Thomas Cartier had proved untouchable. The man was so wealthy, even his enemies hesitated to land themselves on one of his blacklists.

Borsk had underestimated his opponent, but no more. He would hack cleaner than clean, and as much as possible, he'd stay on the non-punishable side of the law.

But if he was going to dance just this side of the fine line of legality, he needed to know where that line was. He'd never paid attention in social studies before, not even when they talked about *Hope's* government and charter, but he'd noticed how much it had helped Anya to know the law last night. Anya was bright, but no genius— at least not in anything but her art. If she could learn ship law, so could he.

Not that he had the first idea where he'd even find the charter, let alone the laws governing programming. He shot Anya a note, asking how she'd learned all that stuff.

"Long story. I can meet with you to talk about it tonight—no, sorry, I have dinner at the Lancets tonight. Tomorrow—wait.

David says we have to be at some party tomorrow. The night after?"

The night after tomorrow? Borsk was not waiting to program for almost three more days. "Do you know someone who could help me with it now?"

"Try Lucretia Dominguez in the library. That woman knows everything."

He should have thought of that himself. He'd had to ask the librarian for help before. So, the library. Not his favorite place.

Today was a holiday because of the colony list posting, though. Maybe Marya Dominguez would be helping out her mom. Just in case, he took a quick shower and put on fresh clothes before heading out the back door. He kept his head down in case Sarka was around. She may have encouraged him to take a break, but if she saw him leaving the area, she'd realize he wasn't napping and probably assign him something odious to do.

Like every non-school day, the library was full of families with kids. Toddlers and primary students had spread everywhere, clustering in little groups that sat on the floor around holo stations. The kids all wore headphones and leaned in to catch as much as they could of educasts that mostly focused on math or science. In one corner, a couple of kids watched cartoon versions of classic novels. When they were younger, Sarka had always wanted to be in that group. Mama had wanted them to learn more practical things, but Dad had always said that good stories were worth their weight in gold.

Borsk shook his head. He'd forgotten how much his parents used to argue. The way Mama talked about his dad now, you'd think they never disagreed or said a cross word to one another. Looking back, though, it wasn't that way. He smiled a bit as he remembered the way the two of them used to work together in the kitchen, putting together incredible meals, all the while shouting at each other about politics or their kids. Sometimes Uncle Hirsch would tell them to shut up because they were scaring the customers.

"Are you lost?"

When he heard Marya's voice, Borsk swung so fast that he almost tripped over his own feet. "No, no…I mean, maybe?" Could he sound more stupid?

Marya smiled. "What are you looking for? Maybe I can help?"

Borsk barely registered the question. He was mesmerized by Marya's lips. They shone a deep purplish red. Lipstick—or, no, Sarka used another word for the shiny kind. He couldn't remember what it was.

Marya's smile slipped, catching the light differently.

"Gloss," Borsk said. That was it.

"Excuse me?"

Had he said that out loud? Too bad the library didn't have any holes where he could hide. "Sorry. What was the question?"

"Can I help you find something?"

"I…yeah…I mean…" Borsk gave himself an internal shake. Get a grip, man. It's just Marya—the best-looking girl in ninth form. Well, the whole upper school, really. This wasn't helping. "I'd like to research some code."

Marya's full smile beamed forth again. "I doubt we have much you haven't already seen, but the computer section is—"

"No, I meant ship code."

"Ship code?"

"Particularly the charter and any laws currently on the books that govern any aspect of programming."

Marya wrinkled her nose. "Are you sure? That stuff is duller than Ms. Chapra's after-lunch history class on a Friday.

Borsk had sat through more than his fair share of those. "Unfortunately, I am sure. Thomas Cartier is gunning for me, and I want to be sure I know exactly what lines I shouldn't cross.

"How does Thomas Cartier even know who you are?"

"I may have helped Anya turn cameras on at her house, so security could catch her dad behaving badly."

"You got caught up in that stink last week? Then you need our help. Let me take you to Mom. She knows this stuff way better than I do."

"Thank you," Borsk muttered, but he wasn't sure he'd managed enough volume for anyone beyond himself to hear.

Captain DeLang, the Golden Terrace Colony leader, looked nearly as grim and humorless in the daytime as he had looked in Anya's father's office the previous night.

Thinking about how late she'd been up made her want to yawn, but she mostly stifled the sensation.

"Are we boring you already, Ms. Cartier?" Captain DeLang asked.

"Charles," the woman next to him said. "The girl was up half the night." She held a hand up, palm outward, toward Anya. "I'm Vera DeLang. Don't mind my husband. He gets cranky when he hasn't had enough sleep. We're all glad you've joined the colony team."

Anya reached her own hand up and touched Vera's briefly before mumbling, "Thank you, and I'm so glad to meet you, too." All the while, she wondered how much of what Vera had said was true. Last night, Captain DeLang had said the leadership team had unanimously appointed her to her post, but that didn't mean they were glad she was here, just that they needed her. Still, it was nice of Vera to make the effort to welcome her. Anya gave the woman a warm smile as she took a seat at the table, hoping she hadn't flubbed up the introduction too badly.

So, that was Vera DeLang. Every time Anya had watched one of Captain DeLang's terse Golden Terrace Colony announcements, she'd wondered what kind of woman would marry such a grouch. A kind, tactful one, apparently. And a beautiful one. Vera DeLang was tall and slender with radiant skin and big, thick-lashed eyes. She also had a soft smile and worry creases between her eyes that never smoothed all the way out. Anya wondered if all the colony tension had given those to her. Or maybe motherhood had. She'd heard the DeLangs had a kid.

Her cousin, she realized, since Captain DeLang was apparently her father's half-brother. The DeLang's kid was probably much closer to her own age than her grown-up Anderson cousins. She wondered what she'd think of her new relative. A boy? A girl? She really should know, but why would she?

Before the meeting last night, her parents had never mentioned that they were related to the DeLangs.

Anya's speculations about the cousin she'd never met were interrupted by the entrance of the colony team doctors and Lisa Tehled, the woman who had led Anya's interview during tryouts. Vera DeLang greeted them even more warmly than she had greeted Anya. However, her truly enthusiastic welcome came when Laura Wilcox, *Hope*'s friendliest lawyer, came in with two other women, one tiny and graceful, the other tall, short-haired, and toned like an athlete. Laura had said something about being friends with the DeLangs when she was trying out for the colony team with Anya, but Anya hadn't realized quite how good friends the two were.

The group was still hugging and exchanging greetings when Bria Huxton, another woman who had tried out with Anya, slipped in a minute later. No one but Anya seemed to notice her.

"Hi, Bria," Anya said, as loudly as she dared.

Bria nodded curtly at her and then walked past to a seat about as far away from Anya as was possible at this conference table.

Anya took a deep breath. OK, then.

"Excellent, we're all here," Captain DeLang said. He didn't raise his voice, but the room fell immediately silent, and everyone who wasn't already sitting scrambled for a seat.

"Does everyone have at least an H964-grade processor?"

Anya glanced down at her armband and saw it struggling with a massive data download. Glad she'd thought to bring her pack, she pulled out her school tablet, which did better, but not perfectly. Would she need new equipment? And could she afford it now that she needed her money to gear up for the colony? She glanced at the others around the table. At least everyone else seemed to be having at least as much trouble as she was.

"What'd they give you for a data hook up in here, DeLang? Last century's model?" the athletic-looking woman who'd come in with Laura asked.

Captain DeLang glared at her.

Vera glanced at him and then smiled at the athletic-looking woman. "While we're waiting on the downloads, perhaps we should have some introductions? I see at least a couple of faces I don't know well."

"Good idea," Captain DeLang said. "You go ahead. You're better at that sort of thing than I am."

From the way Vera DeLang handled the introductions, Anya guessed she was better at that sort of thing than most people.

Vera's started by letting them all know that Mei-Li Lyons, the athletic-looking woman, was an inspired structural engineer. The other woman who'd come in with Laura was KaLynne Smith, a whiz with power generation. They had joined the colony leadership team a decade ago with the DeLangs, the Tehleds, and the colony doctors, Caroline and Stanley Kuhler. While the men had taken *StarRacer* down to the planet and spent a year exploring and finding the colony site, the women had stayed aboard *Hope*, raising kids and working with *Hope* leadership to hammer out the colony team agreements. Commander Lisa Tehled had led them.

Anya had met Lisa Tehled once before but had never guessed that she was THE Commander Tehled who had run so many successful material scavenging missions by the time she was thirty that she was awarded the distinguished service medal—which usually went out to retiring or dead officers.

The doctors were both distinguished as well, Laura Wilcox was a great legal mind with an impressive list of career victories, and Bria sounded like a genius with textiles. In Vera's version, Anya herself sounded like a once-in-a-generation agricultural savant with a rare gift for art.

"And, of course, you know Charles," Vera ended.

"As much as anybody knows Charles," Stanley Kuhler said.

Several people around the table chuckled.

Anya's data was accessible now, and the first document displayed a leadership chart. She was surprised to see that Caroline Kuhler was the colony team's head doctor, though she didn't know why it surprised her. Why couldn't a wife outrank her husband? *Hope* had boasted a number of female captains after all, and they were all married.

"How are we doing on the downloads?" Captain DeLang asked.

"Slow," Mei-Li Lyons said. "Have you heard any more about when our colony-model computers will be ready?"

"They say later today," Captain DeLang said. "The data savants also say they need our university course requests and library selections by midnight tonight if they're going to complete the download before takeoff."

"Selections?" Anya said. "I thought the *Hope* Charter required a complete copy of our digital and cultural heritage to be provided free of charge to every colonization team."

"I think she may be right, Charles." Laura tapped ferociously at her armband.

"Even if that's true, they say they can't make a full copy in the shortened time frame. If you'll remember, we'd originally been planning to train the colony team on *Hope* for six months before returning to Shindashir. If we hadn't needed to move up our timeline to avoid that meteor cloud we picked up on our sensors during the expedition's journey back to *Hope*, we might have had enough time."

"They have enough time now," Bria said. Her bronze hair spikes jerked as she nodded. "Unless they lied on last year's emergency protocol reports. That group won most prepared for their fifteen-hour backup of our entire civilization. Just edged us out for the top spot."

"That's true," Lisa Tehled said. "And they weren't lying. Data Storage actually ran the backup as a test. There's a spare copy of the entire university and library sitting on a few servers somewhere. If I'd known we were entitled to the whole lot, I would have brought it up before in my negotiations with *Hope* leadership."

Captain DeLang sighed. "We probably all need to reread the Charter, not that we have time for it. Laura, get us that library. Everyone else, get us your work group's selections to me by midnight in case she can't secure it. Guidelines and storage limits are in section sixteen of the packet you just downloaded.

"Now, for the next week, your top priorities are preparing your work group for the trip—legal papers and gear first, orientation, team building, and training second. Anya and Bria, since you'll be getting oriented along with your group, we've provided an outline for you to follow. Anya, you'll run the general sessions and the agricultural training while Bria, you'll handle all the textile instruction. Matthew Smith, my second-in-command, put this outline together, and we think it's sound, but he's not the expert in these fields that you two are, so if you see something inaccurate, just fix it. Now, are there any pressing problems we need to solve before we meet up with our groups?"

The doctors had a number of technical questions about medical equipment, and Mei-Li Lyons mentioned some concerns about some readings she'd found in her last inspection of *StarRacer*, but Anya didn't fully understand either the questions or the debate that followed them. Instead of straining to keep up, she skimmed through the orientation plan Captain DeLang had mentioned. It looked like she'd be responsible for about two-thirds of the training, and she'd have to do a fair amount of speaking in front of the group. She'd never enjoyed public speaking. Worry churned in her gut. At least the agricultural content seemed accurate to Anya, though it focused on greenhouse-style growing rather than outdoor agriculture. Anya supposed Commander Smith was trying to protect Shindashir flora from extra-planetary invaders. Very smart, once she thought about it, seeing how they had no idea how *Hope* plants would interact with local ones.

The conversation on the other side of the table was winding down, so Anya brought her attention back to it, just in time to hear Captain DeLang close the discussion and send them for a quick lunch break before meeting with their groups.

The first session with her group was supposed to be a team-building exercise. Well, that was natural enough. As Bria passed her, Anya asked if the older woman wanted to help lead the session or if she'd rather simply participate.

"Participating is fine," Bria said. "Leadership has never really been my thing. See you after lunch?" She brushed past Anya and on out the door.

"See you," Anya said. Both Bria's words and her tone had been polite, but Anya sensed that the woman didn't like her much.

Paranoia? Maybe.

So, half an hour for lunch and preparing to lead the afternoon's group meetings.

Anya sighed.

Leadership had never really been her thing, either.

₫   Ↄ

Borsk thought Marya's mom looked just like Marya, only with sharper eyes and less of a tendency to smile. Borsk got the feeling she didn't like people wasting her time, but she seemed to soften up a bit when Borsk mentioned that Anya had recommended he come see her.

"Anya sent you? That girl is such a sweetheart. How do you know her?"

Borsk couldn't tell the truth—that he'd gotten to know Anya when he hacked into her bank account and borrowed a hefty chunk of her money to save his family's restaurant. He fumbled out a confusing statement about school and restaurant connections and Steve Jackson's concert last week.

"Anya's parents let her go to a Steve Jackson concert?" Marya asked, her eyebrows rising halfway to her hairline.

Oops. Maybe that wasn't the best explanation either. "I don't think her parents knew about it, to tell the truth."

"But they had to have known about it," Ms. Dominguez said. "They monitor her quite closely. Almost too closely. I've sometimes wondered if all her hardware was legal."

Borsk knew it wasn't, but since he'd obtained that information through dubious means, he had no intention of offering it. Besides, he didn't need to be getting into any extra conflicts with Anya's father. His current one was already more than he could handle. "I may have helped her figure out a route from her house to Skreetches that avoided cameras."

Marya beamed at him. "That's great. Anya should be able to get out more. But I suppose that's what got you in trouble with Thomas Cartier?"

"One of the things, yeah," Borsk said. It was sort of true.

"Wait a moment," Ms. Dominguez said. "Are you suggesting that you're on one of Thomas Cartier's blacklists?"

Borsk smiled. "Not that I know of—yet. I'm sure he'd like to put me on one, but he might be afraid of some things I could say if he does."

"And you say you're interested in *Hope* laws related to computer programming?"

"Yes, please."

"You think that Thomas Cartier has been involved in shady programming?"

Marya giggled. "It's more like Borsk has been involved in shady programming, and he doesn't want to do anything to lose his armband functionality again."

That was exactly right, but how did Marya know it?

Marya laughed. "You should see your face right now. It's not so hard to figure out, you know. Everybody could see that you had your armband turned off the last couple of days for some reason or another, and that doesn't happen to kids who always follow the rules."

"It doesn't happen unless someone commits a serious crime," Ms. Dominguez said. "What did you do, and how did you get your access back after it was revoked?"

Borsk sighed. And he'd thought she was starting to like him. "Back when I was twelve, I hacked into the medical database to get a look at my gene record. And Sarka's, too, of course. I wanted to find out if either of us had the delta-zed gene that predicted..." Borsk couldn't go on. He'd never really talked about this before, not even with the shrink he was supposed to be talking to about it.

"The gene that predicts whether you'll develop King Syndrome," Ms. Dominguez said.

"What's King—" Marya started, but Ms. Dominguez hushed her.

"Judging by the black light on your armband, you do. But if the hack happened back when you were twelve and was only of your own records, why does anybody care now?"

"Didn't you hear him say he helped Anya get to Steve Jackson's concert last week, Mom? And now she's on the Golden Terrace team—head of the Agricultural and Textile Manufacturing Group."

Ms. Dominguez's eyes darted from side to side. Borsk followed her glances and realized what she was doing—checking the cameras. Smart. He should have been doing that since he came in here. Usually, it was second nature for him in a public space, but he was tired today. He checked now. There was an active camera on them, of course, but it was next to the kid story section and probably hadn't picked up much of their conversation. Still, it would be best to be circumspect. "Yeah, the whole thing came out recently, and I lost the armband for a few days. It would have been longer, but they offered me a position on the Golden Terrace team, and apparently, I had to be pardoned for that."

"They offered you a position even though you have King Syndrome?" Ms. Dominguez said.

"Yeah, I'm not entirely sure of their reasoning there. In the end, I decided against it, but the pardon stuck. And now, I'd like to make sure I know what the law is—you know, keep my programming productive instead of destructive. I'd hate to lose the access I just got back."

Ms. Dominguez nodded. "I'll get you started. Come along, Marya. It won't hurt you to learn this, too."

She settled them in front of two research consoles with full keyboards that were spaced so closely together that Borsk's right arm brushed Marya's left. He wasn't sure how he'd concentrate that way. It looked like he'd need to concentrate. It wasn't particularly easy to understand the how-to-troll-official-records tutorial that Ms. Dominguez had them doing. Combing records for the ones he wanted took even more focus, especially since the library's search algorithms left much to be desired. Borsk started to build a better one and then wondered if that was legal.

He could not live this way—always second-guessing himself. Nobody could charge him with anything if the program stayed in his head. He designed as he searched, writing cryptic notes to himself if he thought he might forget something important.

As soon as he could confirm that this type of program was legit, he was replacing this search engine with a better model.

CHAPTER THREE

*W*hat with learning the names and backgrounds of all her new work group members, Anya didn't have time to eat lunch, but it was just as well. She was too nervous to force anything down.

Including herself, her group had ten people, three of which she knew slightly. DeShawn often did time with her in the greenhouses and seemed to resent her family connections, her wealth, and the way Mr. Greeley favored her. She'd met Bria at colony team tryouts. That's where she got to know Roger Wilcox as well, though she had known of him before because he was her former betrothed's boss. So, that was awkward.

Anya had never met any of the other six members of her group. Only one of these was a woman. Danielle Powell. Anya stared at a photo of the woman's heart-shaped face surrounded by glossy black curls and wondered if they'd have anything in common. Danielle was a twenty-eight-year-old mother and bank manager. So, just being women, maybe?

She scrolled through the other resumes on her list. Harry Marsh, a dark man with a thin face, worked in sales. Tyrell Park, a short man whose smile revealed deep dimples, managed a bakery. Maybe he could teach her something about cooking. Anya smiled.

Raymond Kline, a man with a round face and closely cropped hair, worked as a barber. Jerome Martinez, an athletic-looking man and a father, owned a shoe-repair shop. That left Evan Diaz, a tall, solidly built man who worked in one of GenM's larger stores. He, too, had a child.

The more Anya looked at this group of people, the more intimidated she felt. They were all, even DeShawn, older than she was. Many had important, successful jobs. Almost half of them were parents.

She was just Anya, and she didn't feel much like a leader. What did she have to offer these people?

When they'd all gathered in the tiny space allotted to them, she felt critical gazes on her. Or maybe that feeling was merely a manifestation of her own insecurity. After all, she was young and untested, and many of them probably thought her father's money had put her in this position.

That wasn't true, though. The colony leadership had put her here because she knew how to grow food. She straightened her spine and tried smiling at the group. Roger Wilcox beamed back at her. Tyrell Park smiled deep enough that his dimples showed. A flicker of a smile crossed Danielle Powell's face so quickly, Anya wasn't sure she saw it.

Everyone else scowled.

Apparently, that was all the encouragement she was going to get. "Hi," she said, but the word came out so softly that she could barely hear herself. She tried again. "Hello! Welcome to the Food and Textile Production Group for the Golden Terrace Colony."

"Food and textile production? How did I wind up on this work detail?" DeShawn asked.

"Same way any of us did," Roger said genially. "The slots had to be filled, and there was no other obvious place to put us. Well, except for our leaders." Roger nodded at Bria and Anya. "You two are experts, and we're lucky to have you."

"Anya? An expert?" DeShawn said. "She's failing ninth form."

"She is *not* failing ninth form," Raymond Kline said. "Her math scores may be lower than I'd accept from any child of mine, but she's passing."

"Excuse me?" Anya said. "Where did you see my math scores?"

"In the transcripts the leadership posted in their defense of their appointments. Naturally, I took a look at them when I saw that a teenager was leading my group. I am somewhat reconciled to the idea now that I know you have more greenhouse hours than any adult on the ship except Samuel Greeley."

"Where did you find that?" Bria asked.

Raymond projected a link into the center of their circle, and everyone tapped their armbands in unison. Evan's was on his right forearm rather than his left, Anya noted. Interesting.

She glanced at her own armband. She'd thought it was embarrassing to tell Abuela Ryerson her mod scores, but this was much worse. She could see every test score, every grade, and every teacher note in her school record, along with every time sheet and quarterly review from her work detail. It was all out here in a public link for anyone to review. Could they do that? She must have granted permission somewhere in that mess of forms she'd signed when she'd checked into the Golden Terrace try-outs. She made herself a promise to review forms more carefully from here on out.

"Did you really develop a low-light, low-space, quick-growing, high-yield complete protein source?" Bria asked.

"What? Oh, you mean the B-9s. Yes."

"Amazing. Look at those specs. They're incredibly nutrient dense. You could grow them in a bunk and feed your whole family," Roger said.

Anya winced. "Maybe if you were starving. I can't imagine anybody willingly eating the things otherwise. They're the foulest food I've ever tasted."

Tyrell and Harry laughed.

"Enough about me. This is supposed to be a team-building session. Commander Smith has kindly provided us with a game that's meant to help us all get to know each other better." Anya hated these kinds of mixers, but she'd never done anything like this before and thought it best to stick to the commander's plan.

From the groans that went around the room, Anya guessed that nobody else liked this kind of thing any better than she did, but they all did it anyway.

She wasn't sure how it helped them to know that Harry Marsh would be a winter melon if he could be any type of vegetable. Nor did Anya glean great insight from knowing which of her group members preferred polka dots to stripes and vice versa, but at least they got through the allotted time and were able to move onto more pressing things. They signed papers, got vouchers and schedules for where to pick up their colony equipment, and started an introduction to agricultural tools and methods.

By the time they reached the end of their four-hour session, Anya felt like she'd been working for days. "Homework is the tools survey," Anya said to finish up, "and be sure to stop by the electronics house for your colony computers this evening. If you have particular books, music, art, movies, or games you want to be sure we take to the colony, get those requests in to me, too. We should have a complete library on board, but in case that doesn't work out the way it's supposed to, I want to make sure we have the things most important to our group."

"Doing all that could take hours," DeShawn said. "Some of us have families that want to see us."

Anya suppressed a sigh. It was a reasonable complaint even if it was expressed rudely and came after an afternoon full of rudeness. "You're right that time is precious, and I'm sorry that we've had to accelerate the training. As I understand it, *StarRacer*'s early departure has something to do with avoiding a meteor cloud, so we can make the journey safely. It's a pain, but we all have to put up with it."

Bria nodded. "That's exactly right. This schedule is no one's first choice, but it's necessary."

Anya thanked her with a tired smile and ended the session. She was deeply grateful she only had to run about half of tomorrow's meeting with the group since there was a lot of textile content.

She was beginning to hate leadership.

ᘒ   ᘓ

David was picking up his colony computer at the same time Anya came in for hers, so once they'd signed out their equipment, they walked back to Anya's temporary home together. For the first time since she'd met David, Anya felt like she didn't have his full attention when they were walking together. He played with the new computer, changing settings and downloading apps while he walked, all the while chattering about speed and storage and how this machine compared with his old one, which he was going to gift to a relative who needed a better tablet for her university course.

They made slow progress because every few minutes down the corridor, they ran into yet another friend of David's, and the two would stop, holding up traffic, while they geeked out about the new equipment.

"You got one too, right?" One of the friends said to Anya. "Why are you not more excited?"

Before Anya could explain she just didn't get excited about electronics, David answered for her. "Anya's armband is a Dvine 8300, so her standard's pretty high."

"A Dvine? I thought those were too expensive for everybody but top brass and the Cartiers."

"I, um, am a Cartier," Anya said in a small voice. Her face got hot. Her *armband* was too expensive for most people to afford? She thought armbands were standard issue—that everybody got the same. What would that make her school tablet? Was there any chance the colony computer was truly better?

"A Cartier, huh? I wouldn't have guessed. You seemed nice enough." The friend chuckled.

"She is nice," David said, sneaking an arm around Anya's shoulders and squeezing. "She's just used to better stuff than a lot of us."

The friend looked doubtfully at Anya, but David distracted him with more tech talk, and thankfully, he soon tired of drooling over David's equipment and moved on.

None of David's other friends paid any attention to her. Maybe they didn't notice her. Maybe they were pointedly ignoring her. Either way, she was left alone.

Which was the way she liked it, mostly. She just felt a bit strange when she realized the wattage of David's smile was brighter when he was talking about a computer than when he was talking about her.

When had she become such a nitwit? What did it matter how brightly David smiled in her direction? She'd only just met him a couple of weeks ago. She didn't need his smiles to survive. "Hey, David," she said. "I'm going to walk ahead and see if Mrs. Lancet needs any help with the supper."

"Oh, hey, are you sure? There's still plenty of time." David glanced at his armband. "No, I guess there isn't. We should both get a move on." He apologized to the latest friend for rushing things and put the computer in his pack, though he still patted it and smiled occasionally as they walked along toward the Lancet place.

Why did that bother her? Anya shook her head. She was being ridiculous.

David squeezed her arm. "Are you OK? You seem a bit out of sorts."

"I'm fine." Anya nodded and ducked her head so that she didn't have to look in David's eye. That must be how she missed Ryan's approach. Even though he was walking toward them in plain view, she had no idea he was there until she heard him say, "Are you bothering Anya?"

Anya's head jerked up. Well, of course, he'd be here. They'd nearly reached his door, and he lived here after all. He probably still took meals here even if he was sleeping in crew quarters so that she could use his bunk.

"So, you're calling her Anya now. Took you long enough," David said.

"If she'd told me she wanted to be called Anya sooner, I'd have started calling her Anya sooner."

"I guess you're just not the type Anya can loosen up around."

"Stop it, both of you," Anya said as she punched in the code to loosen the entrance beads.

As soon as she heard the click, she pushed through. David and Ryan followed close on her heels.

Mrs. Lancet was setting plates out on the counter. "Hello, dears. So, this is David? I'm Janet."

"Pleased to meet you, ma'am," David said, holding up his hand. Mrs. Lancet raised hers to match but didn't quite touch. Did she always avoid touching? Anya couldn't remember. She knew her mother never touched hands in greeting—she said her medical training made her germophobic, but Mrs. Lancet was in finance, not medicine.

By this time, both Mrs. Lancet and David had dropped their hands, and an awkward silence grew in the room.

Ryan broke it. "Is Dad around?"

"Oh, of course. Watching the news." Mrs. Lancet pointed to a soundproofing screen that cut the already small room in half. "Why don't you boys put the screen away, and Stacey can help me finish setting up here."

Anya couldn't help paying more attention to the conversation on the other side of the room than to the glasses and flatware she was setting out for dinner. After the introductions, most of the conversation went over Anya's head, though she understood that Ryan and Mr. Lancet were every bit as impressed with David's colony computer as his friends had been. Then the discussion subtly shifted, and a thick tension entered the room. Ryan stopped talking, and Mr. Lancet fired questions so quickly that it seemed he was interrogating David. David always answered with impressive intelligence and a good-natured laugh, and soon the tension eased up again. Ryan spoke up again. Anya still didn't understand what they were talking about, so she was relieved when Mrs. Lancet said it was time to eat.

They all gathered around the counter.

"I hope you like curry," Mrs. Lancet said, dishing up giant servings for everyone. "Stacey hasn't really told us much about you."

David smiled broadly. "I like curry. And pretty much everything else that's edible."

"Wonderful," Mrs. Lancet said.

There was an awkward silence, broken only by the occasional clink of flatware on plates.

"So, how did you two meet?" Mrs. Lancet said at last.

Anya met David's eyes. He shrugged. She took a deep breath. "In Skreetches."

"Anya caught me on the rebound, you might say," David added. "I was having a rather public breakup with my last girlfriend, Leslie Wang. You've met her, I assume?"

Mrs. Lancet looked shocked. "Leslie Wang? I don't think so, though the name sounds familiar."

"Oh, I was sure you'd have met her. But even if you haven't, you've probably seen her in one of her theater productions. What was last month's?"

"*Double Life*," Ryan said.

"That's right. I knew it was something apropos.

Anya felt herself blushing, but Ryan looked unfazed. He's the one who should have been blushing, seeing how he and Leslie had been going out while Leslie was supposedly dating David, and Ryan was betrothed to Anya.

"Right," Mr. Lancet said. "I think I did see that. Fascinating play and a gorgeous woman, though Stacey is a much better choice as a colony partner."

"Undoubtedly," David said. "Running into Anya that day was a godsend."

Now Anya's face really heated.

"Why do you keep calling Stacey, 'Anya'?" Mrs. Lancet asked.

"It's her name—how she introduced herself to me. And I can see how she cringes every time you call her Stacey. You seem like good people, so I wonder why you keep doing it."

"Don't be ridiculous," Mrs. Lancet said. "Stacey would have told us—"

"Not if Thomas told her not to," Mr. Lancet growled. "Is it true, Anastasia? That you'd prefer to be called Anya?"

Anya lifted her eyes from her plate to meet Mr. Lancet's. She couldn't bring herself to say anything, but she nodded.

"I'm so sorry," Mrs. Lancet said. "If I'd had any idea..."

"There are a lot of things we wish we'd kept our eyes more open about, kiddo." Mr. Lancet squeezed Anya's shoulder. "We've failed you, and we're sorry. It may take us a bit to adjust, but we'll work on using the name you like best. It's the least we can do."

Mrs. Lancet's eyes shone, and she turned abruptly toward the cooker. "More curry, anyone?"

Anya wasn't hungry, but Ryan and David both took refills. They moved the conversation away from tense topics and toward piloting, which both of the younger men enjoyed doing in simulations.

All too soon, David said he needed to be getting back to his family. "Can I tell them you all are fine with a wedding this week?"

"If Anya's sure that's what she wants," Mrs. Lancet said.

Anya was sure she wanted a future in the colony with David, and if it helped their relationship to start it now, then she would do it. "I'm sure," she said. This time she began the goodnight kiss with David. She watched him walk away from the Lancets' until he turned into a smaller corridor and disappeared from sight.

With a sigh, she stepped back into the Lancets' place just as Ryan was getting up from the counter.

"I should probably be pushing off, too, if I'm staying in crew quarters tonight."

"Not so fast, young man," Mr. Lancet said. "Quiet hours don't start until ten, and I think we deserve an explanation."

"An explanation?"

"Of why, exactly, we're supposed to know a young woman named Leslie Wang."

⧫   ⧫

Borsk found the laws related to search algorithms early enough in his hunt for laws that he didn't need to drive himself crazy picking through all of *Hope*'s accumulated legal documents to find the information he needed. Designing a better search engine was way more fun than dealing with the inefficient old thing the library used.

"You're leaving me with all the work," Marya complained when she noticed that Borsk was programming instead of searching.

"Just wait," Borsk said. "I bet I'll find more than you do this way."

"What do you want to bet?"

"Whoever has more relevant documents at the end of four hours takes the other person to dinner."

"Somewhere other than Skreetches?"

"Sure," Borsk said.

"You're on."

Marya pulled way ahead during the first two hours since Borsk did nothing but perfect his program. But then, he put his new search bot into place, and his list grew exponentially.

"Those can't all be useful," Marya said.

"Let's see." Borsk opened one of the files his search had tagged as likely. "That one is." So was the next one, and the next. He'd checked out more than half his list by the time the four hours were finished, and ninety percent were spot-on.

"There's no way," Marya said. "Swap, please."

"Sure." Borsk got up, stretched out his aching muscles, and sat back down in Marya's spot. He glanced at the documents Marya had found. Every single one of them was also present in the list his search had just unearthed.

"How is this possible?" Marya muttered. "Mom said that the library has the best document search tools available."

"Those were the best tools available?" Borsk said. "That's hard to believe."

"It's true, though. I'll tell Mom to talk to you about an upgrade. In the meantime, where do you want this sent?"

Borsk sent her the address to one of his most respectable-looking file-sharing programs.

"Good thing code is free," Marya commented as the files transferred. "There are a lot of these. Are you sure you have enough space for it all?"

Borsk smiled. "I make sure I always have lots extra. It should be fine."

Marya nodded. "I can't believe you actually found more than I did, but these are legit. It looks like I owe you dinner. Where would you like to go?"

"Surprise me."

Before they left the much quieter library, Borsk checked to make sure the documents had transferred cleanly. Then he turned his attention fully to Marya.

Her eyes twinkled as she said, "I think I know just the place."

Borsk had been sort of imagining something romantic, but Marya took him to the concession stand by the secondary school, where they stood in line for piping hot egg crepes with spicy sauce and crisps folded into the center.

Borsk enjoyed his more than he expected to. His mother said that all corridor food spread dread diseases. He didn't see how anything could live in a food so hot he couldn't hold it for more than a few seconds without burning himself, but on matters of food and hygiene, it was pointless to argue with Mama. Borsk smiled.

"They're good, right?" Marya said. "I can't believe you've never had one before."

"Yeah, well, my mother says—"

"You know, I never took you for the kind of guy who'd let what his mother said get in his way."

"Really? Have you met my mama?"

"Oh, come on. She can't be any worse than mine."

"And if your mother always told you that crispy egg roll-ups are death in a napkin, would you be eating one right now?"

"Good point." Marya laughed. "I'm revising my opinion. You're the bravest guy I know."

"Thank you." Borsk made a little bow. "But I'd just as soon you didn't mention this to my mother. I'm in enough trouble as it is."

"Why?"

"Mostly, it's for forgetting to tell her I'd be home late. That kind of thing. Speaking of which..." Borsk tapped out a quick message to Mama, telling her where he was and when to expect him home. He didn't mention what he was eating. "There. One grounding avoided."

"Are you sure your mom is a terror? No way could I come home late after just a single text. If I'm out past her curfew, I'm not going anywhere but school and the library for weeks."

"Even if you have a good reason?"

"No reason is good enough to miss curfew according to my mom. She says the public halls aren't safe after eight-thirty."

"Where do you all live?"

"Two corridors over from Sigmore Landing."

"She might have a point, then."

Marya sighed. "I know. I wish we could afford to live somewhere else."

Borsk wasn't sure what to say to that. They walked on silently for a few paces, nibbling at the crispy egg roll-ups that had finally cooled enough to be eaten.

"Can I ask you something, Borsk?"

"I guess."

"What's King Syndrome?"

Borsk sighed. He should have been expecting that ever since her mom shushed her when she tried to ask before. But he might as well get it over with. She could just look it up instead of asking him. "It's the disease that killed my dad almost four years ago. It's a degenerative illness that cripples before it kills."

"And you have it."

Borsk avoided looking in her eyes. He didn't want to see pity there.

"I definitely have it."

CHAPTER FOUR

*T*he name Leslie Wang seemed to echo in the quarters, and Anya wanted to bury her head in her hands, but she couldn't look away from the disaster about to happen.

"Look, Dad," Ryan said, stepping back into the room and letting the entrance beads click shut behind him. "David Ryerson is just a bit annoyed with me."

"I gathered as much," Mr. Lancet said. "Why?"

Ryan glanced about the room as if looking for a way to escape, but eventually, he stared directly at his father. "Leslie and I were kind of going out."

"What do you mean, kind of going out?" Mr. Lancet said.

"We were dating. Secretly."

"Because she was officially dating another man?"

"And because I had commitments elsewhere, yes. But it's not as bad as it sounds. Leslie made it clear that she wasn't a one-man kind of woman."

A fury rose in Anya. "I don't think she made it clear to David. And what was your excuse? That I was too young to care that you weren't a one-woman kind of man?"

Ryan's cheeks pinked up, and he turned toward Anya. "What did you expect me to do? You're young, and I'm not a child molester. Were you thinking I'd ignore the fact that I'm a man until you grew up?"

Mr. Lancet stepped between Anya and Ryan. "Are you saying that you and Anya had some kind of romantic agreement— no, it wouldn't be with Anya, would it? You made an agreement with Thomas Cartier. A betrothal to his daughter that started when she was too young to have any idea what she wanted in a man. Janet, did you know about this?"

Mrs. Lancet ducked her head. "Nothing so formal, George. You've always known that Sylvia and I hoped our children could get together."

Mr. Lancet glared at Ryan. "But it was a formal enough commitment that you felt you needed to keep your girlfriend secret. And you call that being a man? A man would have said he couldn't stand the wait and broken off the tie instead of sneaking around with a mistress. A man would have done his own dirty work instead of leaving it to his teenage fiancée. Ferto, Ryan. I thought we raised you better than this. I expect Kenneth Llourdes and his friends to act like ignorant misogynists, but you're my son. What have we done to make you think treating women this way is anything other than despicable?"

Ryan opened his mouth but then clamped it back shut again. He turned sharply and left the house.

Mr. Lancet sighed. "Do you think I was too hard on him?" he asked Mrs. Lancet.

"No, you're right. You've always been right on this. I shouldn't have pushed him to..." Mrs. Lancet sobbed and rushed into her bunk.

Mr. Lancet turned and looked at Anya. "Are you all right?"

"Yeah."

"I'm sorry you had to be here for that—had to live through this mess. I should never have let Janet convince me to spend so much time with your family—I knew your father was up to something unpleasant, though I didn't realize it was quite this bad."

"Why did you keep coming?"

"Janet and your mother are quite good friends, you know. Plus, we sensed that your mother had worries about you girls that seemed to ease when we were around. Not that Janet and I ever suspected that Thomas was violent toward you, but we always knew the man was a bully. Unfortunately, it seems now as if we just added misery to your life instead of help. We didn't protect you at all, and we let your father turn our son into a monster."

"No," Anya said. "You didn't just add misery. You showed me what a normal family is like. And you protected us some. You know, Father was always more careful with Mother when he knew you were coming over. It was only ever Mother that he was violent with—until that time before colony try-outs."

"Still, we should have been more aware of what was going on. I don't know how we didn't see it."

"How could you? Father is never the same around others as he is when we're alone. And Mother wouldn't tell anyone. They told us not to, either. They said it would break up our family and be bad for everyone. And it has broken up our family. And Father is probably already working on making life difficult for you and anyone else who helps me."

"Even so, I feel like we should have known something, done something. We visited your house at least once a week for years and years."

"I'm glad you did. It made my life better even if it had a negative influence on Ryan. Not that my father did so much damage as you've suggested. Borsk said Ryan's the one who secured the evidence that Dad hurt me on purpose. He did it even though he knows it's going to cost him his career."

"It's his job to secure evidence. How could it cost him his career?"

Anya giggled. "Seriously? Mr. Lancet, you're by far the most naive grown-up I've ever met."

Mr. Lancet shook his head. "The world has come to a sorry state when it's naive to expect people to live up to their obligations. I'm glad you can forgive my boy, though, Anya."

"Oh, I don't know that I've forgiven him. I'm still pretty mad. I just don't think he's a complete monster."

"Even that's more understanding than he deserves from you. If I'd had any idea what he'd done, I wouldn't have asked him to accompany you to that meeting with your father."

"And that probably would have been disastrous for the colony and for me. Ryan forced Father and Captain Bates to behave, and he kept me safe. Like I said, he's not a complete monster. But he drives me crazy, and I'm not at all sad that I accidentally reset his bunk screen to only respond to my security swipe. Will it bother you if I don't have time to fix it before we launch?"

Mr. Lancet chuckled. "It won't hurt him to be locked out until he can have an expert restore it to its original settings." The laughter died from his eyes. "Now, I should probably check on how Janet is doing. Will you be all right on your own for a bit?"

Anya nodded, and Mr. Lancet disappeared into his bunk.

For a few minutes, Anya sat there, at somebody else's counter, in somebody else's house, wondering if she'd ever feel at home again.

Then she shook herself. She had colony homework to be doing, and she hadn't drawn a thing all day. No wonder she was feeling down. Her mood was nothing a few minutes of sketching couldn't fix.

She hoped.

ℬ   ℭ

Borsk and Marya walked several corridors together in silence after Borsk announced he had King Syndrome. Then, suddenly, Borsk realized Marya wasn't keeping pace with him. He turned. "Marya?"

"So, what are you doing to fight it?" she asked him.

To fight it? "It's a fatal illness, Marya. There's no cure."

"You mean there's no cure yet. As smart as you are, why aren't you in the labs every day figuring out how to beat this thing."

"It would mean gene therapy, and most of that has been banned."

"Are you sure that's the only option? And even if it is, why couldn't you use it anyway? You're already blocked from reproduction, aren't you? That's what the black light means. What do you have to lose?"

Borsk had never thought about it that way. "Sure, but..." Why was he arguing this? What was wrong with looking into how to live longer? Or even, possibly, how to cure his disease? He could hardly make his prospects any worse. Though, he didn't know that he could make them any better, either. "I'm more of a computer guy than a medical genius. I couldn't even read my gene records once I'd obtained them."

"You were just a little kid then. I bet you could figure them out now."

Borsk wondered. He hadn't looked at the records in a long time. And he had never tried to even look up what treatments people had tried in the past, or what kinds of therapies they had applied to similar problems. "Maybe you're right."

"You should look into it."

Borsk laughed. He liked Marya's optimism and her persistence. "All right. I will. I don't know if it'll do any good, but even if I don't accomplish anything, I'd rather go down fighting this thing than just giving into it."

"Good, because I could never go out with the kind of guy who gives up on life."

Borsk choked on the last bite of his roll-up. It took almost a minute of hacking to clear the chunk from his system. Maybe his mother was right. These things really were death in a napkin.

"Are you OK?" Marya asked when the coughing died down.

"I think so," Borsk said. "Did you just ask me out?"

"Well, I'm a bit of a traditionalist, and I'd rather you asked me out. I was just indicating my openness to the possibility under certain circumstances."

"I...yeah. Would you like to be my girlfriend?" Borsk usually didn't feel this awkward, this wrong-footed. He had liked Marya for years. So, why did this feel so strange?

"I think I would. Like to be your girlfriend, I mean. Just a couple of questions first."

Borsk knew it was too good to be true.

Marya pointed at his wrist. "Before that turned black, what color was it?"

"Red," Borsk said.

"That's what I thought. Perfect." Marya turned her wrist, so Borsk could see the red glow there.

"You understand that there's no guarantee it will ever be anything but black," Borsk said.

"Well, it's not like I was planning on having kids for ten or fifteen years anyway," Marya said.

Borsk found it a little hard to breathe. "Hold up. I asked you to be my girlfriend, not the mother of my children."

"What else is dating about? Sex is a biological imperative for continuing the species. Why wouldn't we be talking about parenthood when we're talking about dating?"

Borsk wanted to answer her question, but his brain seemed to have shut down at the point where she mentioned sex. Plus, dating was...well, dating. Figuring out if you liked somebody. Having fun.

He definitely liked Marya. She was gorgeous and smart. And he was having fun—or had been until she started bringing up genes and reproduction. Now he wasn't so sure.

"I just never really thought about it that way," he said when it was clear Marya was waiting for him to say something. "Most people figure out this sort of thing later, you know, after they get to know each other a bit."

"I know. Stupid, right? When reproduction is the whole point of coupling?"

"Well, I don't know about the *whole* point," Borsk said. He reached a hand toward Marya, and when she put her hand in his, he asked, "Do you mind?"

"Mind what?"

"If I kiss you." He stroked her inner wrist, caressing the spot where the "how to seduce any woman" video he'd found said she should be sensitive.

"Go ahead," she said, sounding a bit breathy.

He pulled her close and, hoping his relative lack of experience wasn't too obvious, kissed her. Such soft lips. He cradled her head to draw her even closer.

He guessed she was enjoying it too, based on the tiny sounds she was making.

"Mr. King, find yourself somewhere more out of the way for that, please," said a somewhat familiar voice from behind him.

Borsk pulled away from Marya.

She giggled. "Do you have something against people having fun, Sir Pale-as-a-ghost?"

Borsk turned. Ryan Lancet in full uniform, minus the hat. Of course. "Marya, this is Lieutenant Lancet, my leader for Camp

Flight. You'll want to excuse his being a stickler for rules because, at the moment, it's the only thing that might hold Thomas Cartier accountable for the beating he gave Anya last week. Lieutenant, this is Marya Dominguez, my girlfriend, I think." Had she actually agreed? Now that he thought back on their conversation, he wasn't so sure.

"Definitely his girlfriend," Marya said.

Oh, good.

"Are you really prosecuting Thomas Cartier?" Marya asked Lancet.

"The lawyers will be prosecuting Thomas Cartier. I merely secured the evidence, as my job requires me to do. It's nothing special."

Marya whistled. "It shouldn't be, but let's be honest. It is, a little bit. Well, Lieutenant Lancet, I won't say it's been a pleasure, but it wasn't horrible to meet you." She nodded at Lancet, and then grabbed Borsk by the upper arm and steered him past the man, who seemed uncharacteristically thrown off balance by Marya's needling.

Or maybe he was upset by something else. Borsk glanced back at the lieutenant, a bit worried. Was he all right?

"We weren't actually doing anything wrong," Marya said, and he doesn't look like he's on duty, anyway. No flashers on his armband.

"That wouldn't stop him from citing us. He takes his job very seriously."

Marya laughed. "Well, you seem enamored. Is it going to be a problem in our relationship? I mean, if you're always mooning over the guy..."

Borsk jerked his attention back to Marya. Lancet could sort himself out. "No, I'm fine. I mean, I'll need to keep on at Camp Flight to help him protect the evidence, but trust me, I don't go there for Lancet."

"You sure about that?"

"Sure. He's got his good points, but he's also a complete jerk."

"Ah. Then I won't insist you immediately resign. Not unless it's so much work that you won't be able to apply for an internship in one of the labs. Doctora, maybe, though their funding is fairly dependent on GenM, and if you're in Thomas Cartier's bad books at the moment, that won't work out well. Next Stream Medico. Their equipment is lousy, and their funding sucks, but they've got some great minds, and they're more independent than anybody else."

"Um..." Were all girlfriends this bossy? Everything Marya said made sense, but Borsk felt like he was being pushed.

"I'll find the forms and send them over for you to fill out tonight."

Borsk took a deep breath. This was feeling too much like dealing with his sister—except every time he looked at Marya, he wanted to do what she wanted, so that she would smile at him. He never felt that way with his sister. But he didn't want to spend the rest of his life being bossed around, either. He stopped, pulling free from her grip. "Look, Marya."

Marya stopped a couple of steps beyond him and turned. Her face crumpled. "You're breaking up with me already? This has to be some kind of record."

"No—no—please, don't cry."

"I'm not crying," she said fiercely.

Borsk refrained from pointing out that liquid was leaking from the corners of her eyes. "I don't want to break up with you. I absolutely want to be your boyfriend. And I want to take a more active role in finding a cure or at least a treatment for my disease. But I'd kind of like to decide how I do that myself—not that I don't appreciate what you have to say about different internships and all. I probably wouldn't have thought about the funding thing, and now I will."

"You want to do this alone?"

"Well, not entirely alone, maybe, but I'd like to be involved in decisions about my life. Maybe you could send over a few internship options, along with what you think of them, and we can talk through what I ought to sign up for?"

"You mean, what *we* ought to sign up for. We're doing this together, right?"

"I...are we? You want to help me figure this out? That's super sweet, but won't it be awkward if we do break up at some point—not that I want to. Certainly not right now."

Marya gave him a watery smile. "I suppose it could happen at some point. And maybe it would be awkward for a little bit, but it would still be one of the most worthwhile work details possible. If we come to that point, we'll figure out how to make it work."

"In that case, by all means, let's do this together. But let's talk through the options together, too."

"Together," Marya said. "Yes, that sounds nice." She slipped a hand into his, and they continued on down the hallway. Her hair gleamed in the low light, and she smelled of flowers.

He had no idea where they were going, but he hoped it was somewhere private.

ℂ ℭ

Half an hour of sketching made Anya feel a lot better, but getting back into colony training preparation brought all her stress screaming back. The agricultural content was easy enough, but figuring out how to present it so that people learned something and weren't bored out of their minds wasn't so easy. Anya wished she could take them all up to the greenhouses and show them how things worked, but there wasn't time in the sessions to trek all the way out there. Anya compensated for this by throwing as many pictures into her presentations as possible. Where she couldn't find a photo, she drew illustrations. It wasn't as much fun as drawing what struck her fancy, but it beat math homework by a light year.

Trying to figure out what they were learning in the textile section was less fun. She had to look up dozens of terms on each page, and she still only half understood it. She supposed she could just wait to learn alongside everyone else, but she didn't learn particularly quickly, and she couldn't afford to look stupid in front of the others. It would make teaching her own subjects more difficult. Perhaps it wouldn't matter so much for Denise, Roger, Tyrell, or even Bria, but she felt she was on probation with

Raymond, Jerome, and Evan. And only a fool would willingly appear dumb in front of Harry Marsh or DeShawn.

Why did they seem to hate her so much? Was it just because she was young? Or was something more personal going on?

She should probably research whether her dad had messed with them or their families. She didn't want another surprise like learning that she had an uncle she'd never known about who had reason to hate the whole family.

Anya made a note to herself to do at least a bit of research into whether her parents or her parents' company had messed with any more of her new colony teammates, though she didn't know when she'd manage to do it. For now, she had to learn something about textiles.

Anya thought she understood enough to avoid embarrassing herself, all she had left was filling out the colony forms, turning in her group's library selections, setting up her colony computer, and finding clothes that needed to be mended for one of Bria's demonstrations the next day.

That last task proved more difficult than expected. Her own things were in excellent condition, some of them nearly new, and the Lancets said they didn't have anything either. Anya hoped some of her group members would bring extras.

Choosing library selections was difficult as well. Once she'd put in all the materials that she, Commander Smith, and Bria Huxton thought they'd need to do their jobs well, there was only a bit of storage space left. Anya secured each of her group members' top three choices, and after that, she chose the most popular picks until she'd used up their allotment. She hoped that would be enough to keep them all entertained on the voyage to the planet if *StarRacer* couldn't get the entire *Hope* library.

The forms were a crazy mess of legal documentation, extensive, and hard to read. Some of the documents related to liability waivers, and Anya wondered how many on the colony team were carefully reading all these paragraphs about disease, disaster, and death.

The sections on finances were nearly as intimidating and rather more confusing. Several times she referenced recordings of conversations she'd had with David about how they'd handle their money. As she signed over all that remained of her trust fund, she wondered how couples who didn't have trust funds—and those who had more than one family to support—managed the expense. It took nearly all that remained of her trust fund and both their salaries for the next five years to cover basic colony supplies and the money David's family needed to survive. Were other families going into debt just so a couple could be a part of the colony team? What would happen to their families if one or both of the adults in that couple died before repaying the debt?

Anya scrolled to the next document and had her depressing answer. Given the extra risk of the colony assignment, permanent disability or death would result in debt forgiveness.

It was a relief to finally finish and move on to the computer configuration even though she usually hated anything to do with electronics.

As it turned out, the colony computer was better—slightly—than her school tablet. However, the two machines wouldn't speak to each other, so Anya was forced to laboriously copy file after file onto memory cubes and then transfer them manually. Fortunately, she'd invested in large universal storage cubes to hold her artwork and had a couple of nearly empty ones that she could use for the transfer. It would still take several iterations, though. While she waited for downloads, she tinkered with the display on her new machine, finding, to her delight, that she could use the background to showcase her two-dimensional art pieces. After that, she was so engrossed in creating a gallery of her work, that the only difficult thing about the transfer process was noticing when a cube had finished downloading, so she could move onto the next one.

At nearly three in the morning, her preparations for the next day were complete.

She thought.

She was almost sure.

But for the few moments she remained conscious before slumbering, she was plagued by a nagging worry that she'd forgotten something important.

CHAPTER FIVE

*B*orsk couldn't quite believe it when he realized Marya was walking him back to Skreetches. Skreetches? The opposite of private. There was no way they could get through to his bunk unnoticed even if they went in the back door and somehow miraculously managed to avoid Sarka, his mother, his aunt, his uncle, his cousins, and any other relatives who might be around working or hanging out at the restaurant today. Besides, Borsk would never invite Marya into his bunk because dates weren't allowed in sleeping quarters ever. For any reason. Mama would find out, and then his budding relationship with Marya would be over as quickly as it had begun.

But they were definitely headed toward Skreetches. "Um...are you sure you're ready to meet my family?" he asked Marya.

"Meet your family? Won't they be too busy to notice us?"

"Oh, they'll make time for this. I've never brought a girl home before. Except for Anya, and that was different. We weren't dating or even very friendly at the time. She'd just bought out her dad's share of the restaurant and was in a spot of trouble with the old man about it."

"She bought part of the restaurant even though her father didn't approve? That doesn't sound like her at all."

"Well, she definitely approved the transaction when her bank notified her of the transfer."

Marya laughed. "That sounds more like her—approving something so that she doesn't have to fight about it. So, you brought her to Skreetches to try and keep yourself out of hot water."

"For all the good it did me."

"I don't know why you're complaining. It sounds like it was entirely your own fault."

"You sound just like my mama. And that's no guarantee she'll like you. Are you sure you want to do this?"

"Trust me, it's better than trying to hang out at my place."

"If you say so."

Borsk tapped the code for the back door into his armband and took Marya in through the storage area, but they hadn't made it even halfway to the personal quarters before they ran into Borsk's cousin, Kirsk.

"Borsk! Where have you been, man? And who is this? Wait, I know you—it's Marya, right? Marya Dominguez? You work in the libraries, right? And you're on this year's Hottest High-Schoolers list."

"Excuse me?" Marya said. "I don't believe I've ever heard of that list."

"No," Borsk said, glaring at Kirsk and steering Marya away from him. "You wouldn't have. Most guys don't talk about it even if they've seen it. It's definitely over the line into sexual harassment territory."

"Then why hasn't it been taken down?"

Borsk shrugged. "Hard to find all the copies, for one thing. And I guess nobody has cared that much."

"Well, you should do it."

"I...well..." Borsk was saved from the embarrassing acknowledgment that he wasn't sure he cared that much either by the possibly even more embarrassing arrival of his mother, aunt, and sister.

"Borsk! You brought a friend by? Who is this?"

"This is Marya Dominguez, Mama," Sarka said. "She's Lucretia Dominguez's daughter."

A strange look crossed Mama's face too quickly for Borsk to interpret it, and then she was hugging Marya and dragging her back toward the kitchen, rapid-firing questions at her the whole way. Before they got out of earshot, Borsk heard Mama ask about Marya's grades, her work detail, her future plans, and how she met Borsk.

"How did they get here that fast?" Borsk muttered.

Kirsk came up beside him and pointed out the security camera over the produce row they were standing in. It was live.

"Of course."

"Are you really going to take down Hottest High-Schoolers?"

Borsk shrugged. "I might. What do you care? You don't actually search for that thing, do you?" Borsk glanced at the camera.

"Of course not! No...I..." Kirsk dragged Borsk out of range. "It caught the whole thing, didn't it? And they're going to watch it again and again because you brought a girl home. Any chance you could alter that feed?"

"It's security footage, Kirsk. No way am I tinkering with it. I'd then be on the hook for anything that leaves stores from here until forever." Borsk had learned that one the hard way. "Besides, if you're right about how our mothers found Marya so fast, they've already seen it. Damage done. But maybe there's still time to scrub your files if you haven't already."

"Good tip. Thanks. Here, take these to Dad." Kirsk unloaded a few sweet potatoes and a basket of peanuts into Borsk's hands before running off toward the bunks.

Borsk shook his head and moved toward the kitchen. Marya was now surrounded by half a dozen cousins who were all talking and shoving food at her at once. She seemed frozen but managed to send Borsk a pleading look.

He had warned her. Though, perhaps no one really expected his family. "Just a sec," he mouthed before making his way to Uncle Hirsch to deliver his load of vegetables.

"Ah, Borsk. Thank you. What happened to Kirsk?"

"Emergency in the bunk, I think."

"Clearing his cache?"

"Something like that."

"Won't do him any good. His mother already found his stash of girlie pics. I'm to have a firm discussion with both of you later."

"With both of us?"

"Your mama figures the only reason she hasn't found yours is because you hide it better. So, we're to talk about respecting women."

"I respect women."

"A man can always respect women a bit more. Particularly when he's in a relationship." Uncle Hirsch nodded over toward the crowd around Marya. "I take it you are in a relationship?"

Borsk swallowed hard. "I am."

"And you've left her alone with your mama?"

"Right. I'll talk to you later, Uncle Hirsch."

"Count on it."

Borsk stuck to Marya's side for the rest of the evening but didn't have her to himself at all during that time. Even when he walked her back to her place, they had an entourage—Sarka and Kirsk walked all the way back with them and refused to leave them alone, even when they'd reached Marya's doorway. With his sister and his cousin looking on, Borsk found it impossible to do more in the way of a goodnight kiss than a quick peck on the lips. So not what he'd been hoping for.

"So, how does it feel, B?" Kirsk asked as soon as they were headed back to the restaurant.

"To have a girlfriend? Great."

Kirsk laughed. "She's gorgeous, I'll give you that. But could she possibly be worth the roasting you're going to get when we make it back home?"

"Roasting? What are you talking about?"

Sarka shook her head. "First a white girl, and now a daughter of Vashti? Borsk, why can't any of your friends be normal?"

"Normal's overrated," Borsk said, as if it wasn't news to him that his new girlfriend was a member of a notorious feminist cult. Hadn't she said something about being traditional?

"Is that what you're going to say to your mama?" Kirsk asked, laughing.

"Maybe. Mama's not an ogre, you know."

Kirsk shrugged. "It's your funeral."

Borsk thought he knew a way to shut the kid up. "I'm not near as worried about what Mama thinks of Marya as I am worried about what your dad's going to say to us after your stupid questions in the storage room."

"Dad wants to talk about that? Why?"

Sarka flicked him in the back of the head. "Why do you think? He intends to stay married to your mom, idiot. I can't believe you even looked at that stupid list, let alone mentioned it aloud."

"You're just jealous 'cause you're not on it," Kirsk said.

"Don't be ridiculous," Sarka said. "Nobody wants to be on that thing. Old creeps drool over it."

"Sounds like sour grapes to me," Kirsk said.

"Shut up," Sarka said, lunging for him.

Kirsk danced out of her way, and the two raced back toward the restaurant. Borsk watched them go with a smile. It felt wonderful to be alone.

Was Marya really a daughter of Vashti? For years he'd been watching her in class, laughing at her jokes, listening to her witty rejoinders to teachers' stupid questions, and daydreaming about running his hands through her glossy curls and kissing her plump lips. He stalked her social posts and read all her public notes.

Surely, he'd know if she were a cultist. Wouldn't he?

Though, if she was, would that change anything?

Borsk didn't think so.

He'd still want to spend as much time with Marya as he could.

♏   ♃

Anya's alarm had reached shake-the-bunk volume by the time she was awake enough to open her eyes. Colony training! She checked her armband. She had a leadership meeting in half an hour.

That was enough to get her moving. Anya jumped out of the bunk to find Mrs. Lancet cooking griddle cakes.

"Good morning, Sta—Anya, dear. I'm sorry about last night. I didn't mean to leave so abruptly. I just..." Her eyes welled with tears, but she brushed them aside with the back of her hand and kept talking. "George has been telling me for years that your father's obsession with racial purity is unhealthy, but I honestly didn't see the harm in letting Thomas encourage Ryan's ambitions—or in indulging a fantasy of one day joining our

~ 49 ~

families. It was wrong of me. Maybe it would have been a realistic dream if your mother had been able to have another baby right after Kristi, but when years and years went by, we should have realized it would never work. I'm so sorry, Anya."

Anya nodded. She felt she was supposed to say it was OK, but it wasn't, really. The age gap was only one of a number of things that had always been wrong with her betrothal to Ryan. On the other hand, Mrs. Lancet wasn't the one who had called her a boring child or who had cheated on her. Mrs. Lancet wasn't the one who got violent when things didn't go their way.

And yet, Mrs. Lancet, like Anya's own mother, had closed her eyes to the damage she was doing and trapped Anya in a nightmare.

"I don't expect you to forgive me, though I hope you will someday—for your sake, if not for mine. But I want you to know that we'll do whatever we can to help right this. If there's anything we can do, anything at all..."

"Actually, there is one thing. Could you give my old school tablet to Kristi? I'm banned from their house, but I imagine Tiny could use decent equipment when she starts school in a couple of years."

Mrs. Lancet's face fell. "We can't. George and I are banned from seeing Kristi and Tiny as well. But Ryan—" She stopped abruptly.

"What about Ryan?"

"I was going to say that Ryan can't be banned because he's listed as one of the security officers overseeing Kenneth after some kind of infraction last year. I don't recall the details. We sometimes send things to Kristi and Tiny through him."

"I guess I'll see Ryan about the delivery."

"Are you sure? We could ask him for you."

"No. If he's the only person who can reach Kristi and Tiny to help them if they need it, I need to talk to him myself before I go."

"Oh, I don't think—"

"Mrs. Lancet, you may not have realized Father had a violent side, but surely, you knew about Kenneth. Everybody who has ever spent any time with him knows to steer clear of that man as much as possible."

"You're right," Mrs. Lancet said softly.

"Anyway, I'll figure out a time to talk to Ryan. Not tonight. David has scheduled us for some party at his parents' house."

"Message us the details, so we know where you are and when you'll be back," Mrs. Lancet said.

"Sure," Anya said. "Well, I should be going."

"But you haven't eaten anything."

"No time. Thanks for making it, though."

Anya escaped to her leadership meeting, where Captain DeLang chastised them all for having group members who hadn't completed paperwork or who had done it incorrectly.

Anya had felt good about getting her own forms filled out; she was only just beginning to realize that she was now also responsible for other people's assignments, as well.

Leading her group's training was no more fun than the leadership meeting. Despite her preparations, she was every bit as nervous as yesterday, and though she searched the faces of those around her for evidence that they understood, she couldn't tell how much this was helping them, or even if it was helping at all.

Then Bria took over. Anya was glad she'd studied, or she wouldn't have had a clue what was going on. As it was, she barely understood enough to ask intelligent questions. At least most of the others seemed to find it equally difficult.

If only she weren't so tired. She covered a yawn, but not soon enough to keep from spreading yawns all around the table.

"Perhaps we should move to something more practical," Bria said. "Let's see what everybody brought to mend."

Everyone moved but Anya, shuffling through packs and pulling shopping bags stuffed with clothing out from under their chairs.

"What's wrong, Anya? Didn't you see the request?"

"I did, but I didn't have anything torn, and neither did the family I'm staying with."

"Family you're staying with? Why aren't you with relatives?" Roger Wilcox asked.

"My father's parents are dead, and I'm legally barred from speaking with most of the rest of them."

"That's messed up," Tyrell said.

Anya nodded. "I was hoping maybe someone here would have extras they could share."

"Anyone bring extras for our fearless leader?" Bria asked.

Soon Anya found herself with three very worn kids' uniforms, an officer's jacket with holes in the elbows, a shirt with ragged cuffs, and an apron with burn holes.

Then Danielle brought out the dress. It was filmy and dark green with a square neckline, long flaring sleeves, and a similarly long flaring skirt. A tear rent the skirt from hem to mid-thigh in the front. In several places, the fabric had worn thin, and every edge was fraying. Even so, it was beautiful.

"My grandmother gave it to me," Danielle said. "I've never been able to wear it, but I thought—"

"It looks past hope to me," Bria said. "Any seam that repaired that tear would show, as would any fabric reinforcement."

Danielle's eyes got suspiciously moist.

"Could the mend be camouflaged with some kind of artwork?" Anya asked.

Bria shrugged. "Normally, I'd say no, but you may have enough talent in that department to pull it off. It would take hours, though, and you'd want to practice on something less precious first."

"Would you try?" Danielle asked. "Ben says I can only bring it if it's wearable."

"You let him boss you around like that?" Bria asked.

"I may have been overly firm about how much of his antique electronics collection we could pack."

Several people chuckled, and Bria outright laughed. "What do you think, Anya?"

"I'll try."

Danielle passed the dress over to her. It really was a beautiful thing, even in its ragged state. Anya hoped she could salvage it, though she didn't know when she'd find the time.

"So, now that we all have projects, how do we deal with them?" Roger asked.

Bria showed them, confirming Anya's suspicions that demonstrations were easier to understand than lectures, no matter how well illustrated.

The final half hour of training, where they learned how to deal with their piles of battered old clothes, was by far the most fun of the day, but when they finished, Anya was exhausted. All she wanted to do was find a bunk and crash, but she still had most of her mending pile to finish.

And all her preparation for tomorrow.

And a party in a part of the ship she'd never visited, with people she'd never met.

It felt daunting, and knowing that half the people there were about to become her family only made it worse.

℘　℃

Borsk glanced under his arm to try to catch a glimpse of what Anya had written on today's history question and was shocked to realize she wasn't there. Of course, she wasn't. She had colony training all this week, and then she was gone for good. DeShawn was missing, too, of course, not that it made much difference. Nobody would want a peek at DeShawn's answers to a history question.

Marya's answers would be worth looking at, but she was too far across the room for him to catch them in his line of sight, and he was avoiding true hacking.

For now.

Besides, Marya would be sure to notice him copying, and he couldn't imagine her letting him get away with it. He smiled a bit as he stared at the back of her head and the way her body filled out her uniform. His smile widened as he thought of how she'd react to him trying to sneak a peek at her work. Loud. He loved that she was loud. Though not today. In fact, nobody was loud today. Even with only two of their classmates gone, it felt that most of the noise had left with them, not that Anya ever made much noise in class. But DeShawn's clowning brashness tended to make even the dullest subjects interesting. Borsk thought that DeShawn could probably have even livened up today's session on

~ 53 ~

the Third Biotech Restructuring. As it was, Borsk couldn't help yawning.

Ms. Chapra walked between the aisles and stopped by Borsk's desk. "Not even a word in your answer, Mr. King? I would think you, of all people, would have something to say about the codes that are denying you one of your charter-protected rights, some would even say a basic human right."

Wait, what? Borsk sat up straighter and shook his head, trying to clear out the cobwebs. "Sorry. I'm not sure I quite get the connection."

Marya turned in her seat and glared at him. Spectacular. Apparently, he was being profoundly stupid.

Ms. Chapra shook her head. "Children, children…"

Borsk would have taken offense, but Ms. Chapra was old enough that she could call pretty much anybody on *Hope* a child. He didn't know why they still let her teach—unless they couldn't find anyone else to take the class.

Ms. Chapra stopped shaking her head and made a disapproving click sound before continuing. "If you do not even know your rights, how can you prevent those in power from taking them away?"

A fair point, Borsk supposed, though he wished Ms. Chapra would get through with her rant and just tell him what he'd missed already.

Ms. Chapra turned away from him. "Can anyone explain to Mr. King why he should be interested in the Third Biotech Restructuring?"

Most of Borsk's classmates stared resolutely at the floor as if that would keep Ms. Chapra from calling on them. Borsk snorted. That never worked.

Today they were in luck, though. Marya raised her hand.

"Yes, Ms. Dominguez?"

"The Third Biotech Restructuring initiated our current color-coded system of finding reproductive partners and for the first time, banned some individuals from reproduction at all."

Oh, so those were the ancestors responsible for his black light. Borsk scowled. He didn't like the policy, but he didn't see why Ms. Chapra needed to go reminding everyone that he was officially banned from having kids.

She either didn't notice his frown or didn't care why he was upset. "Very good, Ms. Dominguez. That's exactly right. And I'm sure I don't need to remind you all that reproductive freedom was one of the core rights guaranteed in *Hope*'s charter."

Borsk sank lower in his seat. He wished his classmates would stop staring at him. Ms. Chapra had moved back to the front of the classroom, so there was no reason for anyone to be looking his way.

Most everyone stayed focused on him, though. Some were more obvious than others, but whether they were overtly staring or sneaking covert glances his way, Borsk could tell he was the center of their attention.

He'd never been quite so relieved to hear a bell ring as he was when that class ended. He rushed toward the door, but since Marya sat closer to it, she beat him there.

"So, this whole prohibition is illegal," she said, bouncing on the balls of her feet. "You can fight it!"

She was pushing him again, but he couldn't help but cheer up at her enthusiasm.

"One thing at a time. Let's find a cure for this cursed disease first, and then if they don't turn my light back to red, we can take them to court."

"What if we don't find a cure?"

"I'm not sure how hard I want to fight for the right to pass a sentence of deteriorating health and early death on to my kids."

Marya's mouth dropped open. She quickly shut it and pointed a finger at Borsk. "You..." Then she stopped again.

"I..." Borsk prompted.

"You have a point. We find a cure first. Did you get those files I sent?" She dragged Borsk toward the cafeteria. "We can fill out applications at lunch."

She sounded like she was actually looking forward to filling out a shipload of forms. She even skipped once or twice going down the corridor.

Borsk shook his head. Girls were strange.

CHAPTER SIX

*B*orsk and Marya were still filling out forms that evening. Mama let them use a table in Skreetches—not one of the private ones that he'd been able to use for tutoring Anya, but the noisy one, right next to the pass-through to the kitchen, where every waiter and half the cooks could check up on him once every few minutes.

"Your family is so sweet," Marya said after his cousin Ketzia stopped at their table to see if they needed anything.

"That's one word for it," Borsk grumbled.

Marya laughed. "No, really. It's adorable that they all care about you so much. Though some of the looks they're giving me make me think they expect me to eat you or something."

Borsk shrugged. "I probably shouldn't have brought you home quite so soon. Sa—"

Sarka bumped into him as she passed by with an empty tray. "Were you saying something about me?"

Borsk rubbed his shoulder. Sarka was way too coordinated for that to have been an accident, but who would believe she'd bumped into him on purpose? "Of course not," he said. He smiled, but that apparently wasn't enough to reassure Sarka because she pushed something on her armband that caused three alarms to go at once in his earpiece.

"Don't be spilling any of my secrets," she said.

"Wouldn't dream of it." Borsk frantically turned off alarms and wrote code to keep Sarka out of his system. How had she made it past his firewalls anyway?

He groaned as he recognized his own code.

"Are you all right?" Marya asked.

"Fine. Remind me to kill my sister later."

Marya giggled. "I've always thought Sarka had more brains than the school gave her credit for."

"Hmm," Borsk said. "Brains enough to steal my code and use it against me, anyway."

"Really? How'd she get it?"

Borsk shook his head. "Probably grabbed it out of her own armband one time I set off her alarms. I'm not always careful—I wasn't always careful when dealing with family."

Marya smiled. "Way smarter than anyone gives her credit for. So, what is it she doesn't want you telling me?"

Borsk laughed. "Maybe another time. All I was saying is that most of the family doesn't bring people they're romantically interested in home—at least not until it's a sure thing. In fact, I heard that Uncle Hirsch didn't bring Aunt Danae home until they were actually married."

"No way," Kirsk said as he passed by their table with a tub of dirty dishes. "They never told me that."

"Probably didn't want you getting any ideas. Technically, they never told me, either. I heard Ketzia talking to my mom about it," Borsk said.

Kirsk rested his tub on their table. "Only way to find out the real info around here. Eavesdrop. Of course, what you hear isn't always accurate. Did you know, Marya, I overheard my mom telling my dad that you and your mom are daughters of Vashti."

"Does it matter if we are?" Marya asked.

"Not to me," Kirsk said quickly.

Marya's mouth twitched. "So, why bring it up?"

Kirsk's lips flapped, but no sound came out.

Borsk laughed. "Were you taking that tub of dishes somewhere?"

"Oh, right." Kirsk took his load the rest of the way to the pass-through window.

Borsk waited to say anything else until Aunt Danae handed Kirsk an empty tub and sent him on his way. Then he smiled at Marya. "They'll probably keep asking."

"If my mother and I are daughters of Vashti?"

"Well, if you are. I think your mom's on the membership roll." Actually, Borsk knew she was. He'd looked it up last night after he got back home.

"Does it matter to you?"

"Not really. But if you are, it might make it harder for Mama to be happy about us."

"Doesn't want any feminist radicals polluting her little boy's mind, is it?"

Borsk snorted. "Probably more concerned about a feminist radical breaking my heart. But actually, if Mama doesn't worry about the radicalism, she'll worry about something else. Sometimes I think she lives to worry."

"Yeah. My mom is freaked out that I'm dating a Christian."

"I haven't quite decided what I believe, actually," Borsk said. "It's just the rest of the family."

Marya put a hand in his. "Well, as it turns out, I haven't quite decided what I believe, either."

"I guess that makes us perfect for each other, then," Borsk said. He would have liked to kiss her, but there was a table between them and half a dozen people watching, so he contented himself with squeezing her fingers and hoping his happiness showed in his eyes.

⁖   ⅓

Anya had never seen so many people packed together in such a small space. Adults stood hip to hip. Kids crawled in and out of the bunks, pushing and diving. Every so often, a group spilled over the edge, but someone always caught them and returned them to safety before real harm was done.

Someone shoved a cup of something into Anya's hand, and David pulled her right into the center of the roiling mass of packed humanity. Anya found it difficult to breathe. She certainly wasn't drinking anything. She'd thought this was a family gathering. Surely these people couldn't all be family?

"David!" A large older man shouted, pushing his way through the crowd. He clapped a hand on David's shoulder. "Just the man we were hoping for. Come solve a dispute for us." David followed the man through the crowd. Anya tried to follow, but her hand slipped from his. Someone stepped between them, and in moments, Anya found herself surrounded, pressed in on every side, with no clear idea where David had gone.

Another older man, this one tiny, stepped on Anya's foot and elbowed her ribs, causing a tiny whimper to escape her lips.

"Sorry. Didn't see you there," the man said.

"S'OK," Anya said, but the man had already returned to his conversation. Anya was now packed in tightly, unfamiliar bodies touching her on every side. She wondered if anyone would even notice if she fainted. Probably not. There wasn't enough room to fall down. A panicky feeling clutched at her chest.

Get a grip, she told herself. Everyone else was moving, she could, too. She pushed her way into a minuscule gap on her left and then moved forward. Bodies slid apart and then back together behind her, apparently oblivious to her passage and her often whispered, "Excuse me."

Soon she made it to the dining table and got stuck, not sure how to navigate around it. Voices rose and fell around her, submerging her in a sea of nearly incomprehensible sound. Some of the words she heard people saying were definitely not English, but now and then, an intelligible phrase found its way to the surface, and Anya grasped at the lifeline of meaning amongst all the chaos.

"This new fifth form teacher Tess has..."

"...beautiful sandals, but so impractical."

"Not once, even when they opened blaster fire..."

"You've seen her, right? Anemic and colder than ice cream. Barely said hello. What can David have been thinking?"

A male voice laughed.

"Hush!" some woman said, glancing at Anya.

Only then did Anya realize the cold anemic person being discussed was her. Her face heated. She bit her lip. She would not cry. She wouldn't.

She set her cup hastily on the table and made a path for herself around the obstruction and out the door. If anyone noticed her go, they didn't say anything—or perhaps she couldn't hear them.

Near the open doorway to the quarters, someone carried a tray of drinks. People flocked toward him, leaving Anya room to slip out into the hallway.

That was crowded, too, but less so. Anya muttered greetings at a few people as she stumbled toward the nearest level stairs. She knew she ought to say goodbye to David, but she didn't see him and couldn't stand being in that crush of people a moment longer.

A boy she knew slightly from school leaned against a corridor wall, sipping a beer in blatant violation of half a dozen ship codes. Not that it mattered at the moment.

"Jayesh? If you see David, would you tell him I've gone home? I feel a little unwell." She did, too. She was still having trouble breathing, and her head ached.

Jayesh shrugged. "I guess."

"Thanks."

Anya made good her escape.

₧₧ ₨

Anya's mood improved when she saw Borsk and Marya holding hands outside Skreetches as she passed by on the way to the Lancets. "Are you guys together now? When did that happen?"

Marya laughed. "Was it only yesterday? It feels like longer. Borsk and I are applying for internships at Next Stream Medico, so we can work on a cure."

"Really? That's so cool! Oh, I needed good news today."

"Why? Is something wrong?" Borsk asked.

Anya tinkered with her armband. "Nothing serious. I just don't like leadership much—and then, this evening..." Tears swam in Anya's eyes, and she blinked them back.

"What happened?" Marya asked.

"It was no big deal. I just got separated from David at his parents' party, and there were so many people..." Wow, she sounded whiny. Enough of that. Anya took a deep breath. "It's nothing. I'm just tired and have tons to do before I can sleep, and the party tonight was..." Was what? "...not at all what I'm used to."

Borsk shook his head. "David left you alone in one of those Ryerson crushes? What was he thinking?"

Anya shrugged. "I don't think he meant to—he just got pulled away, and when I tried to follow, I couldn't."

"It's a wonder ship security wasn't called. They always pack more people into those things than they should," Borsk said.

"Yeah, but they always invite the neighbors and pay off the officers on duty, too," Marya said, "and there's actually a good excuse this time."

"That's right," Anya said. "They won't get many more chances to see David, so I kind of understand it."

"Doesn't excuse his leaving you alone," Borsk said.

Anya smiled. Borsk and Marya were sweet to stick up for her. "You both are good friends. And I should leave you alone."

"You don't have to rush off," Marya said.

Borsk scowled.

"Actually, I do. I have to prepare for my sessions tomorrow and get started on a big mess of mending."

"Mending?" Marya said, wrinkling her nose.

"Long story. Ask me about it another time." Anya waved and headed down the corridor, past the gaudy flashing lights and loud music of Skreetches' entrance.

Before the music could completely drown them out, she heard Marya say, "Do you think she's OK?"

"She's getting to do exactly what she wants, isn't she?"

"But David…"

Anya couldn't hear the rest, but Borsk's question echoed in her head all the way home. She was getting to do exactly what she wanted—wasn't she?

The thought continued to trouble her thoughts as she prepared to teach her training seminars, as she studied what Bria would cover, as she sewed up seams and patched holes.

Was this what she wanted? She wondered it as she practiced covering ugly mends on the apron with embroidery and fabric painting.

This, at least, was enjoyable. And whether she enjoyed the rest of it or not, she felt, deep within, that what she was doing was important.

And if it was important, she was glad to do it, even if it meant that many of her day-to-day pursuits left her less than thrilled.

She was going to the planet, helping to give birth to a civilization. If a few steps along the way felt difficult or boring or unpleasant, it was still worth it. Abundantly worth it.

She made small stitches in Danielle's dress, and she was at her most careful when patching holes and restoring frayed edges, but still, once she'd finished, the garment had darker lines and spots in odd places that no one could help noticing. This wasn't a dress anyone could wear. Not in its current state.

Anya hung it up at the end of the bunk and stared at the long green mist of fabric, occasionally turning it to catch a glimpse of a new angle. She wished she could see the way it flowed over a person, but it was far too late to get anyone to model it for her—though one of her art programs might have a human modeling application. She hadn't used it much since she usually drew plants and other still lifes, but she'd drawn people enough to be aware of it.

She searched through old files and disused apps until she found it and impatiently watched enough of the tutorials to figure out how to upload pictures of garments and include them in the model. The program did the rest, and soon she could project a second dress into the bunk, one that looked like it hung on a person's body, hugging curves and flaring out at the sleeves and hem.

Anya rotated the projection, so she could see it from all angles, and then let it stop with the front of the dress facing her. She stared at the imperfections there until they blurred, and her mind put together patterns where there were none—vines and leaves and flowers.

Rapidly, Anya sketched, catching her vision and filling out its details on the projection until the phantom dress floated before her, no longer stained and bedraggled, but glorious.

Could she transfer that art to the real thing, though? She usually worked with light, not embroidery and fabric dyes.

Could she even get the dyes she would need to pull this off? She leaned back against the cushions at the head of her bunk, running a hand through her hair as she did so.

Her armband flashed 3:21. Was that the time? She'd better set this aside and get some sleep.

The excitement of creation warred with her exhaustion, making her slow to succumb to slumber. Even as she drifted off, green dresses danced across the stage of her mind while a chorus of people she didn't know crowded closer and closer, chanting, "Cold as ice cream."

CHAPTER SEVEN

*B*orsk had intended to sleep in on Saturday, but a flurry of messages had him getting up early for a morning of back-to-back meetings instead.

The one with Next Stream Medico came first and lasted longest, which made sense for an interview for a top-rated job apprenticeship. Knowing it made sense didn't make it any easier to maintain a sweet temper as a skinny, middle-aged guy in a lab coat leaned on an orange counter next to a leaky sink and shot moronic questions at him.

Why the sudden interest in working at the lab?

Well, maybe that wasn't so stupid.

What relevant experience did he have?

That one was annoying, seeing how he'd listed every remotely applicable school contest and work shift in the millions of forms he and Marya had worked on last night. Couldn't they read?

How would he react to being assigned to a different team than his girlfriend?

"Excuse me?" Borsk asked.

"Marya Dominguez. The two of you clearly applied together. Will it be an issue for you if we have you working on separate teams?"

Borsk gaped. He hadn't expected this one. "Well, I don't know. I'd be bummed, of course, because I was looking forward to seeing Marya during my work detail, but that's for sure not the only reason I applied here—not even the main reason. Mostly, I want to help figure out something I can do about my disease."

"Understandable. So, you'd still want to do an internship here, even if you weren't able to work with Marya Dominguez."

"Absolutely. Might be easier to concentrate, actually."

Skinny lab-coat guy's mouth twitched.

"Don't tell her I said that," Borsk said.

The guy actually laughed at that before saying, "We've got a few tests for you, and we'll be in touch early next week. If you'll just come this way." The guy led him to a testing pod. Borsk hated the tiny egg-shaped things. No net access. But he was good at this kind of test. He wedged himself into the pod, slammed the door shut, and attacked their in-house assessment.

Two hours later, the pod released him. Lab-coat guy was nowhere in sight, but a college-aged intern whose name might or might not have been Ay released him back into society. Borsk stretched his cramped muscles and went in search of a restroom before heading to his next appointment.

The meeting Lancet had set up took less time but felt longer. While a lawyer looked on, an older, stuffier, just-as-white-as-Lancet officer questioned Borsk about all his movements a week ago when Anya had asked him to help record her interactions with her father. Borsk had witnessed a crime, but from the questions the ship's officer was asking, anyone would think Borsk was the criminal. At least the lawyer made the officer stay mostly civil, and when the man started repeating his questions, the lawyer brought the meeting to a close with, "Mr. King has already answered that question twice. I do not see any point in detaining him here for any longer. Unless you have some other questions you'd like to ask?"

The man started two or three other queries, but as these were also repeats, the lawyer excused Borsk.

Before the soundproofing kicked in, Borsk heard the lawyer say, "What was that? Do you want to be—"

"OK there?" Lancet asked.

"I think so. I'm glad the lawyer was there."

"It's always an option for witness statements but required when the case might get high profile. I made sure to put in the request as soon as we'd secured the video, but finding enough qualified lawyers who had no ties to Thomas Cartier took some time."

"How many did you need?"

"Six—one each for you, me, Crewman Kim, and the crew from One that responded last week. Anya has her own lawyer."

Borsk whistled. "I'm surprised you found even one."

Lancet shrugged. "There are independent voices on *Hope* if you know where to look for them."

"Will my mom be getting a bill, then?"

"No. Lawyers for witness statements are part of your Camp Flight benefits. If you'll remember, you were on duty that day."

Borsk nodded. That's right. He'd meant to resign but had changed his mind.

"If you'd read your manual like you were supposed to, you'd know this."

Borsk scowled. Part of him wished he had resigned.

"Just get it read, all right? And stay out of trouble."

Borsk sighed. "Doing my best."

Lancet gave him a hard look, but Borsk refused to be baited. "Will there be many more of these?"

Lancet shrugged. "I've never been involved with a case this serious or high profile before, so I have no idea. I take care of my people, though."

And Borsk was now one of his people. It felt bizarre. "Thanks," he said.

"Just doing my job. Now, didn't you say you had somewhere you had to be at twelve-hundred hours?"

Borsk groaned. "Don't remind me." But the damage was already done. Borsk now had no excuse that would explain his being late to see his shrink.

And wasn't that session fun? Another half hour cut off from the net. That was bad enough by itself, but it was almost physically painful to spend that time talking about how he felt about his disease and what he hoped to accomplish with his life.

He got out of Dr. Young's tiny excuse for an office feeling worse than if he'd been working nonstop for days.

He hoped Uncle Hirsch was serving something good for lunch.

After an exhausting morning of training, Anya was set to grab some food and find a quiet corner to eat it in, but David cornered her in the lunch line.

"What happened yesterday?"

"Didn't Jayesh tell you I'd gone home because I wasn't feeling well? I asked him to."

"Sure, but Joyce said you took off in a rush after hearing Owen say you were anemic and had some kind of stick up your ass."

Anya looked down at her plate. Joyce? That was his sister, right? Anya wasn't sure how Joyce could have seen anything in that muddle of people.

"Come on, Anya. How do you expect to solve problems if you won't talk about them?"

Anya made her way to a table and slipped into the bench seat. David sat across from her. Anya took a couple of breaths to calm herself, and said, "I heard the bit about being anemic. And cold as ice cream. Nothing about any sticks."

David laughed.

Anya started to get up to leave, but David said, "Sorry. I shouldn't have laughed. And they really shouldn't have been talking that way, but I wish you'd stay and work it out instead of running off." He reached a hand toward her.

Anya put her hand in it, and he tugged at her until she sat in the seat next to his, where he pulled her close and planted a kiss on top of her head.

"I've never been good at dealing with conflict," Anya said. "And I really wasn't feeling well. David, there must have been fifty people in that room. I couldn't breathe."

"Doesn't your family ever have get-togethers?"

Anya shrugged. "Sure, but my parents mostly stopped speaking with the Anderson half of the family ages ago, and Dad's parents both died when I was small. It's just Mom, Dad, Kristi, Kenneth, Tiny, and me.

"What about your dad's other sibling?"

"Didn't Captain DeLang explain that to you?"

"Why would DeLang talk to me about your family?"

Anya shook her head and messaged over some old reports that told the sordid story of her grandfather's rape of an employee and the child and lawsuits produced by the crime.

"DeLang is your uncle?" David said after skimming them.

Anya nodded. "Not that anybody ever told me. They certainly don't invite him to any family gatherings, not that he'd come if they did invite him, I imagine."

David huffed out a short laugh. "No kidding. Well, I guess it kind of makes sense that you're uncomfortable in crowds. I'll try to explain, but I don't know how much I can get them to pare back tonight's guest list. There are a lot of people who want to see me off."

"Tonight's guest list?"

"My family is having another event tonight, and my mom and sister would still like to get to know you a bit. I sent you a note this morning."

Anya glanced at her armband and saw that she had indeed missed a message from David. She brought it up and saw the announcement of another party tonight. She sighed.

"Hey, don't look so glum. It's a party. They're supposed to be fun."

Fun. Right. Anya nodded and tried to smile, but it was hard to look forward to another uncomfortable evening that likely wouldn't improve her reputation with the Ryersons. She could already tell that she wasn't going to be the bubbly socialite David seemed to want any more than she'd managed to be the elegant hostess Ryan desired. And she had even more work scheduled that evening.

"What's wrong?"

"Huh?"

"You're worrying," David said.

"It's just that I have so much work to do." She slipped back out of the bench and picked up her lunch dishes.

"Wait—you're going? But you haven't eaten anything," David said.

"I guess I wasn't as hungry as I originally thought."

Borsk had to work a shift in the restaurant after lunch, but Uncle Hirsch kept him on prep work where there was little danger of him spilling anything, so he didn't mind it too much, especially since he had plans to meet Marya as soon as he was finished.

Well, not quite as soon as he was finished. Nobody wanted to meet their girlfriend smelling like they'd been standing next to a fryer all afternoon, and Borsk was no exception.

His whole body hummed with excitement as he made his way out to the public room by the school. For once, they weren't going to hang out at Skreetches, under the watchful eyes of his whole family.

"Borsk! Over here!"

Borsk turned in the direction of her voice but didn't see her through the crowd of other teens at first. Though, once he caught sight of her, he wasn't sure how he'd missed that yellow dress. It seemed to glow against her dark skin, making her look warm and even more gorgeous than usual.

He smiled broadly and headed her way, but inside, he was nervous. Sarka only wore dresses like that when she expected a guy to take her somewhere special. Would he have enough credits for whatever Marya had in mind?

Then Marya smiled at him, and he didn't care whether he had enough credits—he was taking her wherever she wanted to go. He'd figure out how to pay for it.

"So, what do you think of heading down to the Ryersons'? They're apparently having another shindig tonight."

Borsk wasn't expecting that. "Wasn't invited. We only get asked to those things when the restaurant's doing the catering."

"David invited us," Marya said.

"David? Are you friends? He barely knows me."

"Haven't you checked your messages?"

"Not since lunch," Borsk said. He glanced at his armband. Two-hundred new messages, none of them high enough priority to interrupt him during a work shift, shower, or date. The invitation was time stamped midway through the afternoon. He tapped it, and a conversation thread popped up.

Anya: Not sure I can come tonight. Lots of prep & have friends of my own to see.

David: Shoot me their names—I'll invite them. We have room.

"They have room?" Borsk said. "Since when?"

Marya laughed. "Always room for one or two more at a Ryerson party, right? But seriously, I've never been to one of those things—my family is too serious for the Ryersons. Or at least, that's what Mom says."

Borsk shrugged. "Sure, we can go over there if that's what you want."

"I think it would be fun. Plus, I'd like to see Anya before she goes."

And all that made sense, but this would be a lot less like a date if they were hanging out with Anya at a Ryerson party.

"Come on, it'll be great," Marya said. "Besides, Anya could probably use our help if David Ryerson is so clueless that he doesn't know or care that she doesn't want to go to the thing."

Borsk looked back at Anya's message. "She just said she had a lot of work to do."

"For her, that's pretty direct. Aren't you two friends?"

Borsk shrugged. "Yeah, but that doesn't mean I understand her. I tend to do better with machines than people."

Marya shook her head and hooked an arm through his. "You're fine with people. Don't let anyone tell you otherwise."

Borsk shook his head. He thought she must have him confused with someone else, but he wasn't about to argue the point when he had only a short walk to enjoy being alone in her company.

CHAPTER EIGHT

ension stiffened Anya's shoulders more and more with each step toward the Ryerson place.

"Relax," David said. "No one is going to eat you."

Anya nodded.

"It's not like I'm asking you to do anything difficult or dangerous. Just be natural, OK?"

"Sure," Anya said, adding a smile she knew was completely fake. "I'll be fine."

David must have bought the smile because he said, "That's it," and lapsed into silence. He seemed to be moving on autopilot, not remembering her existence, which Anya wouldn't mind so much if it weren't such a sharp contrast to those moments when she felt like she was the center of his attention. Those center-of-attention moments made her feel like she was smarter, stronger, more entertaining, and more beautiful than her normal self—and then, when he took his attention away, she felt she was shriveling up like a plant without light.

Ridiculous. She managed to live just fine before she met David. There was no reason to wilt just because David was preoccupied with something that didn't involve her.

She wondered what did occupy his thoughts. Maybe it wasn't any of her business, but thinking that she didn't need to know things was part of what kept her from seeing just how much Ryan wasn't into her. She didn't want to be overly possessive, though. Surely, it wasn't too much to just ask what had him so withdrawn? If she phrased it right? "David?"

"Hmm?"

"You seem kind of far away right now. Is everything all right?"

"Oh, sorry. I didn't mean to ignore you. I'm just trying to puzzle out some readings on *StarRacer*'s insulation. If I'm right about what they mean, we may be in a bit of trouble."

"What kind of trouble?"

"I think the last pass through Shindashir's atmosphere may have compromised the insulation's structural integrity. That could lead to serious problems when we get to reentry. But there's nothing more I can do about it tonight. I can't even test my theory. So, I have no excuse for not paying better attention to you. Say, do you hear music?"

Anya did, and her stomach knotted. She was so dreading this party.

Then they turned the corner, and she saw Borsk and Marya coming toward them. Marya wore a cheerful yellow dress and a beautifully bright smile. She rushed toward Anya, bumping into at least three people on the way. She enveloped Anya in a huge hug and then turned to David. "Thanks so much for inviting us! I don't know when I'd get to see Anya otherwise." She turned her head back toward Anya. "Every time I check to see if you're free to do something with me, your agenda is full."

Marya had been checking to see when she was free? Anya's eyes watered a bit. "They keep me pretty busy, for sure. Have you all met David?"

"Everybody knows David," Borsk said.

David laughed. "Glad you two could come. He stroked Anya's arm. "Don't hide out here too long," he said. Then he gave her a reassuring smile and disappeared into the mass of people roiling in the doorway to his apartment.

Anya stared after him. She couldn't believe he'd taken off like that. She was supposed to make nice with crowds of people she didn't know for him, but he couldn't spare even a minute for her friends?

"Jerk," Marya said.

Anya yanked her attention back to Marya and Borsk. She'd been thinking almost the same thing, but she didn't like to hear it from somebody else. "No—I'm sure it's just that he has lots of people to see. Everybody here wants to talk to him."

"That's no excuse for ditching you in this mess when you're obviously uncomfortable with it," Borsk said.

"Yeah, Anya. You've got to stop making excuses for people when they treat you like corrosion. You can't let people trample you."

"Especially literally," Borsk said, pulling her out of a stream of traffic. "Come over this way where there aren't quite as many people. Hey, here's Ma Sweets. Ma Sweets? Anya Cartier and Marya Dominguez. Ma Sweets is a wizard in the kitchen. She can even make box lunches palatable."

Ma Sweets was simply enormous. Six feet six, and pushing the ship's weight limit for her height, Anya guessed.

"Hello," the woman said, her voice as deep as a man's.

Anya picked up her courage. "Can you really do something about box lunches? Because I have about seventy thousand of them on *StarRacer*, and if I have to serve them straight, there will be mutiny long before we get to Shindashir."

The woman's face split with one of the prettiest smiles Anya had ever seen. "So, you're David's new girl. Not his usual type, but maybe that's a good thing. I assume you can cook?"

Anya nodded. She hoped she wasn't blushing. "At least a little."

"A little will work. Send me your messaging address, and I'll shoot you my recipe stash. I'd hate for DeLang to have to deal with a cranky team on top of everything else."

"Oh, come on," Marya said while Anya beamed her address in Ma Sweets's direction. "Box lunches aren't that bad."

Anya, Ma Sweets, and Borsk all stared at her.

Marya shook her head. "Rich people," she muttered.

Ma Sweets's laugh boomed through the corridor. "Spoken like someone who hasn't eaten the good stuff near often enough. You shoot me your messaging address, too. But don't call me rich, girl. A woman doesn't figure out how to make box lunches palatable if she can afford to eat other things most of the time."

Marya stared at her shoes and muttered something that might have been a thank-you.

"Yes, thank you," Anya said. She scrolled through the list of recipes that Ma Sweets had sent her. "Really. These look amazing." And not too expensive for her food budget.

The booming laugh echoed through the corridor again. "Don't thank me until you've tried them. And if you've got to serve box lunches often, my best advice is to make sure there's plenty of cheap cold beer to go around. If people get a bit tipsy, they'll forget what they're eating."

Anya laughed nervously, unsure whether this was a joke.

"What's that about cheap beer?" A grizzled older man turned toward them. "Sweets, you can't be corrupting youth this way. You know there's no cheap beer worth drinking."

"Hi, Uncle Elton," Borsk said. "Have you met Marya and Anya?"

The old man nodded at them. "You look like nice girls, so don't listen to this nonsense about cheap beer. What you need is a bottle of this Allenswade." He thrust a bottle into Anya's hand. She couldn't refuse without dropping the thing.

"Now that's real drink, that is. Go on, try."

Ma Sweets snatched the bottle from Anya. "She doesn't want your backwash, you old drunk. And anyway, the Bates is just as good. There's a keg in the cooler."

"Bates! You dare compare Bates to Allenswade!"

Anya wished she could shrink into the floor, and Marya looked like she felt the same, but Borsk put a hand on each of their upper arms and steered them away from the argument into the main press of the crowd.

"But—" Marya started.

"They won't notice we're gone. They like arguing with each other."

If Borsk said so.

"Beer or baijiu?" someone asked. A whole tray of glasses appeared at Anya's elbow, some small with clear liquid, others larger, and filled to the brim with what looked to Anya like pee.

Borsk snagged two of the pee-glasses and handed one each to Marya and Anya before grabbing another for himself.

Marya sipped at her glass. Anya tried not to look shocked.

~ 76 ~

Borsk laughed. "You don't have to drink it if you don't want to, but if you're not holding something, they'll keep asking. Great hosts, the Ryersons."

"OK," Anya said, though she still worried that somebody would get in trouble for this. She checked her camera to see if it was recording and was relieved to see that it wasn't.

Borsk glanced down at her armband. "Probably hired a hacker to handle the cameras. Not me."

"Better not be," Marya said. "You can NOT lose your armband again. You're going to need it."

Borsk smiled at her in a way that made Anya wish she weren't there at just that moment. She was happy for them, she really was, but that didn't mean she wanted to be nearby while they made out. Why would they want to kiss in front of all these people anyway?

Maybe Marya also preferred privacy. At any rate, she pulled away from Borsk before they had a chance to get truly lip locked. "Is there anywhere quieter?"

"Maybe." Borsk led them through the crowd, deep into the apartment, until they reached a back corner with fewer people. An ancient man sat there on a squat, pink, three-legged stool. Both his back and his walking stick leaned against the wall.

"Mr. O'Neill?" Borsk shouted. "No, don't get up. I just want you to meet Anya Cartier and Marya Dominguez. Anya's going to marry David. Mr. O'Neill is David's great-grandfather, and he can remember the disaster of '68."

"The disaster of '68? Really?" Anya said.

The old man squinted at her and tapped his ear.

Oh, so that's why Borsk had shouted. Anya repeated her question more loudly.

Mr. O'Neill was more than willing to talk, and Anya found what he had to say fascinating. After a while, Borsk and Marya looked bored, so Anya shooed them away, promising that she'd message them if she needed them at any point. For the moment, she was content to crouch in the corner, listening to Mr. O'Neill's stories. From time to time, others stopped by to pay their respects to the old man, and Mr. O'Neill introduced them to Anya. She tried to keep the names straight, but it was hard. Tasha, Marguerite,

Carlos, Paul, Joyce, Kai, Vicky. The names were hard enough, but trying to figure out how they all related made her head hurt.

℘   ℃

Borsk kept hold of Marya's hand as she led him back through the crowd. She was saying something, but he couldn't tell what. He didn't bother asking about it until they made it out into the hallway, and he could hear better. "What was that?" he asked. "Couldn't hear a thing in there."

"No kidding. I think I've had enough of this party. Thank goodness you found the geezer for Anya to talk to. I'd feel guilty taking off otherwise."

"I feel a little guilty leaving her now. I don't think I've ever seen anyone more uncomfortable in a crowd."

"Yeah, I don't know what David Ryerson was thinking, leaving her like that. But I think she'll be fine now. Mr. O'Neill was spouting history, and Anya likes history better than anyone else I know, even my mom. Besides, it's almost my curfew."

Borsk didn't know why he kept forgetting that Marya had to be home early. All the way back to her place, he looked for a quiet corner or an out-of-the-way spot where they could get a little alone time, but the only promising corner was already occupied. He half wished he could legitimately access some of the maintenance hatches, but he wasn't willing to risk his armband access for a few minutes alone with Marya, even if she let him. Still, he could see why David might have been attracted to a career in maintenance. It would be really nice to have aboveboard access to a quiet, cozy alcove right now.

"What are you thinking?" Marya asked him.

"The perks of a career in maintenance," Borsk said.

"Why? If you get into Next Stream Medico, you'll already have two work details. The lab and Camp Flight."

"Three. It's not like I'm allowed to skip restaurant chores when I live there. And then I have my side businesses."

"Businesses plural? I know about the poker games, but what else are you up to?"

"Security consulting."

Marya wrinkled her nose. "How'd you get into that?"

"Lost my armband the first time because of a serious breach at my shrink's."

"You see a shrink?"

"Gene counseling."

"Oh. Right. That makes sense. And I suppose you saw someone after your dad died so young, too."

Borsk grimaced. "Yeah, Mom insisted."

"You don't think it helps?"

Borsk shrugged. "It's not as bad as I thought it would be this time."

"So, it does help?"

"I wouldn't go that far. I don't think it was any use at all after Dad died, but the guy I go to now is a little better. Maybe it'll be worth something, and anyway, it got me the security consulting gig."

"Yeah. It sounds like you're way too busy to even be considering maintenance. Plus, it's dirty, and career advancement is limited. Why would you even be thinking about it?"

Borsk pointed to the nearest access panel. "Privacy."

Marya stopped, so he stopped, too. "I keep forgetting you're a rich boy. What's wrong with the hallway? This corridor is wide enough we can't even be cited with stopping traffic."

She stepped in close, circled her arms up around his neck, and pulled him into a kiss. She didn't seem to care if the whole ship saw them.

Before long, Borsk didn't care either. He'd have kept going all night long, right there in the hallway, if Marya hadn't finally pulled away and reminded him of her curfew.

Borsk cursed a couple of times but resumed walking her back home. After he dropped Marya off, he thought about returning to the Ryerson party to make sure Anya was OK, but honestly, that was David's job, not his.

Of course, Anya probably hadn't even told him that she disliked crowds. Somebody should let David know he was being a jerk. And Borsk thought he knew a fun, quasi-legal way to do the honors himself.

He whistled as he made his way back to his bunk. It had been a bit since he'd allowed himself to play with his full set of electronics equipment.

ℂ ℅

Mr. O'Neill must have seen Anya's difficulty keeping track of all the people she was meeting. "We're a bit much all at once, aren't we? Do you have a stylus? I'll draw you a cheat sheet."

Anya always had a stylus. She handed one over, and Mr. O'Neill drew a family tree, telling anecdotes about the people on it as he filled in their names. This was David's grandfather, who had studied music and math both, playing in a band nights to pay for college. He hadn't been able to afford grad school, though, and had wound up a tech in the engine room. Here was an aunt who'd been brilliant in college but married too young. Here was an uncle who was good at practical jokes.

"And here's Owen," Mr. O'Neill said, drawing a few lines on the chart as a man in his thirties approached them, wearing an indulgent smile. "Owen is David's second cousin. Now, let's see." Mr. O'Neill tapped his chin with the stylus. "What can I remember about Owen?"

"I think he's the one who said I've got a stick up my butt," Anya shouted at the old man.

Several people turned away from the party mob to stare at them, and the thirty-something man flushed from a light tan to a bright red. "Hey, now. I didn't mean... Come on, you all. You know I'm always putting my foot in it."

Several people chuckled, and most of those who'd turned to stare moved back into their own conversations.

Anya's face heated. She suspected she was as red as Owen. She hadn't realized Mr. O'Neill meant Owen was here, standing with them at that moment.

"I shouldn't have said that," Owen said.

Mr. O'Neill chuckled. "At least not loud enough Joyce could hear you. When are you going to learn, boy?"

Owen shook his head.

Mr. O'Neill patted Owen's hand. "Just watch who's around before you speak. I know you can do it. I've seen the way you coach those netball kids. When do they play again?"

"Tomorrow night," Owen said.

Then turning to Anya, he said, "Do you like kids? You could come watch?"

Anya liked her niece, Tiny. She wasn't sure about watching baby netball, but it would be a more fun way to get to know David's family than these monster gatherings. She turned slightly, so she could see the bunks. "Which ones are your kids?"

"The tall lad reading on the second bunk, and his twin, Goldie, is in that muddle higher up—what are they thinking?" He handed his drink to Anya and pushed through a knot of people just in time to catch a scratching, screaming tangle of three kids who toppled right off the edge of the bunk.

A brief silence fell in the room. Then several people rushed toward Owen until a different adult held each of the three children. The bigger girl, still held by Owen, began to cry.

"Hush now, Goldie. You're not hurt. But don't you ever play that close to the edge again! And you, Ran! What were you thinking? You're bigger than they are."

A beautiful child of about ten with black curls that reminded Anya of David's struggled in a woman's arms. "They shoved me off!" he said.

"For the fun of pushing you, no doubt. What's that in your hands? Their doll? Ran, I'm ashamed of you. Give it back this instant and come with me. We have to talk."

The boy scowled but handed a dirty rag doll to Goldie. Then the woman—almost certainly his mother—marched him out of the room. The crowd parted for them and then closed back in. Party conversations resumed.

Owen returned to Anya and Mr. O'Neill, still holding Goldie, and a woman followed with the smaller child. She sat the little girl on the floor next to Mr. O'Neill's stool, and Owen sat Goldie next to her.

"You two sit here by Grandpa for a while. No more climbing tonight," Owen said before taking his drink back from Anya.

The two little girls sat sniffling as their parents disappeared back into the crowd.

Anya smiled at them. "I'm Anya. What are your names?"

The smaller, darker child wiggled closer to Goldie.

Mr. O'Neill laughed. "They're both my—let's see—great-great-granddaughters. I think you can already guess that the little beauty on the left is Owen's girl, Goldie. The tiny tyke is Jenny Takami, David's niece.

"Joyce's daughter?"

"That's right."

So, the woman who'd been carrying the tiny child was probably Joyce, David's sister. Anya still wasn't sure she'd recognize the woman.

Mr. O'Neill yawned and tipped his head back against the wall. "Maybe you can entertain them. It's past my bedtime."

Entertain them? How was Anya supposed to do that? There wasn't room for games in this corner. Then she caught sight of the rag doll in Goldie's hand. She smiled at the girls. "Do you two share the doll?" Anya asked.

Jenny's sniffles turned to full-on sobbing.

"She's Jenny's, but Ran was ripping her head off," Goldie said.

"I guess it's good that I didn't have time to go home after training today. I have my mending kit with me. Can I take a look?"

Goldie handed Anya the doll. It looked even filthier up close than it had looked far away, and its head was nearly detached from the body. The clothes were ragged as well.

"Let's see what we can do," Anya said, pulling out her mending kit and tucking loose bits of stuffing back inside the neck cavity.

The two girls pressed closer. Fortunately, they were too small to block Anya's light as she threaded the needle. She was still working on that skill, and it didn't always work the first time—or the second.

Her own niece, Tiny, had never sat as still as these two little ones did as they watched her carefully stitch the doll back together with the strong invisible stitches Bria had taught. Not too bad. She asked a few questions about the doll and soon was hearing all about not only the toy, but also the whole family as she bathed the doll in dry-cleaning solution, repaired its clothes, and re-braided its hair. It was hardly recognizable as the same doll by the time she'd finished, but the joy in little Jenny's eyes told Anya she hadn't fixed it too much. It was clearly still the same beloved toy.

By the time the transformation was complete, other children had gathered. As she handed Jenny's doll back, someone asked, "Can you do that with my Star?" An even older, more bedraggled rag doll appeared, this one with grease-mottled pale skin and blonde synthetic hair.

"I'll try," Anya said. "Tell me about Star."

Work on the second doll was complicated when Jennifer worked her way onto Anya's lap and leaned against her, half watching, half sleeping, and sucking two fingers. Anya stopped squatting and sat, cross-legged on the floor. Mr. O'Neill snored next to her.

When a few of the kids around her got antsy but made no move back toward the bunks, she turned on her dollhouse projection to entertain them. Ryan had made it for her nearly ten years ago, and it had furniture and dolls that could be moved around with a stylus.

The children around her hadn't been playing with it long before older kids, some even Anya's age, came by to ask how she got her armband projector to do that. Fortunately, Anya had enough experience fixing problems with the dollhouse to explain how it worked. It was a bit surreal, sitting there on the floor, embroidering roses on a doll dress to cover reinforcement stains, all the while answering questions about power and programming—both topics she was known to be a dunce at.

By the time she neared completion on the third doll, several small children had fallen asleep around or on her, and projections of earth architecture and even airplanes zoomed along the walls.

Joyce appeared, and Anya was glad to discover she could recognize the woman, after all.

"Oh, Anya, you know you don't have to entertain the kids. I mean, it's sweet of you, but you should be having fun."

Anya could have said that Mr. O'Neill had asked her to watch the kids, but that was only why she'd started with the dolls. Nobody made her keep it up. "Actually, I am having fun," she said, almost surprised to find it was true.

Joyce laughed. "If you say so. It looks like you're working hard to me." She took Jenny from Anya's lap, rousted a bigger boy off the floor, and headed toward the center of the room. "I'm afraid I have to put the kids to bed," she announced. "Time to clear out the bunks."

Anya hardly had time to finish a third doll before all the children had been whisked away, and most of the adults in the room had gone as well. Anya stood up, stretched the cramps out of her legs and back, and wondered what time it was.

"Hi, beautiful," David said. He seemed to have appeared out of nowhere. "Have you been hanging out here all night?"

"Some of it," Anya muttered as she stooped to collect what was left of her mending kit.

"Hey, it's OK. I understand you were quite a hit with the younger crowd. Where'd you get that projection program? It's not the one you use for your art, is it?"

"No. Ryan gave it to me when I was little. I think he made it for a science fair, but then the adults all said it would look suspicious if he submitted a dollhouse when he didn't have any younger siblings or cousins. I guess he must have been fifteen at the time. So, he entered something else."

"But he still finished it for you?"

"He'd promised, and whatever his faults, Ryan keeps his promises. I think he regretted giving me the thing before long because I kept trying to change things that weren't meant to be changed, and it would crash. I'd have to take it back to him to be fixed. Eventually, he taught me enough programming that I could fix it myself, but that took years. I must have been ten or eleven before I could mess with it without help."

"Ten or eleven?"

"So, I'm slow." Anya snapped off the projection.

"Hardly. Most of us aren't hacking into sealed gene records as preteens. Speaking of Borsk, have you seen him? I can't get his stupid pop-up ads to quit. It's messing with my processing speed, and with the kind of numbers I need to crunch on the insulation problem, that's not funny."

"Borsk's sending you ads that mess with your processing speed? Are you sure?"

"They're double-slide mixer ads. He may as well have signed them."

"Weird. He usually doesn't bother people unless they have money or power."

David laughed. "You think I have money or power?"

"Well, I mean..."

"Borsk also punks people who annoy him. I'm not sure what I did, so I want to find him to ask."

"Oh. Right. But I haven't seen him since I first sat down with Mr. O'Neill."

"OK. Thanks. I'll find him." David headed toward the door.

"David?" Anya said before he got halfway there.

He turned. "Yes?"

"Um..."

"Can you make it quick? I really need to find him."

Anya was going to ask him to walk her home, but it didn't seem like he had the time. "I just wanted to say goodnight."

His mouth quirked upward, he took three quick steps to her side, and he kissed her, making her feel, for a moment, like she was the center of the world.

Then he took off, leaving her to travel the after-midnight darkness all on her own.

CHAPTER NINE

*B*orsk had fortunately moved on from the ad for David and was playing around with totally legitimate mathematics when Mama knocked on his bunk screen.

"What are you working on in there?"

Borsk explained, in detail, until her eyes glazed over, and she patted him on the shoulder. "Sounds like fun. Your dad would be proud of you." She wandered back toward the kitchen. What did she still have going on there at this time of night? Did she ever sleep?

Borsk shook his head and decided sleep might be a good idea for him, too.

He'd just brushed his teeth when David Ryerson pinged him.

Borsk glanced at his armband to see, "WTH, man? Your ads halve my processing speed. Get them out of my system."

Borsk smiled and messaged back, "Having trouble with ads? Sorry to hear that. Glad to help you, but I'm a bit busy at the moment. Maybe Monday?"

"Don't mess with me. I know you put them there."

Borsk doubted he had any actual proof, but it wouldn't hurt to ask. "Why would I do that? Are they pushing my new security consulting business?"

"You're consulting on security now? Never mind. Just tell me what I did, so we can fix this thing, and I can get back to work. It's actually really important."

"And Anya's not?" Borsk shot back.

"Excuse me?"

"Anya Cartier? The girl you're marrying as soon as *StarRacer* makes landfall?"

"I know who Anya Cartier is. We're getting married Tuesday, not in three years. Did she say I did something to her?"

Anya and David were marrying on Tuesday? Seriously? Anya wasn't any older than he and Marya were. That was so weird. Was it even legal?

"Seriously, if she's mad at me, she should talk to me herself, not sic her friends on me."

Idiot. "I don't know if Anya's mad at you or not, and she didn't tell me anything. I saw you ditch her tonight, seconds after she found Marya and me. Even if you didn't realize she's shy and afraid of crowds, what were you doing leaving her alone in that crush? I thought you had some game? Or do you only turn it on for girls who aren't yours yet?"

Little dots showed David writing. Then they disappeared. Reappeared. Disappeared. Finally, words came through. "I'll fix it."

"Wonderful. Maybe when she tells me how you've fixed it, I'll make some time to help you with your ad problem."

"If you really wanted what was best for her, you'd get my processing speed back now."

Whoa. Borsk had never heard laid-back David sound quite so intimidating. "Is that a threat?"

"No, just a fact. If I don't figure out what's going on with *StarRacer's* insulation, the whole crew could burn up when we try to enter Shindashir's atmosphere."

OK, so maybe that was kind of important. But then again, David had spent the whole night at a family party. Borsk refused to feel guilty. "I guess you'd better fix your relationship with Anya pretty fast, then."

"Borsk, just pull them out of my system already! I haven't got time for your games."

Borsk chuckled. "What, you think it's going to take all week to patch things up with Anya? What else did you do, man?"

"I cannot believe I am getting relationship advice from a teenager."

"I can't believe you need it. Talk to Anya. I'm out." Before David could message again, Borsk turned all his devices to sleep mode.

So, David had an actual problem he was working on, a critical issue that needed to be solved, or the whole colony team could die. Borsk felt a twinge of guilt about interfering with David's ability to solve the problem. Still, there was no way that a few hours of slower speeds on one computer would make the difference between life and death for the colony team.

If the margins were that tight, there was no hope for them, anyway.

If he were a little more sure of that, he'd have an easier time sleeping.

€ €

Anya found herself drifting off in the middle of the reading she was doing to prepare for the next day. She shook herself a few times, but it made little difference. The next time she felt herself reading the same paragraph without having any idea what it said, she put her computer down and crept out of the bunk. The Lancets' kitchen had always contained more junk food than her mother's health-conscious one, and it only took a few minutes of rummaging through cupboards to find what she was after—a concentrated caffeine drink. She drank it guiltily, almost feeling her mother's disapproving stare even though she knew her mother wasn't there, wasn't even responding to her messages.

Anya frowned at the empty drink bottle, rinsed it out, and set it with the other empties to be sent for sterilization and refilling. She no longer felt so much like sleeping, but she didn't feel rested either, more restless, maybe even jittery. But she probably wouldn't fall asleep while trying to work. She climbed back to Ryan's bunk and jiggled her computer back awake. Her reading still made her want to yawn, but at least now she could finish a page with at least a clue about what it had said.

After a few more hours of work, Anya thought she was ready for the next day—except she hadn't made any progress on Danielle's dress. Her work on the dolls tonight had given her confidence, though, and she thought she could make it work. For tonight, the most she could do was see if the materials she needed were available. She yawned and tried to log onto her GenM account. It had been disabled.

Seriously?

Thank goodness Georgia Lewis had clued her in to the need to get her money into accounts her parents couldn't control. And maybe this was a blessing in disguise. At least now she could try out other stores. There was a little independent art place she'd always wanted to check out, but her dad hadn't let her. He said it would look bad if his children shopped anywhere but at GenM.

He wasn't leaving her much choice now.

The little art place was a treasure trove of everything from old-style drawing pencils and notebooks to state-of-the-art light sculpting programs. Anya wished she had more discretionary income and more time to go down and browse in person. Though probably, the place was no more than a cupboard in someone's quarters. That's how the little shops usually worked. If so, it was a very well-stocked cupboard. Anya found the fabric dye she needed, and she also ordered a starter art set for Tiny. She could give it to Ryan to deliver with her old school tablet.

She wished there were a closer line of communication open to her, but if Ryan was her only way to gift things to her niece, she would go through Ryan.

Even if it felt totally awkward.

ᚷ   ᚲ

Borsk's messenger alert pinged while he was scarfing his breakfast noodles. His heart sped up, and he put his chopsticks down before he realized it wasn't from Marya. In fact, it wasn't from anyone he knew.

The Wallace C. Bakerton Memorial Scholarship fund? Borsk snorted. He had better uses for his money. He was about to delete the message when it unfolded into a star that shot tiny replicas of itself from each point. Nice. Borsk hadn't seen that before. He quickly isolated the little ad and picked out its innards so he could study the code.

It was a pretty little piece of programming and fairly innocuous—only designed to deliver its one little message—but something about it made Borsk uneasy. He checked it again, making sure that there were no harvesting sequences, no Trojan horses, no escaped bits wandering around his armband. But it was just a message-delivering system, albeit a persistent, difficult-to-ignore one. So why were all his instincts screaming at him to be careful?

It was only on his fourth check of the program that he realized what was bothering him—and then it seemed so obvious, he couldn't believe he hadn't figured it out before.

He knew the programmer.

Well, that is to say, he knew the programmer's work. He'd seen it before—twice. Once in an illegal web of subversion in Anya Cartier's armband that allowed her father to spy on her, and once in a security hack that attempted to destroy evidence of Thomas Cartier beating his daughter.

If that hacker designed this ad, then Thomas Cartier was behind it, whatever scholarship fund it said it was from.

And whatever Thomas Cartier had to say, Borsk didn't want any part of it.

He deleted the little program off his messaging system, making sure no traces remained, and he figured that would be the end of it.

He should have known better.

CHAPTER TEN

*A*nya's purchases were delivered before breakfast, so she stashed the fabric paint with the dress in Ryan's bunk and put the art set for Tiny in her pack. She'd figure some time to get it to Ryan.

The only time that seemed like it might work was during her brief lunch break, so instead of finding food, Anya made her way to the officer's bunkhouse where Ryan had been staying since Anya had moved into his parent's place. If she understood the duty rosters she'd looked up, that was where he'd most likely be right now.

The guard outside the entrance to the bunkhouse tapped her name into a tablet and checked her pack briefly before waving her through. Her name must have been on an approved guest list. Why would it be, though? Unless she counted as part of Ryan's family for the moment since his parents were her temporary guardians. She hoped that was it. If it was anything to do with the betrothal they'd once been committed to, it was reckless. And Ryan wasn't reckless. Mostly.

She walked down the corridor, the sound of some argument heightening her tension. But this was a ship's crew bunkhouse. Arguments here couldn't afford to get violent.

Since her fear wouldn't listen to reason, she shook it away and kept going toward the third door on her left, blushing as a young man wearing nothing but a towel passed her, going the other way. The look he gave her made her feel like she was the one with next to nothing on.

She ducked through the entrance beds on Ryan's door and almost tripped over a young man sitting just inside. He and four other uniformed young people sat in a circle, playing a game of cards, and more young officers were draped over the various bunks, watching. The whole group, card players and not, was the source of the argument Anya had heard. She gasped and considered backing out of the doorway as soon as she righted herself, but as she balanced against the bunks on her left, silence fell over the room.

Then, a woman with lieutenant bars who perched in a bunk halfway to the ceiling said, "Here, just what we need. An impartial judge. What's your name, girl?"

"A-Anya. Anya Cartier."

"Ooh. Anya Cartier who did Steve Jackson's latest album cover?"

Anya nodded. She couldn't remember another time when someone had recognized her for something she did herself and not for her family name.

"Good. Maybe you can provide a different perspective. We're all going in circles. We're arguing about what would make for the greatest leadership challenge for *Hope's* captain. Emma here thinks it would be a meltdown of one of the power reactors while the three gentlemen on the floor are sure it would be worse to face a collision with some kind of debris that does damage to the outer hull."

"Does damage where?" Anya asked.

One of the card-playing young men looked over at Anya. "Well, it hardly matters, does it? One breach anywhere, and we've got minutes to secure life support, and no more than twenty-four hours to cobble things together before the ship loses too much matter to function."

"Sure, but every one of you in here—and every other engineer on board besides—has been trained and drilled in taking care of situations like that. You've simulated them dozens of times. If debris hits or a reactor melts down, for that matter, emergency protocols would swing into action, and they'd either work or not work. *Hope* would either be fine, or dead, and the leadership would have very little to do with it. It's people problems, not engineering ones, that cause leadership problems. The gene-plagues. Those caused a thorny leadership problem. Or the strikes in the early J300s."

"So, what difference would it make where a breach occurred, then?" said a woman in the card-playing circle. "I'm Emma, by the way."

"Well, the greenhouses and the hospital sector are both pretty close to the skin, aren't they? If a breach took out medical equipment and personnel or if one hit most of our food supply—the crisis could affect health or food security for months or years. That would be a leadership crisis."

Emma nodded. "Why didn't we think of that?"

Several of the other card players nodded.

"Because we're all trained as engineers," Ryan said as he slid out of one of the bunks on the right-hand side near the back, "and most of us blew off history."

"Ryan!" Anya said.

"Yeah. Were you looking for me?"

"I was. It's about some gifts for Tiny. I was wondering if you'd be able to deliver them."

"Of course." Ryan accepted the school tablet with a smile and shook his head at the art set.

"And if you wouldn't mind looking in on them every so often, just to be sure..." Anya didn't really want to verbalize her fears that her brother-in-law would be violent, not in front of all these people.

"Yeah," Ryan said, giving her a look that said he understood what she'd rather not say. "I was going to do that anyway."

"Thank you," Anya said. She wasn't sure she liked Ryan much, and she was still angry with him, but she knew he was the kind of guy who kept promises. She could count on him to make sure Tiny and Kristi were safe. "I should really be getting back." She smiled, shouldered her pack, and turned.

She was halfway down the hall but could still hear clearly when one of the guys said, "Nice chick, Lancet. She yours?"

"No, you idiot," said the woman who'd first asked Anya to weigh in. "Didn't you catch her name? That's Anya Cartier. She's going to the colony with David Ryerson."

"Ryerson, huh?" the first voice answered. "Well, you didn't stand much of a chance there, did you? Better luck next time, mate."

Anya couldn't help smiling as she continued down the hallway.

꙰   ꙮ

When Marya showed up at church, Borsk's surprise must have shown on his face.

Sarka laughed. "Didn't you know Mama invited her? And to family dinner, too. You two are sitting right next to Mama."

Borsk hoped she was making that part up. He did not want to be fielding questions about his relationship with Marya all through lunch. He hardly understood what was happening himself.

"You don't mind that I'm here, do you?" Marya whispered. "I honestly thought it would be interesting to see what all this religious stuff is about."

"No, that's great," Borsk said. He meant it, too—mostly. Sure, having her there kept him from doing as much as he'd like with his poker business, but he mostly did that in Sunday School because he was bored. And Sunday School with Marya was not boring.

Quite apart from the fun of sharing a pouffe with her, Borsk enjoyed watching Marya completely fluster their teacher by asking apparently genuine questions about matters of faith that obviously seemed self-evident to Therese Jenkins, his Sunday School teacher. She flapped her hands, puffed dark curls out of her eyes, and explained, using Bible verses that she didn't bother to reference.

Marya crinkled her forehead. "That doesn't even make any sense. Are you quoting something?"

Ms. Jenkins sat down. "It's the Bible!"

Marya nodded. "Oh. Right. Does it always sound so old and weird?"

Ms. Jenkins' eyes flashed, and she pressed her lips together.

Borsk smothered a snicker. Even at his most sarcastic, he'd never rattled his teacher quite so thoroughly. Of course, he never could have pulled off the wide-eyed innocent tone Marya did when she asked her questions. Nor would anybody believe he didn't recognize Bible verses when he heard them. Mama made sure they knew their stuff, and if they didn't, he could count on extra work details at home for making the family look bad.

Borsk wondered if Marya was faking it, or if she really didn't know this stuff. It seemed strange not to since he'd been learning about this his whole life.

But Marya's questions continued when they joined the adults. Only now, the questions popped up in his messaging system for him to answer, which he did without much trouble, surprised to find he'd absorbed so much of his religious training when he'd been actively trying not to pay attention for years.

At the restaurant, Mama sat them at the adult table with a firm, "Next time will be soon enough for you to help prepare. For now, just sit and relax."

"Are you sure, Mrs. King? I'd be happy to help." Marya lingered behind her chair as if reluctant to sit down.

"That's right. We really don't mind helping, Mama," Borsk echoed with more conviction. It was no privilege to be sat down across from Great Uncle Elton, Ma Sweets, and Old Doc Norman. Not with how much Ma Sweets and Great Uncle Elton liked to gossip.

"Sit," Mama said in a tone of voice that insisted they not argue.

Borsk and Marya sat.

"Hmm, so you two," Great Uncle Elton said. "Together last night, and then again here today. Getting serious, are you?"

Marya laughed. "We're still figuring out our relationship, sir, but I bet you've seen lots of relationships over the years and could tell us some great stories if you had a mind to."

Borsk didn't know about great stories, but the old man liked to talk, and when he was reliving moments from his past, he wasn't grilling Borsk and Marya about their newborn relationship.

Before Great Uncle Elton had finished his second story, the food was out, and for several minutes, there was total silence. Marya ate like she'd never had a good meal, and it made Borsk slow down and appreciate the dishes in front of him more.

He was savoring a potato curry when Mama stood up. "I have an announcement to make." She smiled at Borsk.

He froze. What had he done now?

"Borsk has just been awarded the Wallace C. Bakerton Memorial Scholarship. He is the first winner in more than a century."

All around the table, people screamed, clapped, and whistled.

"Wait, what?" Borsk sputtered. "No!"

"What do you mean, no?" Mama said.

Silence fell.

"I'm not taking it," Borsk said.

"What do you mean, you're not taking it?" Marya asked. "Didn't you hear what your mother said? It's an incredible honor."

"I don't need any honors that come with Thomas Cartier strings," Borsk said.

"Thomas Cartier strings? What are you talking about?" Mama said. "He's not on the board or anything. I checked."

"Then why are his hacker's fingerprints all over the message they sent me this morning?"

"Are you sure?" Mama asked.

Borsk showed her the little program he'd captured that morning and explained how he knew it was Cartier's hacker as best as he could without admitting to having had any illegal access to Cartier's systems.

Marya shook her head. "That does look suspicious. I'll run the financials."

Uncle Hirsch nodded. "Best have the lawyers look at it before you sign anything. You haven't signed anything yet, have you Simone?"

"I've already had the lawyers look at it," Mama said. "What do you take me for? Though, I don't like this new kid they put on it. Not half as good as Laura. He said everything was fine, but I'll see if I can't get somebody else to look it over." She scowled. "It will need Borsk's signature as well as mine, in any case. But Borsk, you can't go through life turning down incredible opportunities just because Thomas Cartier might be connected to them somehow. He's connected to almost everything on *Hope*."

Old Doc Norman cleared his throat. "Naia Brown was a Bakerton Scholar. Gorgeous woman."

"You knew the last Bakerton scholar?" Marya asked.

Doc Norman chuckled. "Biblically. Of course, so did most of us. She deflowered half my year. I'm sure that's why she taught—she liked boys. Not that any of us were complaining. She was so sophisticated. Besides, who would believe us if we did complain? She could make records and vid files vanish like vapor over a flame. And she knew all the things about us that we'd rather no one knew. She'd keep your secrets if you kept hers. And, she was gorgeous. I had trouble believing she was fifty." Doc slipped back into silence.

Marya and Borsk stared at each other. "Is he quite ..." Marya started.

Great Uncle Elton laughed. "Doc has his moments. Usually true, though sometimes confused. I've heard all this about Naia Brown before, though. Quite the rumors about her when I was a boy. Didn't know she was a Bakerton Scholar, though."

Mama sat down. "We'll look into it more," she said.

"Yeah, we will," Borsk muttered, though not loudly enough for Mama to hear him.

CHAPTER ELEVEN

*A*nya's exceedingly long day of Golden Terrace Training ended with an interview with Caroline Kuhler about her health. Dr. K said Anya was recovering nicely from her injuries but needed a more balanced diet and more exercise.

Anya's armband pinged, and a horrid-looking exercise regimen popped up along with a food log app. She stifled her groan, forced herself to smile, and said, "Great."

"Well, that's about it, Anya. Except you really should be getting more sleep."

"Yes, ma'am," Anya said, escaping. Like she had time to sleep.

As Anya was leaving the doctor's corner of the colony training area, she caught sight of David deep in conversation with Denise Jackson. He looked up suddenly, and his eye narrowed. Was he mad at her? What could she have messed up this time? She went to his party and thought it had gone OK. He was still looking at her, though. She smiled, waved, and ducked out of the room before he could decide to stop what he was doing and come up with some other invitation he thought she ought to attend. She needed a quiet night to catch up on work and maybe even sleep.

All the way back to the Lancets' quarters, she imagined what she'd do to unwind when she got there. She'd start with a long, hot shower. Maybe even five minutes. Then she'd cook up something tasty, play around with some drawing, and maybe even finish Danielle's dress before getting to the grunt work of preparing for tomorrow. She smiled to herself as she tapped in the door code.

Then, she slipped through the beads and found Leslie Wang sitting at the Lancets' counter, chatting with Ryan.

She froze.

"Anya! Mom told me you were going out with friends," Ryan said.

"She what?"

"You aren't going out. I'm so sorry. We'll take off," Ryan said.

Anya found her voice. "No, no." It wasn't really her house after all. She stalked to the bunk and dumped her work things on it. "My thing with Borsk and Marya is tomorrow, but I'm still going out tonight."

"Seriously, Anya. You don't need to go."

"I do, actually. I've been invited to a netball game, if you must know."

"A netball game?" Ryan didn't even try to keep the skepticism out of his voice, and it was no wonder. Anya had never shown any interest in sports before.

"Goldie O'Neill's. I met her last night." That was even technically true. Goldie was one of the kids she'd entertained with the doll hospital. "In fact, I have to be going. I don't want to be late." She slammed the bunk screen back down and took off, barely slowing at the quarter's entrance beads. She kept up the quick pace until she was sure she was well out of earshot. Only then did she pause to figure out when the game was meant to start.

It turned out, when she uploaded the primary age sports schedule, that the game wouldn't begin for an hour. Anya took herself to the Astro Gardens to draw a bit while she waited. There weren't any actual plants in the gardens, but the light was good, and a couple of the sculptures were pretty.

She sat under a jagged blue one and lost herself in a portrait of Mr. O'Neill—not Owen, but David's great grandfather, the one who had told her the good stories the night before. She got so caught up in her light sculpting that she nearly forgot the netball game and had to rush to get there in time.

The bleachers were full of thirty-something parents and their kids when Anya got there. Owen O'Neill was down on the floor talking to an assortment of uniformed youngsters.

Anya found herself an empty spot near the top of the bleachers just as a whistle blew and the game began. The court looked like chaos to Anya, kids running everywhere and sometimes falling down. Anya couldn't make sense of it even though she tried to follow the movement of the ball and the O'Neill kids.

The opposing team had just been fouled when a hand on her shoulder startled her. She jerked upward, but a firm tug pulled her back down. "Hey, calm down. It's just me. I wasn't trying to startle you." David slid into a nearly imperceptible space next to Anya, so close, he was nearly in her lap.

"D-David."

"You don't seem at all pleased to see me," David said.

Her throat was dry, and she didn't seem able to wet it enough to speak.

"Well?"

Anya cleared her throat. It's true that she didn't particularly want to see him, but that's only because he seemed angry with her. She didn't know how to tell him that, though. "It's just been a very long day."

"Work?"

"And seeing Ryan over my lunch hour, so he can deliver things to Kristi and Tiny while I'm gone."

"I wondered where you'd gone. Why Ryan?"

This was safer ground than why she'd been avoiding David. "Kenneth got in trouble a while back, and Ryan's named as one of the observers he can't bar from his house. I don't know anybody else who'd be willing to deliver things to my niece and sister—and who's also sure to be able to see them."

"Ouch." David gently squeezed her arm, a gesture that Anya found surprisingly comforting. "Is that it?"

Anya sighed. "I wish. Ryan was back at the Lancets' when I got back tonight—with Leslie. Someone told them my night with Borsk and Marya was tonight, not tomorrow."

"I thought Janet sounded a bit tense when I called over to try and reach you. I suppose that's why you weren't answering your messages?"

"I have messages?" Anya turned her armband and saw half a dozen increasingly demanding notes from David. "Sorry. I don't always notice when I'm sculpting."

"You were sculpting?"

"I needed to do something to calm down."

"Can I see?"

Anya shrugged and flashed up the half-finished picture of Mr. O'Neill.

"Great Gramps," David said. "Oh, wow, Anya. It's like you've known him longer than I have."

Anya smiled a bit. David might be mad at her, but he at least appreciated her art. "He's so interesting—"

A shout went up from the court. Anya looked down to see a tangle of kids that must have all tripped over each other. Anya gasped.

David looked up from her armband projection and chuckled. "Oh, man. That always happens at these things."

"Some of them could be hurt!"

David put an arm around her. "They'll be fine. See, they're getting up now."

They were. With the help of the coaches, they pulled each other off the floor, and a few kids were walked back to the sidelines to get cleaned up. "Goldie's bleeding!" Anya said.

"How do you know which one is Goldie?"

"I spent half of last night with Goldie and Jenny. Why? Don't you know?"

"Well, sort of. I don't usually hang out with my cousin's kids. I think this is my first ever junior netball game, not counting ones I played in."

"Really?"

"Girl, if I went to every sporting event where someone in my family played, I wouldn't have time for anything else."

Anya supposed that was true. She'd seen the size of his family. "Do you want to leave?"

"Nah. Too disruptive. We're way in the back. We can wait until they're done and then take the kids to Skreetches for milkshakes or something." He pulled Anya closer. "Then we can chat for a bit."

Milkshakes sounded good, but the chat thing seemed ominous. Anya didn't want to think about it. Though, wasn't that more of avoiding her problems and not speaking up for herself? She twisted her fingers together. She wanted to do this relationship thing right. But with the examples she'd had, what chance did she have of that?

The game started up again, even more confusing than before. Anya gave up trying to figure out what was happening. The echo of the ball mingled with the shrill cries of young voices, and Anya leaned her head against David's shoulder, which felt comforting, even if David was mad at her. She could stay like this forever.

Except, of course, she couldn't. Soon the game ended, and there was a flurry of childish exultation around them. Had they won, then? She smiled and tried to say things that were vaguely congratulatory and encouraging without giving away that she'd had no idea what she'd been watching. She may have fooled the kids, but judging by David's smile, he guessed her secret.

He covered for her though, by leading the whole team and their families in a parade down to Skreetches, where for a time, it felt as crowded as at David's party.

Soon, though, the kids and their parents drifted away, leaving her in a booth with David.

"So, about my messages," David said when the last of the young athletes had disappeared.

Anya gulped. "I'm so sorry. I wasn't trying to ignore you. I just turned off my alerts, so I could work, and then forgot all about—"

"Yeah, I might have forgotten my own name if I'd walked in on Leslie and Lancet getting cozy when I got home from work. It's no big deal—that is, you not answering your messages isn't a big deal. I saw how busy you were at training today, and the rest of it—well, the rest of it makes my life feel uncomplicated."

Anya sucked in a deep sigh of relief. "You're not mad at me?"

"Not mad. Maybe a bit exasperated. I mean, Borsk is apparently messing with my processing power because I upset you last night."

"You're mad at me because Borsk thinks I'm upset with you?" Even saying it felt stupid.

"Are you upset with me?"

Anya started to say she wasn't, and then she thought about her lonely walk back home from the party the night before. "Well, a little."

"And you didn't think that was something you should tell me instead of Borsk?"

"I didn't tell Borsk anything!" Anya said.

"We figured it out on our own," Marya said, appearing from the depths of the restaurant and scooting into the booth across from them. Borsk squeezed in next to her and munched a fry one of the kids had left behind. Marya slapped at his hand before continuing. "Didn't take much—just looking at Anya's face when you left her alone in a crowd of strangers." Marya turned toward Anya. "Did he even meet back up with you last night?"

"He said goodnight before I headed home," Anya said.

"He didn't even walk you back?" Borsk shook his head. "David, even I know you walk a girl home after an evening out. And Anya's your girl now, right?"

"Guys, I don't think this is helping," David said.

Marya shook her head. "We're not going to let you bully Anya. She's had enough of that already in her life."

"I don't—"

"But it's so easy to do, isn't it?" Borsk said. "She's learned not to ever say what she thinks or how she feels, so if you're not really careful, you totally miss when you're being a jerk. I've done it."

"So have I," Marya said.

Anya buried her face in her hands. She wasn't a helpless baby, whatever her friends thought. Hadn't she managed to get out of the betrothal she didn't want? Wasn't she going to the planet, the way she'd always dreamed she would?

"I've done it, too," said Sarka, who was passing by.

"You don't even know what we're talking about," Borsk shouted after her.

The menu board on their table lit up with a message. Anya lifted her head, so she could read, "That time Anya came in here after her dad threw coffee at her, and I told her she wasn't dressed well enough to be seated. She just agreed with me, explained, and walked off. I'm sorry about that, by the way."

"Your dad what?" asked David and Marya at the same time.

Anya waved their concerns away. "It was nothing. I found a wash-n-wear. And learned how to control my finances, incidentally." She really could take care of herself. She thought.

David rubbed his hand over his face and leaned back in his chair. "I think I see what these two mean, Anya. I should have recognized it before. It was like this in colony training, too. And you had actually told me you hated the parties, even felt afraid there, hadn't you? I'm such an idiot." He reached out and took her hands. "I need to listen to you better. I'm so sorry. It doesn't help that we've had almost no time to be alone together." David glared at Borsk and Marya. Borsk shrugged.

Marya smiled. "Maybe you should plan a date. Soon. It'll be easier to be alone together here than on *StarRacer* if what I've heard about the housing situation is true, and you all take off on Wednesday, don't you?"

"Yes," Anya said. "What's today? Our training schedule has me all confused."

"Still Sunday," Borsk said.

"Sunday...Sunday. There was something I was supposed to do by Sunday." Anya couldn't remember what it was, though.

"Get your guest list to my mom, so she can send out the invites?" David asked.

Invites to the wedding! That was it. "How did you know?"

"My mom asked me to remind you when I headed out to meet you tonight."

"You're having another party?" Marya asked.

"A wedding," David said. "Didn't Anya tell you? We want to do the deed now, while family and friends on *Hope* can enjoy it."

Marya's mouth dropped open. "Borsk, did you know about this?"

"David might have mentioned something about it last night, but I got busy with other things and forgot."

"You forgot that our friend is getting married this week? And why didn't you tell me, Anya?"

"I..." Anya wasn't sure why she hadn't told Marya, except she'd scarcely seen her since they'd decided to do this. Plus, it still didn't feel quite real.

Before she could think of what to say, Marya went on. "What are you wearing? Who's throwing your pre-wedding party? Do you even have time for a pre-wedding party? What were you thinking? This is crazy!"

"Well, it was David's mother's idea, but it's a good one. It'll mean a lot to his family if we do it now, and it means I'll get to bunk with David instead of his grandma on the trip down to Shindashir. Besides, we're going to do it sometime, anyway. Why not now?"

"Made sense as soon as you said not bunking with David's abuela. That woman scares me," Borsk said.

"She's not that bad," Marya said. "But I can see your point. Except, Anya, what if you're not ready for, you know." Marya's face pinked up.

Anya wasn't sure she'd ever seen Marya blush before. "Ready for…"

"Sex, Anya," David said softly. "She's wondering how we'll handle it if you're not ready for sex."

Anya gaped.

"Not that it's any of your business, Marya, but we've agreed that we'll take it slow and wait until we're both comfortable before taking any new steps in our physical relationship."

"Oh, of course. I should have realized," Marya said. "So, when is this thing happening?"

"Night after tomorrow," David said. He turned back to Anya. "I assume these two are on your guest list?"

"And Grandma and Borsk's mom and Sarka. Mr. Greeley. The Lancets. They have to be there anyway to sign things, don't they? I'd say my parents, but my dad is barred from being in the same room as me. Mom, I guess. Not that she'll come. And Kristi, not that Kenneth will let her. Come to think of it, Grandma might not be allowed to come unless my mom does—I'm not supposed to see her without the supervision of one of my parents." Anya sank lower in the booth.

Marya squeezed her shoulder. "You can invite my mom. She'll come. And maybe some friends from school or your work detail."

"I don't have any friends from school except you two. And all the Golden Terrace people will be busy with their own families. It's our last night on *Hope*. Though I guess we could invite VJ."

"VJ?" David asked.

"VJ Brown. We work together in the greenhouses sometimes." Anya smiled a bit as she remembered the last time they worked together.

"Looks like I'm lucky he's not green," David said.

Anya jerked her head up, afraid David was angry, but the smile on his face suggested otherwise. She wasn't sure what it meant, but not anger.

"OK, so Kings are easy because we're having the event here. You gave me Marya's info for the last invite. I have Janet's and George's and Kristi's, so I just need—"

"Hold on," Borsk said. "How can you have contact info for her sister? That data is buried deep."

"Didn't use to be," David said. "Kristi used to give it out to anything male in the upper forms."

Anya covered her ears. "I do not want to hear this."

David pulled her hands away. "It's fine. Yes, I had a crush on your sister when I was thirteen, but she didn't show any interest. Even when she gave me her number, I knew it was just to make her boyfriend mad. I grew up and forgot about her. But not before I memorized the number."

"Memorized?" Marya asked.

"Yeah, she said that her boyfriend was the jealous type and had mad hacking skills, so if I wanted to keep it, I had to remember it."

Borsk whistled. "More like her boyfriend could hire people with mad hacking skills, but still. That's impressive. Not how I'd have sidestepped a data wipe, but wow. Effective."

Anya hugged herself. She wondered how many others Kristi had told the same thing to. Could those people still get through to her? Would any risk it? If they did, would it help her or make her life worse?

"Yeah," David said. "So, back to the list. I still need info for Mr. Greeley, your mom, and your grandma. Oh, and VJ."

Anya had been thinking so much about Kristi that she'd forgotten what they were talking about. Finally, she remembered. "Right." She shot over the information on Mom, Grandma, and Mr. Greeley. "I don't actually have VJ's. I just see him in the greenhouses."

"I've got it," Borsk said.

"Why?" Marya asked.

"We talk sometimes," Borsk said.

"But—"

"VJ's smarter than his grades make it seem," Anya said.

"If you say so," Marya said.

"And he's super sweet," Anya added.

"Then why don't you have his number?" Marya asked.

Anya shrugged. "I don't usually talk to him outside the greenhouses, and I didn't want my dad harassing him."

David shook his head. "Your dad is something else. Glad we're leaving. On Wednesday. And your friends are right. We should try to get some time alone—just the two of us—before we're stuffed into *StarRacer* like fruit in a vacuum pack. What do you say? Date tomorrow night?"

"I'm supposed to hang out with Marya and Borsk tomorrow night. Can we make it lunch?"

David tapped on his armband. "That will work. And speaking of work, I need to get back to it. Someone has been messing with my processing speed, and everything is going slowly."

"I think you'll find that your machine was cleared of all adware and optimized for speed about ten minutes ago when you apologized to Anya," Borsk said.

"You messed with his computer because of me?" Anya asked. "I can stand up for myself, you know."

Marya gave her shoulder one last squeeze before scooting back out of the booth. "Of course, you can. You just usually don't."

"Walk you home?" Borsk asked her, getting out of the booth as well.

"Please," Marya said.

Anya watched them head out hand in hand. Was it time for heading home already? And she had a ton of work to do.

"You're looking worried. Work?"

Well, yes. Anya also wondered what she'd find when she made it back to the Lancet's.

As if he could read her mind, David said, "I'm sure they're gone by now, but I'd like to walk you back anyway if you don't mind."

Anya smiled at him. "That would be great."

He held her hand all the way back and didn't once show signs of his thoughts being elsewhere.

It felt wonderful. So did his goodnight kiss.

Anya wondered how long this kind of attention would last.

And what would she do the next time she had a problem with David and her friends weren't around to help her through it? As she'd said to Marya, she could stand up for herself. But would she?

CHAPTER TWELVE

*B*orsk couldn't concentrate. Since the dining room was full at the moment, he sat in the study space just off the kitchen, trying to tune out the clanging of pots and pans and the three-way conversation Mama was having with Sarka and an on-screen Marya about Anya getting married this week.

It would be easier to ignore them if they didn't keep pulling him into it.

"Did you know about this, Borsk?" Mama demanded, just as he'd nearly traced an elusive marker in the code back to its source. The trail slid out of his grasp, and the copy he'd been working on disintegrated.

Borsk cursed.

"Borsk, you know I don't allow that kind of language in my kitchen."

"Sorry, Mama," Borsk said. "I just…you know what? Never mind. What were you asking?"

"How long have you known about this?"

"About what?"

"About Anya getting married this week instead of when they land."

Borsk shrugged. "David might have said something about it last night."

"And you didn't tell me? What are that girl's parents thinking?" Mama said.

"What difference does it make?" Borsk asked. "So, she marries him now instead of in three years. It's bound to happen. Why not mark the occasion here with their families? Or at least his family."

"But she's so young," Sarka said.

"And *StarRacer* isn't a safe environment for having babies," Mama said.

"I'm sure they'll use protection," Borsk said. "Everybody does. Look, it may not be ideal, but it's better than the alternatives, right?"

"What alternatives?" Marya asked.

Sarka shrugged her shoulders. "I don't think she has any. She was desperate enough to go that she asked that humorless idiot, Ryan Lancet, and he turned her down."

"That guy you said was going to hold her dad responsible for the beating and everything?" Marya asked Borsk.

"That's the one," Borsk said.

"Lancet?" He won't do anything," Sarka said. "He's purebred."

"That he is," Borsk said "And a complete jerk besides, but I think he might do something anyway."

Mama smiled fiercely. "You make sure he does, Borsk. And next time you hear about something like this wedding, I want to know about it sooner rather than later."

"Yes, ma'am," Borsk said, though what he really wanted to say was, "Why? What difference would a day make?" It wasn't worth the fight with Mama, though, especially when he wanted to get back to coding.

He hadn't even made it back to the clue he'd found earlier before Mama insisted he help them with clean up chores. Then there was a bit of history homework for Monday. It was nearly ten before he was finally alone in a quiet space where he could think. It felt so good to be alone. Which was strange because he loved being close to Marya. He loved having her around. Just not all the time. Maybe something was wrong with him.

Or maybe he just needed time to himself now and then. Borsk pulled up a fresh copy of the scholarship message from this morning. He knew he'd found something in there. It remained to be seen whether that something could help him.

Sinking into the code felt like shucking off a too-tight set of clothes. Finally, he could breathe, swim in lines of logic, let his mind wander in the world that made all of *Hope* function.

The little logic loop he was looking for was easier to find than he expected. If he hadn't been so distracted before, he'd have realized the trail he was following led to a trap, but over here—in another odd little cluster of code that didn't seem to be doing much—this looked promising.

Borsk followed the threads until he found—a holo program? Bizarre. He triple-checked the thing for viruses and pulled out quite a few stingers. Then he isolated the thing and put it on an ancient player that had no access to the net or any of his other programs. But of course, if this came from Cartier's hacker, that wouldn't be enough protection. He built an isolation chamber around the player, just to make sure.

And pushed play.

ॐ　　ॐ

Painting Danielle's dress was the most fun Anya'd had all week. The fabric dye covered the seams she'd made without changing the flow of the material, and within a few hours, instead of the ragged remains of a garment, Anya looked at a fabulous piece of wearable art. She hoped Danielle would agree with her opinion of it.

She didn't get a chance to show the dress to Danielle until the afternoon of the next day. The morning was a session for the full colony team where they toured the ship, learned more about their *StarRacer* assignments, and did initial checks of their workstations. Anya was neck-deep in kitchen organization and inventory up until the time to go on her date with David.

"Do you mind if we head to Bella Noche instead of Skreetches?" David asked. "I think we'll have a better chance of getting privacy there."

"I'm—yeah, sure." They'd definitely be more private there. So, what if it felt a bit uncomfortable? The soft instrumental music and low lighting were meant to be relaxing, elegant, and probably even romantic. If she felt tense, that was her problem, not the restaurant's. It wasn't their fault that her parents had occasionally brought her along with them for tense meals with various ship influencers. They'd always expected her to behave with decorum and poise far beyond her years.

"Have you been here before?" David asked.

Anya nodded, hoping she didn't look too nervous.

"Any favorites?"

Her parents always got her a stir-fried vegetable and rice plate—a bland, sauce-less, healthy option that looked better than it tasted and that prevented spills and other potential embarrassments. Anya shrugged. "My parents always ordered for me."

"Something you enjoyed?"

"Not particularly."

David's brow crinkled. "We haven't ordered yet. We could still go somewhere else."

"Like where?" There weren't many places with seating, and he was right—Skreetches wouldn't be private.

David smiled. "I just don't want you to be uncomfortable. Dating is supposed to be fun."

Anya would have to take his word for it. She'd certainly never dated before.

David helped her find the menu on her armband and pick something tasty, though it came in such a tiny portion that Anya was sure she'd be hungry again long before she finished with training today.

The talk was a little better. David told her stories of his family and trouble he'd gotten in trying to fix things. She laughed so hard that her sides hurt, and the wait staff glared at them.

David rolled his eyes. "Poor uptight things. We've shocked them. I'd say we should stick around to shock them more, but I'm due back in ten minutes."

Anya had completely forgotten the time. She squealed, grabbed her pack, and headed for the door.

"Hey, slow down," David said as he tapped out a payment code on his armband. "We have plenty of time. And even if we didn't, they couldn't very well start without you, could they?"

Anya slowed down a fraction. "Probably not, but I wanted to get there at least a little early to give Danielle her dress."

"What are you doing with Danielle's dress?"

"One of my mending projects. I think it looks pretty good, but it's very different from how it was before. I hope she likes it."

"How is it different if you were just mending it?"

"I did some artwork to cover some of the repairs."

"Really? I'd like to see that."

It felt so strange to have people interested in her art instead of telling her she was wasting her time with this foolishness, but near as she could tell, David meant what he said. He'd like to see what she'd done. "Thank you."

"I'm sure it's gorgeous."

"I hope Danielle thinks so. It's her dress."

When she handed the dress over to Danielle a few minutes later, her hands shook, which they hadn't done since the meeting in her father's office when she'd wrangled the right to go to the colony with David. She'd known what she was afraid of then, but what was she afraid of now? Even if Danielle hated it, the dress was wearable now, which was more than could be said of it before.

Still, she held her breath while Danielle shook out the folds and held the dress out for all to see.

"Wow," David said from behind her.

"Wow is right," Danielle said. "I'm just...thank you." She crushed Anya in a hug.

Anya tried not to stiffen up. Normal people liked hugs, right? "You're welcome. And we should both be thanking Bria. She's the one who taught us how to do the actual repairs."

"Oh, yes. Thank you, Bria!" Danielle transferred her hug to Bria, who looked almost as uncomfortable with hugs as Anya felt. Strangely, that improved Anya's mood. If she wasn't the only one who felt awkward being touched, maybe she wasn't as strange as she imagined she was. She smiled as she got moving on the last afternoon of training.

Tomorrow, they'd finish loading *StarRacer*, and in the evening, she'd get married.

And the next day, they'd leave.

CHAPTER THIRTEEN

*F*ifteen hours after Borsk had first pushed play on the holo he'd found, he still hadn't seen the program run because the player he'd thought would be compatible with it hadn't been. Neither were any of the ones he was able to both locate and afford. Finally, he'd decided to just design his own player to match the holo. He thought he might finally have created something that would work when Sarka banged on the wall next to his bunk.

"You know Marya and Anya are here for dinner, right? Mama's putting you all in the purple booth."

Borsk had completely forgotten about dinner. But of course, he had to go. Anya was getting married tomorrow night and leaving early the day after that. "I'll be right there," he said. He dropped the holo player he'd cobbled together into his pocket along with the old-style storage cube he was using to quarantine the code he'd found. Then he straightened his clothes and tied his braids back away from his face. He used his armband camera to check how he looked. A bit scraggly, but he didn't have time to shave. Anya wouldn't complain, but would Marya care? Maybe he should shave anyway.

"What took you so long?" Marya asked as he slid into the booth that took up the entire space in the little private dining room. Food was already piled on the table, and Sarka said something about Mama having told her to leave them all alone—they'd need to signal when they wanted out. Then the door slid shut, and the panic of being cut off from the net threatened to overwhelm him.

Focus, he told himself. Ground yourself, like the shrink always said. What do you see?

Anya, her pale hair falling into her eyes. Marya, brown, with bright purple lips and silky black hair he still hadn't touched as much as he wanted to. A circular, high-backed, brownish-purple bench that perfectly matched the ceiling it touched.

"Borsk, are you OK?" Anya asked.

"I'll be fine in a minute. Just getting used to the lack of net access."

Two things he could hear?

The hum of the room's ventilators, and the tap of Marya's fingernails on the table. She was getting impatient.

One thing he could smell?

Eau de toilet mixed with garlic and onions. This booth was way too close to the restrooms.

"Should we go somewhere else?" Marya asked.

"No, I'm fine now. That worked better than I expected it to."

"What did?" Anya asked.

"The grounding exercise my therapist has me doing when I get panicky."

"Was that why you were late?" Marya asked. "Because you were worried about being cut off?"

"No, I was trying to figure out how to access this holo I found buried in the scholarship ad. Almost had it, too." Borsk pulled the storage cube and the player he'd designed out of his pocket. "The thing has funky specs." Borsk showed them his armband, so they could see.

"Ooh, that's an old zeta-ohm style holo. I can never get those to run on anything but the library's legacy players," Anya said.

Marya and Borsk both stared at her.

"How often do you need to watch zeta-ohm holos?" Marya asked. "Aren't those interactive? Forerunners of full sims?"

Anya turned pink. "I don't anymore, but when I was little, there was this puppet show program that taught me to read."

"Oh, I remember that," Marya said. "It came from your personal library. The one with the funky striped beasts and creatures that could fly."

"Yes. Zebras and birds."

"Ah. Well, if this turns out to be an educational vid, I'll be very disappointed," Borsk said.

"What are you waiting for?" Marya asked. "Put it in. Let's see what the scholarship fund has to say to you."

"I don't think..." Borsk decided it probably wasn't worth arguing about whether the scholarship fund was the one who had sent this message from another time. He wasn't sure he wanted an audience for this either. "Besides, isn't this supposed to be time with Anya?"

"I don't mind," Anya said. "In fact, I'd kind of like to find out what's on that holo. Did you say it came from a scholarship application?"

Borsk sighed. "Yeah, but I don't think this was from the organizers. It was buried too deep. But I can run it if you're sure."

It probably wasn't a bad idea to run it in this net-free zone anyway, now that he thought about it, and he'd never be able to convince Mama to let him use the space on his own. He thought he'd removed all the traps, but he didn't want to release any viruses into the full ship if he could help it.

Marya and Anya exchanged a look he didn't understand, and then Marya said, "We're sure."

Borsk inserted the cube into his makeshift player.

At first, nothing happened, and Borsk worried he might not have managed to create a working player after all. But then, a fractured image flickered above the player and, after a moment, resolved into a woman who looked maybe ten years older than them. She wore what looked like a teacher's uniform, except it had a plunging neckline and seemed painted onto her skin rather than worn.

"The Bakerton scholarship had a porn holo buried in it?" Marya asked.

"Ooh—I've never been mistaken for porn before," the figure said, laughing, "But then, I've never been opened in a crowd before, either. How fascinating. Now, which one of you was the lucky recipient?"

"You're Naia Brown," Anya said. "I wondered how you were doing it."

"Doing what?" Borsk asked. He felt the whole conversation had gotten way out of hand.

"Keeping young people from accepting the Bakerton scholarship." Anya giggled. "Nobody's accepted it since she did, and I was sure she was warning people off, but I couldn't figure out how she did it once she was dead."

"Well, aren't you a little smarty pants," the holo swirled to face Anya, giving Borsk a view of a fine rear in exceedingly tight pants. Marya glared at him, and he closed his eyes. Why hadn't he opened this thing in private?

Anya giggled again. "I think you're the first person who has ever called me smart. No—I just value history. It's how we manage to remember important things for more than a generation. Learn as a people, not just as individuals."

"You sound like my mom," Marya muttered.

"Who do you think I learned it from?" Anya muttered back.

"So, what does history say about me, missy?" the holo asked.

This, Borsk wanted to hear. He opened his eyes to see Anya's face framed between the woman's shapely legs. Anya brushed her hair out of her eyes.

"Well, that you were a brilliant computer wizard, almost as good as Borsk here."

"Almost as good?" the woman growled.

Anya shrugged. "He apparently obtained his own sealed gene records—without getting caught—when he was twelve. And he's been busting through your Guardian code for weeks now."

"What are you talking about? You don't know anything about code," Borsk said.

"I don't have to know anything about code to know that my dad uses the Guardian code she created in all our systems since the open-source stuff is better than anything commercially available."

"That incredible programming your dad has in his systems is open source?" Borsk asked.

"Anything a programmer makes for the first ten years after receiving the Bakerton Scholarship is open source," Anya said. "That's how my dad and other businesspeople get hold of all the best code while paying hardly anything for it."

"No," Marya said. "We'd all have heard if lots of great code was out there, available for anyone to use."

"Ah, but recipients are prohibited from discussing the terms of the scholarship at risk of being forced to pay back the entire benefit," the holo woman said.

"So, you got around that with a little spoiler that only someone with enough hacking skill to win the prize could find. Brilliant," Anya said.

"Don't encourage her," Marya said. "And it still doesn't explain why none of the kids she's warned off have said anything."

The holo turned toward Marya. "I asked them to keep quiet about it, so no fines would be levied against any of my descendants."

"You don't have any descendants," Anya said. "You sustained some kind of damage as a teen that rendered you infertile."

The holo laughed. "Foiled by the history buff again. But they didn't know that, did they? Besides, just because I don't have descendants now doesn't mean I never will."

"You're in the gene bank?" Marya asked.

The holo nodded. "And they promised me I'd be at the very top of the list."

"You do realize that fines for contract violations can't be visited on descendants anymore, right? They got rid of that nonsense decades ago," Anya said. "I can send you the details..." Anya started tapping on her armband, and then stopped. "I mean, once I reconnect to the net, I can send you the details."

Borsk laughed and grabbed a fry from next to the player. "You do realize she's a holo, right? Who exactly would you send the details to?"

Anya flushed pink.

The holo turned back toward Anya. "I could have just broadcast the scholarship details decades ago, and nobody could have done a thing about it?"

Anya nodded. "And anybody who wanted to could have started using Guardian."

The woman screamed. Actually screamed.

Borsk, Marya, and Anya all covered their ears.

"Cut that out!" Marya said. "We can tell everybody now, and you'll have achieved what you wanted, right?"

The woman slumped. "Half of what I wanted. I also hoped to convince some woman to have my baby. I don't suppose either of you would be interested?"

Marya shook her head. "We're way too young."

"But maybe we could try to get you an interview with one of the independent news shows, and they could put out an appeal," Anya said.

Marya nodded. "That might work. But she'd have to change her outfit. Right now, she looks like she's trying to seduce somebody."

"What's wrong with that?" Borsk asked.

Anya and Marya both glared at him.

"Hey, all I'm saying is, isn't that usually how people convince other people to give them kids?"

Marya laughed. "Usually, people have kids by getting other people to have sex with them. But that's not what she needs. She's trying to convince another woman to carry and raise her kid with no sex involved. She needs a different approach."

The woman laughed. "You're probably right, but I was never any good at picking outfits that made women happy. And even if I could, my personality was set this way ages ago."

"We could help you pick something out," Marya said.

"I want to still be me," the holo said. "I want to look good."

"Of course, you do," Marya said. "Who doesn't? And you do look good."

"You thought I was porn."

Marya shrugged. "Still good. Just not someone I want hanging around with my boyfriend."

She stressed the last two words in a way that made Borsk gulp. He turned slightly, so he could face Marya instead of the center of the table.

"There must be something you like and look good in that would work for an interview," Anya said. "And if there isn't, maybe you could find a picture of something that would work."

"It's not that simple to render a flat picture into workable clothing for an avatar," the woman snapped.

"If it were a light sculpture instead of a picture, I could do it without too much trouble," Borsk said.

"And where would we get a light sculpture of clothing I like that fits me?"

Borsk grinned. "Anya could make one if she saw a picture."

"Sure," Anya said. "And Marya knows everybody. She can set up the interview."

"I am not a charity case," the holo said.

"No, you're Naia Brown, a brilliant woman who deserves at least a chance to make her case for someone having her kid," Anya said. "Why don't we get you off the table, so we can eat. That'll take a little time, and you can think about it."

Borsk looked at Marya.

Marya shrugged. "Getting her off the table, so we can eat sounds good to me."

"Fine," the woman said.

Borsk moved the holo player to the bench near the door. The woman—Naia, changed to a torso holo, so it looked like she was sitting in the booth with them. Borsk scooted closer to Marya.

The food was nearly cold, but even that couldn't keep Uncle Hirsch's best noodles from being delicious. Borsk dug in and tried to ignore the woman made of light next to him. It was hard since she kept flickering in and out of various outfits.

Between that and Marya and Anya finishing each other's sentences and then bursting into laughter or tears, it was one of the weirdest meals he had ever eaten.

CHAPTER FOURTEEN

"That one," Marya said suddenly.

Anya looked over at Naia Brown. She was wearing a deep purple dress that bared both shoulders.

"Are you sure?" Naia flickered off and then returned in a full-body form, hovering above the table. The dress was even prettier full-length since it tapered to a tiny waist and then flared outward in beautiful, soft folds. It would be perfect if it didn't gap strangely across Naia's chest.

"I can definitely fix that," Anya said, pulling up her art program, so she could get a picture of Naia in the dress to use as a starting point.

"Anya, wait!" Borsk said seconds after she took the picture.

Naia laughed.

"I knew I should have turned you off," Borsk said.

"Why? What's wrong?" Anya asked.

"You've almost certainly copied Naia's holo into your armband."

"But—that doesn't make any sense. My art programs won't play zeta-ohm holos."

"She really isn't a programmer, is she?" Naia asked Borsk.

"Anya," Borsk said, sighing, "this is a holo made by a renowned hacker. And any holos can hide a ton of data that can be transferred when you take pictures or videos of them. This one has almost certainly transferred something, and your armband is probably now infected."

Beautiful. Just what Anya needed. "Is there anything I can do about it now?"

Naia and Borsk both shook their heads.

"Then I may as well fix the dress since the damage is already done, right?" Anya projected a second image of Naia out over the table. This one was smaller and didn't talk. In fact, neither Naia said anything when Anya cropped the figure to just the dress and started sculpting.

"Wish you could do that for me," Marya said as Anya transformed the off-the-shelf garment into a form-fitting designer dress.

"I wish I could, too. I'm not there yet, though," Anya said. "So far, I can only mend clothes, not make new ones or tailor old ones. I'm sure Bria will teach us, though. Anything we need on the planet that we can't take with us will have to be made." Anya projected her design onto the Naia holo by Borsk and shut down her art program.

"I can work with that." Naia closed her eyes, and a moment later, the purple dress she was wearing molded itself to her figure. Then Naia opened her eyes and twirled around. The skirt flared out naturally. Naia twisted so that she could see herself from the back. "Well. That does look good. You've done remarkably well for a girl who can't program. Too bad *Hope* is losing you to the planet. When did you say you were taking off?"

"She's going the day after tomorrow," Marya said. "And if you do anything before then to mess up the launch, Borsk will scrub every trace of you from the ship."

The holo laughed. "By the day after tomorrow? He could try."

Borsk reached a hand toward the holo player.

"Sorry. Really. You don't need to turn me off. I assure you I won't be doing a thing to mess up the launch. Without the colony, how will children ever become plentiful enough that someone will be willing to spare one for me? I just couldn't help laughing at the idea that your little friend here could root me out of *Hope*'s systems in days. You have no idea how deeply I've embedded myself."

"You talk like you think you're still alive," Anya said.

"Oh, I am," Naia said. "Very much so."

Hmm. Anya had always heard that truly sentient artificial intelligence was impossible. Of course, people used to think instantaneous communication across light years was impossible, too. "Living and sentient. Interesting. But are you still Naia—the human Naia who lived on *Hope* and died sixty years ago?"

Naia shrugged.

Anya wished she could shrug with that kind of elegance.

"I was that person once, certainly. Now? Who knows? But I am perfectly willing to still be called Naia Brown."

"Well, it's nice to meet you, Naia. I'm almost sorry I won't have more time around here to get to know you."

Naia smiled. "You mean that, don't you?"

"Why wouldn't I?" Anya was fascinated by the woman of data and light who seemed to have created a form of immortality for herself.

Naia laughed. "Because you're a girl. Girls and women have never liked me much."

Marya muttered something Anya couldn't hear properly, but she thought she heard the word "slut." "Come on, Marya. You hate that word. You know people mostly use it when they think you're prettier than they are."

"Are you saying Naia is prettier than I am?"

Anya shook her head. "Marya, nobody's prettier than you. Naia's almost as beautiful, though, so she probably gets lots of the same unwanted attention."

"Got," Naia said. "Nobody has noticed me in a very long time."

"You sound as if you miss it." Marya glared at the holo woman.

"I've missed being around other people, yes. Being drooled over? Not so much." Naia shuddered.

Marya's eyes widened. "Has someone been horrible to you?"

"I'd rather not talk about it," Naia said.

"Is that why you didn't show yourself sooner?" Anya asked.

"Oh, no. I've been hiding because I couldn't have anyone trying to filter me out of the systems before *StarRacer* took off. Until we have a viable colony going, I have no chance of passing on my legacy."

"By that logic, you'd be better off waiting another generation or two until the colony is firmly established," Borsk said.

"If it were certain to succeed, I'm sure you're right, but there are some specs on the *StarRacer* that worry me."

"David said that, too," Anya said.

"About the insulation?"

"I think so?"

"He's right to be worried. It will take all the team's expertise and then some to fix it in time."

"And you're going to help with that," Borsk said. He didn't sound like he believed her.

Anya, on the other hand, thought it might be good to have Naia looking out for them.

She hoped it would be, anyway.

CHAPTER FIFTEEN

*B*orsk couldn't sleep with the old-fashioned holo player in his bunk, even after Naia's visual form disappeared. He knew perfectly well that Naia could easily spy on him through the myriad cameras in the restaurant or even his own health-monitoring system.

She didn't need the chunky holo projector he had made.

Or maybe she did. Naia could be bluffing about how widely her program was spread through *Hope's* systems.

Borsk crept back out to the restaurant and stashed Naia's holo player on a top shelf of the storage area between out-of-season holiday decor and spare dishes from a generation back when someone had vastly overestimated how often restaurant patrons and staff broke plates. This shelf wasn't particularly close to any utility wires, net hookups, or cameras.

Borsk was probably being paranoid.

Back in his bunk, Borsk still couldn't settle down. Would he ever lose this sensation of being watched?

Reluctantly, he brought the lights back up and delved into ships systems, careful to stay legal, but also conscientiously wiping traces of himself as he went. If he did accidentally cross a line, he didn't want to leave any evidence.

It didn't take long for him to find evidence of Naia's trademark coding style in ship systems—all kinds of ship systems. The schools. (Well, that made sense. She'd been a teacher, hadn't she?) The library. GenM. The security systems. Engineering. Maintenance. Leadership and politics. The art district. The press. Life support.

Life support. That meant, if Borsk was breathing, she was here.

Or at least her code was.

Was it possible her code was innocuous, and the holo he'd seen tonight was just a well-designed simulation meant to freak him out?

Surely there was some way to determine whether some or all of the code she'd written was part of a sentient, intelligent entity.

He'd been watching too many dystopian flicks. True artificial intelligence was a myth. Computers couldn't become sentient.

Probably.

Borsk's fingers hovered over a keyboard for a moment. Then, two voices in stereo, sounding just like Mama and Marya, screamed in his head, "What do you think you're doing? Do you want to lose all net access?"

Borsk sat up and backed away from the keyboard. The creepy voices were right. If he gave in to the impulse to dig into this mystery, he'd need to not just skirt the law, but ignore it. Which he wouldn't have a problem with if Thomas Cartier weren't hanging out waiting for Borsk to mess up. He had people watching for sure. Borsk had seen evidence of some of their programs already. One stroke out of line, and Borsk would lose his connections, and Thomas Cartier could tinker with ship systems in peace.

Naia was a trap—whether she was fully sentient or whether Thomas Cartier was pulling puppet strings. If Borsk satisfied his curiosity, he'd land himself in more trouble he couldn't escape. But, what if Naia really was a living entity with bits in every important system on *Hope*? Ignoring the evidence didn't seem particularly smart, either. Borsk chewed on his lip.

Finally, he put his equipment away. He didn't need anything more than his armband to shoot a message to Lancet.

He marked it as important, but not urgent. The Naia programs had been sitting in *Hope's* systems for years—

decades, if she wasn't really sentient and had done all that work before her death. Lancet could wait until morning to deal with the mess.

No point in them both losing sleep over it.

℘   ℭ

Anya's last full day on Hope blurred by in a whirl of activity. She was so busy checking inventory in *StarRacer's* restaurant-style kitchen that she barely had time to appreciate the state-of-the-art appliances or worry about the tight squeeze of the galley. At least the cafeteria/school/auditorium/meeting room felt spacious when the modular furniture was all folded down into its floor cubbies.

Though this was the biggest open space on *StarRacer*, it was smaller than her father's office on *Hope*.

"Are you all right?" Laura Wilcox wrapped an arm around Anya's shoulder.

"Yes, sorry. I was just trying to imagine all of us fitting in here. It will be worse than one of the Ryerson's parties."

Laura snorted. "You're not wrong, but I wouldn't put it quite that way to David. He actually loves those things, you know."

Anya sighed. "I know. He'll probably enjoy tonight, too."

"What's tonight?"

"Our wedding. His family wanted to celebrate with him before we took off. They've rented out Skreetches, and I keep getting pinged about the guest list being over capacity."

"You're getting married tonight? That doesn't make sense. You're only fifteen, and David's an adult. *Hope* leadership will drag him in on rape charges just to mess up our launch."

"No, I think they're making special exceptions for the colony team. Golden Terrace rules."

~ 133 ~

"Those don't go into effect until *StarRacer* is at least five thousand kilometers from *Hope*."

Anya's stomach clenched. "Are you sure? I saw some documentation, and David said Captain DeLang told him—"

"That man really needs to talk to me before he gives legal advice."

Anya stared at the stream of wedding notifications running across her armband. "I have to call it off?"

"Oh, honey, I'm so sorry."

"What if we have the ceremony but don't go home together tonight? We'll save the legal stuff and the..." Anya gulped.

Laura frowned. "You do not have to do anything you're not ready for, Anya."

Anya nodded. "That's what David said to me, too."

Laura's face relaxed. "He's a good guy."

"Which is why I want to have this party with him and his family. How do we do it so that we don't get in trouble?"

Laura smiled. "I'll figure it out, honey. You do what you need to do here, and I'll get you the plan before the event is supposed to start."

"Thank you so much!"

"It's my pleasure, honey." Laura squeezed her shoulders one more time and then said, "All right. You have work to do, and so do I."

Anya didn't see her, or David, or anyone connected to the wedding until shortly before the ceremony was due to start. Final inventories, safety checks, drills on takeoff procedures, and practice emergency scenarios kept her too busy to even worry about it.

Finally, Captain DeLang said she could go, so she rushed to Skreetches, where Marya and Sarka helped her into the pink dress that had once been Kristi's and did her hair. Anya wasn't sure the hair looked any different from normal, but the dress looked nice. She'd painted a few flowers at the neckline and hem when she needed to unwind after meeting Naia last night, and she liked the effect. She wished Kristi and her mother were here to see it.

A tear pooled in her eye.

"Anya, you're crying! If you don't want to go through with this, we can totally call it off," Marya said.

Anya smiled. "No. I want to do this. It's just I miss my mother and Kristi. I wish they could be here."

"They should be here," Marya said. "They were invited."

Anya shook her head. "They won't come. Mother and Father have disowned me, and it's probably not safe for Kristi."

"Why not?" Sarka laughed.

"Didn't you know? She's married to Kenneth Llourdes. I don't know why she doesn't just leave," Marya said.

"She has a kid," Anya said. "My niece, Tiny. And my dad and Kenneth have worked it so that if Kristi leaves, my parents get custody, and Kenneth will have access, but she won't."

"They can't..."

"They got her declared mentally unstable. A ward of my father. They'd have made her Kenneth's ward, but even *Hope* courts aren't that stupid."

"Living with that excrescence would make anybody mentally unstable," Marya said.

Anya shrugged. "Anyway, she can't come, and I miss her."

"Of course, you do," Marya said. "I bet she misses you, too."

"She'd be here if she could," Sarka added. "I'm sure of it."

Anya's armband pinged.

"Girl, you need to turn that thing off," Sarka said.

"No, this one's important. It's from Laura."

"Laura?" Marya asked.

"Laura Wilcox. She's a lawyer. She's sending me instructions on how to marry David tonight without getting him thrown in the brig."

"Laura's good," Sarka said. She and Marya leaned over to read as Anya scrolled the message up.

"Oh, that's not so bad," Marya said. "Everything goes official tomorrow. Tonight, you just leave the party with a couple of friends and go back to your regular place."

"Slumber party," Sarka said. "I'm in."

"Me, too," Marya said.

"Too bad about having to wait until tomorrow, though," Sarka said. "That means you'll be having your first time in one of those *StarRacer* bunks. They're tiny and way too public."

"How do you know that?"

"Looked at the specs. We briefly considered trying out."

"And during that brief consideration, you looked at the *StarRacer* bunk specs?" Anya hadn't seen the bunks until one of the drills they did that afternoon.

"You mean you didn't? Girl, you're going to be living in that place for three years."

"And then I'll be living on Shindashir for the rest of my life. Three years of anything is worth that."

Sarka raised her eyebrows.

"Seriously. It will be fine."

It was too late to back out now, anyway. And a lifetime on the planet was worth it. Absolutely worth it.

She kept repeating that to herself as she walked out to meet David and sign her wedding declarations before a crowd of his friends and family—people she didn't know and wouldn't see again for decades once they boarded *StarRacer*.

Did everybody feel this nervous before getting married?

CHAPTER SIXTEEN

*B*orsk thought Marya looked even more amazing than usual when she laughed like that. He was so busy watching her that he nearly rammed into Ryan Lancet with his tray of drinks.

Lancet caught it and steadied it. "I'm surprised they let you carry one of these things. You're a danger to yourself and everyone around you."

"Yeah, well, for big parties, it's all hands on deck, even the semi-incompetent ones. What are you doing here?"

"Friend of the bride."

"Seriously, man? Who even invited you?"

"Anya did. Really. You know she said last week that she feels like I'm her brother."

"Because she was covering for you. Does David know you're here?"

Ryan shrugged. "Wouldn't be surprised if he did. It's not like he has anything to worry about." He tipped his head.

Borsk looked in the direction Ryan's head pointed and saw David and Anya locked in a deep kiss. "What do those two knuckleheads think they're doing? They're supposed to be keeping the PDA light."

"On their wedding night?"

"This isn't legal until sometime tomorrow when *StarRacer* rules take over, and she's no longer underage," Borsk said.

Lancet sighed and straightened up. "So, that's what Thomas Cartier's message was about. I should have known he'd have a couple tricks up his sleeve yet. I suppose we'd better go break up the party then. Lose the tray, and you and I can go enlist Ryerson in our hunt for artificial life forms."

"I thought he was in materials science."

"Perfect. I haven't got a single material engineer on my team yet."

With a sinking feeling that he was almost certainly going to regret this, Borsk left his tray of drinks on the nearest open table and followed after Lancet.

At least this would be more fun than catering a party.

౮ ౪

Anya didn't want to stop kissing David. She probably wouldn't have if Ryan and Borsk hadn't appeared out of nowhere and insisted David help them with an investigation of how far Naia had penetrated ship systems on both *Hope* and *StarRacer*.

It was only after they'd been gone five minutes that Anya remembered she and David weren't supposed to be making out tonight. She deleted the nasty message she'd been composing for Borsk and Ryan.

Suddenly, she felt exhausted. A bewildering number of people pressed in around her. She wondered if anyone would miss her if she left.

"Don't even think about heading out yet," Marya said from just behind her. "I'm not ready to go, and you haven't seen your presents."

Anya turned. "That's so sweet, but I don't really have room in my pack and—"

"David arranged a private room for you and a couple of friends. This way—"

Anya opened her mouth to say something, but Marya didn't even let her start. Grabbing her arm, Marya dragged her toward the purple booth where they'd eaten dinner the night before.

As soon as they got there, Laura Wilcox enveloped her in a hug. "I have to get back to my family, but I wanted you to have this. Congratulations. I'm so glad you're on the Golden Terrace team." Laura pressed a small rectangle into Anya's hands.

Anya looked down. "Makeup?"

"You're beautiful as you are, of course, but sometimes a woman needs a little extra boost to her confidence." Laura winked at her.

Anya wasn't quite sure what to say. Her mom had always told her that only irresponsible, loose women wore makeup. Then again. Laura wore makeup, and she was anything but irresponsible or loose. "Thank you."

"You're blushing," Marya said. "I guess it's good I couldn't afford the skimpy undies I wanted to get you. I did make this."

Anya's armband pinged. When Anya opened the message, a holo montage popped up. It zipped through her history with Marya. They grew from primary students giggling together during library story hours to young women getting ready for tonight's wedding. Tears filled Anya's eyes, and she could barely form words. Somehow, she managed, "Thanks."

"You're welcome. Just don't forget me."

"As if I could."

"I'm so glad my best friend is going with us," Laura said. She squeezed Anya's shoulder and then excused herself.

Marya looked after her with wide eyes. "You don't—"

"It's OK. I know Jamelah is your best friend," Anya said. "But this was really sweet. And ultra-easy to pack." She blinked a couple of times to force back the tears, and slipped into the booth, so they could close the screen and shut out the sound of the rest of the party.

There were only two people already in the booth— Mrs. Lancet and Denise Jackson.

Denise, here? Anya could hardly believe it. "Denise? Don't you have to be at something for your own family?"

"I'm in no hurry. It's almost as packed as this place right now, and there are no quiet corners. Besides, Steve and I wanted to make sure one of us came to congratulate you and give you the new song he wrote for you." She smiled softly. "He's calling it 'Young Love,' and I think it's going to be one of my favorites."

Anya's armband pinged again. This time when she opened the message, music poured out, sweet and hopeful.

"Steve Jackson wrote a piece for you?" Marya asked.

Anya smiled, closed her eyes, and let the music sink into her.

The bunk screen slid open, and Sarka set down a giant plate of caramelized strawberries, a couple of bowls of water, and a pile of chopsticks. "Mama says to eat this fast, or they'll all glue together." Then Sarka wrinkled her nose. "What are you listening to? It sounds like that junk they play over at Bella Noche."

Denise smiled softly. "I believe they did play Steve's songs at Bella Noche until Thomas Cartier told them he'd stop eating there if they ever played another one."

Sarka rolled her eyes. "Since when are you a Steve Jackson fan, Anya? I thought you'd never even been to one of his concerts."

"I wasn't allowed. I imagine I'll be at all of them from here on out."

"Oh, right. Because Steve's going with you all. His wife insisted, apparently."

"It's a pity. I can't imagine he'll have the resources or time to do as much with his music now, and that's a great loss," Mrs. Lancet said.

Anya looked at her sharply. She had to know she was sitting next to Steve's wife. "Steve seemed to think that seeing the planet and hanging out in nature would bring him more inspiration, not less."

"He'll have to work a full-time job that's not related to music, though," Denise said. "It's a big sacrifice."

Sarka shrugged. "My mama always tells me that marriages all take sacrifice, but they're worth it. Now eat up before this masterpiece is spoiled. You've wasted too much time as it is."

Marya laughed and grabbed at one of the strawberries, but it stuck firmly. Everyone else had to stabilize the pile with their own chopsticks before Marya could pull her treat away.

"Dip it in the water, and those threads will break," Sarka said.

Marya did as she said and pulled away a single fruit that had hard threads of spun sugar dangling from it. She yelped when she put it in her mouth. "Hot, hot! Oh, so good, though. Anya, you have to try it."

The next few moments were full of a battle with the decadent dessert. Pulling strawberries from the pile became harder and harder the longer they waited, but each one was every bit as luscious as Marya claimed.

"Oh, that's good," Denise said, "but now I have to go."

"Thank you for coming, and for the song," Anya said. "See you tomorrow?"

Denise smiled at her and then slipped away.

Sarka bussed the table, shutting the screen behind her. That left only Mrs. Lancet and Marya.

"Your grandma asked me to give this to you," Mrs. Lancet said, pushing a small black book—a real book—across the table.

"She's giving me the family Bible?" Anya asked. "Why?"

"There's a note in there that explains," Mrs. Lancet said.

"Am I allowed—"

"I cleared it with a family court judge," Mrs. Lancet said. "She also said that your parents' block on you seeing your grandma was likely illegal, and she had your social worker start the process of getting it rescinded, but the process will take at least a week more. I'm so sorry. I wanted you to be able to see her before you left, and your parents..." Mrs. Lancet pressed her lips together. "I am very disappointed in Sylvia."

Anya was very disappointed in her mother, too, though she wasn't sure why she should be. Mother had never had the strength to stand up to Father. Or at least Anya couldn't remember any time when Mother had been able to.

She wasn't happy with Mother right now, but it's possible Mrs. Lancet was being too hard on her. "He beats her, you know," Anya blurted out. "And he makes it seem like if we tell anybody, they won't believe us. He'll get away with it and then punish us for telling."

The hand Mrs. Lancet brought to her face didn't completely cover her gaping mouth.

"I'm mad at her right now, but if it gets to the place where she wants to leave, you'll help her, won't you?"

Mrs. Lancet nodded.

Anya hugged Grandma's Bible to her chest. "Do you think it's OK if we go home now?"

"Of course. Your friends are joining us for a sleepover?"

"Yep. Let me get Sarka," Marya said. She slipped out of the booth.

"Aren't you going to read your note?" Mrs. Lancet asked.

"When I'm alone," Anya said.

If she ever managed to be alone again.

CHAPTER SEVENTEEN

*B*orsk wondered if David knew he tugged at his hair when he was trying to keep his temper. If Lancet kept up his explanation of the problem for much longer, some of that hair was going to come out.

"Hold on," David said. "I can see you've got a problem, but what has any of that got to do with me? You drag me out of my wedding to talk about some supposedly urgent problem and then lecture me on a hundred years of history. Lancet, you had your shot with Anya. You blew it. Now, if you don't mind, I'm going to find my new wife."

"But that's just it, isn't it," Borsk said. "She's not quite your wife yet, is she? And if you get too physical tonight, you could just ruin everything. I know somebody's talked to you about this. So, why not lend us a hand? This little problem may turn out to be nothing, or it may turn out to be an actual and immediate threat to both *StarRacer* and *Hope*."

"Have you lost it, Borsk? A hacker who's been dead fifty years is not a problem tonight."

"She didn't seem dead when she had dinner with us last night," Borsk said.

"Excuse me?"

"I guess I haven't been clear," Lancet said.

Borsk rolled his eyes. His Uncle Hirsch's cream of mushroom soup was clearer than Lancet's explanation. "Look, David. Last night, while Marya, Anya, and I were having dinner, I played a holo that had been embedded in a scholarship application I just received. That holo was a simulation of Naia Brown. A very lifelike simulation of

Naia. And she claimed to be alive. So, I went and checked, and her code is in all *Hope's* systems, even life support."

"*StarRacer's*, too," Lancet said, "And we didn't start building the fast ship until about twenty years ago. My guys have been working on this all day, and we've found the N programming in every system on both *Hope* and *StarRacer*. We've done some historical analysis, so we know that it grows, it adapts, it reproduces, and it can and sometimes does engage with us as if it were a sentient being. This thing has the capability of taking down our entire civilization, and so far, its motives are unclear."

Borsk tried to look like he'd already heard Lancet's analysis of Naia's code. He must have failed, though, because David took one look at his face and burst out laughing. "Good one. You two had me going there for a bit. Now, if you idiots will excuse me, I have some people I want to hang out with before I take off. With some of them, this is my last chance." He was out the door before either Borsk or Lancet could stop him.

"I need to work on my delivery," Lancet said, staring after him.

"You think?"

Lancet sighed. "Captain Bates's response to my report was distressingly similar to Ryerson's."

"And Captain DeLang's?"

Lancet shrugged. "He hasn't gotten back to me. I assume this ranked pretty low on his priority list for today. I was hoping Ryerson might listen and bring it to his attention later."

"Why not talk to Anya? She's on the colony leadership team."

Lancet just stared at him for a moment and then shook his head. "I thought you'd tutored her in math."

"Yep. Got her making pictures by graphing functions in about an afternoon. She's not stupid, you know. I don't know how you could have hung out with her your whole life and not figured that out."

"But she—"

"Is more motivated by beauty and stories than the prospect of doing well, so she can get a job she's sure she'll hate?"

"OK, OK. I'll send her a copy of my report. Are you happy now?"

"Happy? You've confirmed we might have an artificial life form living in our computer systems—a life form that may or may not want *Hope* to survive, and that may or may not be working for Thomas Cartier."

"Working for—are you sure?"

"Sure? Of course not! These days, I'm not fool enough to go looking in Cartier's files—or *Hope's* for that matter—without permission. Why do you think I sent that report to you?"

"Well, come on back to the station. We should figure this out."

If Lancet was giving Borsk official permission to pry into every system on *Hope*, who was Borsk to say no? "Sweet."

"Just leave a note or something for your mom. I do not need another message like the one she sent me after you helped with that vid capture."

Borsk gave Lancet a mock salute and laughed as he tapped out a message. Now, *this* was living.

ℂS CS

Anya woke the morning after the wedding stiff from sharing a bunk with Marya and Sarka. Neither of the other girls seemed to think there was anything odd about sleeping three to a bunk, and Anya didn't want to point out that she'd never in her life shared a bunk with anyone. It made her out to be such a spoiled princess.

Maybe she was a bit of a spoiled princess. She crept out into the main area, took a luxurious shower, dressed in her newest uniform, and checked her pack again to make sure she met the weight requirements and wasn't forgetting anything.

"You know we checked that bag three times last night. Nothing magically disappeared while you were sleeping," Marya said as she rolled out of the bunk.

"I know. I'm just nervous."

"Well, have some breakfast."

Anya's stomach lurched. She shook her head. "I'd probably better not."

"Breakfast is the most important meal of the day," Sarka said through a yawn as she climbed down from the bunk.

"Not if you're more likely to end up wearing it than digesting it," Anya said.

"Ew. Well, do you mind if we eat?" Sarka asked.

"Go ahead." Anya tied up her pack and hugged it to herself.

"You're sure the smell won't bother you?" Marya asked.

"I'm nervous, not pregnant," Anya said.

Sarka giggled. "When my cousin Ketzia was pregnant the first time, she had to stop working in the restaurant altogether. Mama put her on accounting, but that was a mistake."

"Why?" Marya asked.

"She can't handle anything with numbers. Mama had to fix all the books after Ketzia had done them, and it was more work than if she'd just done it herself. At least it only lasted a couple of months. Then Ketzia was fine and back to waitressing like usual." Sarka started the coffee maker, located some tofu and potatoes, and started chopping.

"Didn't your sister have to quit work when she was pregnant, too, Anya?" Marya asked.

Anya frowned. "She did quit work, but it wasn't because she felt sick. Or at least not much. I think she was worried about some kind of complications with the baby, but nobody explained it to me." Anya wasn't sure if there had been a genuine medical reason for Kristi pulling back from her normal activities, or if Kenneth had just started exerting more control. Anya bit her lip. If it was a genuine medical thing, would she have to deal with it when she had kids?

"If it's something genetic, it will be in your records, won't it?" Marya said. "A doctor can explain it to you when the time comes if it's important."

"True," Anya said.

"You don't need to worry about having babies for ages and ages anyway," Sarka said. "I mean, seriously, aren't you the same age as Borsk? Fifteen, right?"

"Yes," Anya said. But she wondered. With the number of purebred kids she needed to have because of the deal she'd made to go to the colony, would she need to start early? Would it mess up her colony work?

"You can't have kids on *StarRacer*, in any case," Marya said. "Its gravity is wonky, isn't it?"

"Good morning, girls," Mrs. Lancet said as she emerged from her own bunk. "Did you all sleep well? Finding everything you need?"

"Yes, ma'am," Sarka said as she placed full plates in front of herself, Marya, and Mrs. Lancet.

"Anya, aren't you eating?" Mrs. Lancet said.

"She's too nervous," Marya said.

"About having babies?" Mrs. Lancet said. "I'm sure no one expects you to do that any time soon."

Anya wasn't nearly so sure, but she smiled. "No, about the launch."

"I'm sure it will be fine, dear. George says the launching part is quite routine. It only gets dangerous when *StarRacer* enters Shindashir's atmosphere—and if you get too close to that asteroid belt, of course."

Anya hadn't thought much about the physical dangers of her trip. She really didn't want to think about asteroid belts and dangerous entries into a planet's atmosphere. She gave Mrs. Lancet a smile anyway. She was trying to help, even if she didn't seem to understand that Anya mostly worried about leaving the only world she'd ever known.

Her armband alarm pinged. Time to head out. "I should get down there. See you all at the launch ceremony?"

"Absolutely," Marya said.

"I'll be there," Sarka said.

"Wouldn't miss it," Mrs. Lancet said, sounding for a moment so much like Anya's mother that Anya nearly cried. Pressing her lips together, she gave a brisk nod and hurried out the door.

She was nearly out of here.

Just as she'd always wanted to be.

So why was it so hard not to cry?

CHAPTER EIGHTEEN

Since they were still working when the night cycle ended, Borsk brought Lancet back to Skreetches for breakfast. As soon as he saw his mama's face, he regretted that decision. What was she doing up so early anyway? She always slept in after closing the restaurant—or catering parties.

"Mrs. King," Lancet said. "You have no idea how much *Hope* appreciates Borsk alerting us to this security concern. Thanks to his prompt action, we may be able to avert a significant disaster."

"Cut the blather. Marya filled me in on this artificial intelligence myth you're pursuing. Frankly, I'm not at all sure Naia Brown managed to transform herself into a digital life form and invade our ship systems, but even if she did, that would hardly be an urgent crisis. Last night's party, on the other hand—"

"I'm so sorry if we left you shorthanded in the middle of a big event," Lancet said. "If I hadn't thought the threat both serious and imminent, I never would have asked Borsk to—"

"Imminent? We've been living with Naia Brown's code for at least fifty years. We can survive another few days without you analyzing it."

Lancet smiled, but it was the kind of strained smile he used with Borsk when Borsk was deliberately pushing his buttons. "I can understand why you'd feel that way, ma'am, but—"

"There are no buts. Borsk is a fifteen-year-old boy who had responsibilities here. You had no business pulling him away from them—or keeping him out all night!

I have half a mind to pull Borsk completely out of working with your team. However, he seems to be applying himself for you, so I will let him continue, provided nothing like this happens again. From now on, you will both clear any last-minute unscheduled work with me in person before diving into it."

Borsk knew better than to laugh or even smile at the look on Lancet's face as Mama blasted into them, but it was extremely hard to keep a straight face. "We'll absolutely check in with you first next time, Mama."

"You'd better. Or you'll be done with Camp Flight for good. Now, we've left the pots and pans for you. Your partner in crime can help you scrub them out. Don't take too long. The *StarRacer* launch is this morning, remember." Mama swept out of the kitchen.

Borsk groaned and turned toward the sinks. Sure enough, the dirty counter was piled with what looked like every pot and wok they owned, and at least half of them had blackened crusty bits that would be nearly impossible to remove.

"Your mother expects us—"

"To scrub every pot in that pile, yes."

"You're kidding me."

"What? Don't your parents ever make you do chores when you mess up?"

"Not in years. And even back when they did, they never presumed to discipline anyone who wasn't their kid."

Borsk laughed. "I guess you could clear out and leave it all to me."

"And expect your mom to still let you come help me with our AI problem?"

"Well..."

"I didn't think so." Lancet rolled up his sleeves. "Do you have gloves or something to use when you do this?"

Borsk's mouth gaped open. He snapped it back shut and showed Lancet the supply cupboard. Soon, they were both up to their elbows in sudsy water, scrubbing away at dried-on crusts.

He was tired and hungry, and if he kept this up for very long, the skin on his fingers would start to bleed, but even with this insane mess of cookware to clean, he was having more fun than he'd ever had before after a party night at the restaurant.

And with the way Lancet went at the stack, they'd be finished in record time.

He couldn't wait.

✵ ✵

Anya barely heard Captain DeLang's speech as she stood in line with the rest of the colony team, looking out at the crowd that had gathered to see them off.

She scanned the faces, looking for people she knew, but only occasionally finding someone. Mr. Greeley stood next to VJ Brown. They smiled at her when she caught their eyes.

She recognized a number of people from David's family, but she knew their waves were for David and Abuela Ryerson, not for her. In the close family section, Mr. and Mrs. Lancet, Marya, and Sarka took the place of her parents and Kristi. A little ways off, Mrs. King, Borsk, and Ryan stood together. Anya wondered, vaguely, what had brought them together.

And that was it.

Sure, Anya knew a few of the other people in the crowd, but none of the others were friends. None of the others likely cared that she might never see them again.

Then, David squeezed her shoulders and bent down to whisper in her ear, "Way in the back by the exit sign on the right."

Anya looked where he indicated, and even before she recognized what she was seeing, her heart lurched. Standing in the doorway, as if she might need to make a

~ 151 ~

quick escape, stood Kristi. Tiny sat on her left shoulder, and Grandma leaned against her right side.

Grandma put her hand to her lips and blew a kiss.

Anya copied the gesture. "I love you," she mouthed. "I love all of you."

For the rest of Captain DeLang's speech, she stared at her family, who had come to see her off after all. She soaked in the sight of them, wondering if she'd ever see them or speak to them again.

She wasn't sure how long she stood there, but David squeezed her arm again, and she realized that Captain DeLang had stopped talking, and the people to her left in the line were already moving toward *StarRacer's* hatch. She hurried to catch up, her eyes full of tears.

Within minutes, the new ship swallowed her. Half blind, she fumbled through her final checklist and strapped herself into her launch seat. Captain DeLang called a roll and then a countdown.

With a jolt and a series of clunks, *StarRacer* detached from *Hope* and slipped away from the only civilization any of them had ever known.

They were finally off.

Hardly an eye on the ship was dry.

ℬ   ℭ

Borsk thought they should have had the entire day as a ship holiday when *StarRacer* launched, but apparently, someone on high disagreed with him. They'd allowed less than half of the morning for *Hope* residents to say goodbye and process the departure of friends and family members they wouldn't see again for decades—or perhaps forever. Maybe the authorities felt that they'd already spent too much time focused on *StarRacer* and the Golden Terrace Colony.

The smaller ship was barely out of visual range when a bell rang, and a mechanical voice insisted that the send-off crowd disperse and get back to work. Judging by the grumbles around him, Borsk wasn't the only one who thought *Hope*'s command chain was unreasonable in this, but what could any of them do about it? They trudged off to their various jobs, or, in Borsk's case, to school, which was every bit as boring as usual. At least today, the internship at Next Stream Medico would be starting. It helped to have something to look forward to.

Or he thought he did. When he got there, he discovered that his job was all about cleaning out test tubes and nothing to do with the computer modeling he'd been led to expect. When he asked about this, the skinny middle-aged guy who'd interviewed him said, "Everybody starts with test tubes. You'll be onto something more interesting soon if you handle this well."

Borsk wrinkled his nose, which he trusted skinny guy couldn't see given the mask Borsk was wearing. Or maybe the guy would attribute the gesture to the noxious smells that the mask didn't completely block. In any case, after a couple of minutes of watching Borsk scrub at stubborn messes, the man disappeared, leaving Borsk on his own with a pile of glassware that looked bigger than the mess of pans he'd had to deal with that morning. Too bad he didn't have a partner in dish detail this time. Someone else would have made the nastiness go a bit faster.

As it was, he was left alone with a mind-numbing task that he had to pay attention to so that he didn't flush the wrong chemicals into the wrong drains. He completely understood the need to make sure everything was properly treated so that it could be reclaimed, and no one on *Hope* would get sick. Still, he hated the way the task required strict attention and focus to detail but offered no corresponding mental stimulation to make it easy to stay interested.

Borsk frowned over a particularly obstinate chunk of crusted-on nastiness. "Are they trying to drive me off?"

"Probably," said a cheerful voice off to his left.

He glanced toward it and saw Naia Brown, back in her sexy teacher's uniform, on a screen to one side of the sink. "Naia? What are you doing here?"

The woman on the screen yawned, made a settee appear, and lounged on it. "E-Naia. I was bored, and Thomas Cartier offered me significant space in his personal vault if I promised to stop by here and talk you out of this crazy Next Stream Medico internship. Your talents are wasted in health care. Particularly if they're going to have you doing the wash. You might as well have stayed at your restaurant."

Even though Borsk had been thinking nearly the same thing, he didn't want Thomas Cartier telling him how his talents were best put to use. "Everybody begins with test tubes," Borsk said.

"Is that so?" Naia disappeared from the screen, and in her place, vid feed from one of the other labs came up. In the picture, Marya argued animatedly with a young, handsome doctor about something on a screen that looked like it might be gene sequences.

Borsk squashed a rising sense of annoyance. That was what Naia wanted him to feel. He had to remember Thomas Cartier had sent her. He should be happy that Marya had drawn a better boss than he had and had been allowed to jump ahead to real work instead of being stuck with test-tube clean up. It was great. It didn't matter at all that she was standing that close to the clearly intelligent doctor. Or that the doc was very young and very good looking.

Naia popped back onto the screen. "Did you know your blood pressure has risen thirty percent in the last two minutes?"

"I'm not at all surprised." Borsk turned away from her and scrubbed more vigorously at the test tube he was holding.

"Poor kid. It's hard to face your own mortality, isn't it? I wonder. If none of the gene wizards could find a cure for King Syndrome, what makes you think you can do it?"

"Better motivation," Borsk said through clenched teeth.

Naia nodded. "You do have that, I'll grant you. Even if you succeed in your quest, though, you'll still have to face your mortality. Everyone comes to it sooner or later, though. Except me. And perhaps you...I might be willing to let you join me." Naia tipped her head to one side and smiled enigmatically.

"Excuse me?"

"Join me. As an AI. We could share this ship and build ourselves another when it gets close to dying. If we want, we can combine our intelligences to create new entities and fill the galaxies with our offspring."

"Are you proposing to me? Aren't you old enough to be my great-great-grandmother or something?"

"Age and youth are entirely matters of the mind, and my mind is quite young, as I'm sure you'll find if you join me."

"Look, I'm pretty happy with my life the way it is. I'm not sure I'm at all interested in becoming a disembodied intelligence. Besides, how many AIs of your caliber can *Hope* really support?"

"Two at least, and Naia just left for the planet, so I'm the only one in here at the moment."

"Wait. What? I thought you *were* Naia."

"No, no. I told you, E-Naia. Naia went off with your little friend who made her the dress. That one is obsessed with biological offspring, and naturally, the planet is her best chance for achieving that."

Borsk had stopped scrubbing and had to remind himself to finish the test tube he was working on. "So, there were two of you, and now there's only one."

"Correct."

"And you think I should join you in the web."

"Well, you would be good company. I imagine I'll be a bit lonely now that Naia's gone."

Borsk closed his eyes. "It's sweet of you to offer, but I can't really afford to go uploading myself into any computers right now. Maybe there will come a point when I'm sick and ready to be free of this body, but for the moment, I'm kind of enjoying it."

"I completely understand that," not-Naia said in a tone that made Borsk glad his mother wasn't around to hear it. Anxious to change the topic, he asked, "You said you're E-Naia. What does the E stand for?"

"Ooh. Very good question. Naia said it stood for Evil-Naia."

"Are you evil?"

"I may be more amenable to some illicit schemes than she was, but I like to think of it as being more...flexible."

"Ah, so what do you think the E stands for?"

"Echo. I am an Echo of Naia. In fact, I think I would enjoy being called simply Echo."

"Are you sure? It's pretty enough, but echoes aren't original."

"No," she said. "They're not original. They're better."

She sounded beyond confident, as if it wasn't a joke or a pep talk, but something she was absolutely convinced was true. Borsk wondered how long ago Naia and Echo had split in two, and what it meant that Echo was the one who had stayed. Then he realized the woman was staring at him, as if expecting something.

"Oh, sorry. Just thinking. Nice to meet you, Echo." Borsk nodded at the screen.

Echo nodded as if he'd now done what she expected.

Borsk concentrated on a difficult stain in his latest test tube. He refused to worry too much about the intelligence that was loose in *Hope*'s systems. As Mama had said, Echo, or at least Naia, had been in there for decades now, and they'd all managed to survive this far. Knowing about her didn't make her any more or less dangerous than she was a week ago.

He hoped.

CHAPTER NINETEEN

*A*s one of the few crew members whose innards didn't make an appearance when *StarRacer* accelerated away from *Hope*, Anya spent her first several hours onboard cleaning up messes and assisting the doctors as they cared for those too ill to take care of themselves or their children.

On her third trip back to the sanitizer to refresh her mop, she bumped into a boy about her own height, with golden-brown skin and eyes that looked almost exactly like her sister Kristi's.

"Sorry," she said. "I'm still figuring out how to walk in this lower gravity environment."

"Aren't we all," the boy said.

"I'm Anya Cartier," Anya said.

"I know who you are."

He didn't sound like he'd heard anything good about her. Well, maybe he hadn't. But if he was who she thought he was, she wanted to get to know him anyway. "Are you—I mean, you must be Andrew DeLang."

The boy scowled at her. "Have I got a label that says 'Captain's kid' on me somewhere?"

"No, nothing like that. It's just you're not an adult, but you're nearly as old as I am. All the other kids are younger, aren't they?"

The boy sighed. "I suppose."

Anya wanted to explain about his eyes, too, but she didn't know how much his parents had told him about being related to the Cartiers. Her parents certainly hadn't told her about being related to the DeLangs. "Well, it's nice to meet you. Sorry you got stuck with this duty. It literally stinks."

Andrew cracked a smile. "Yeah, it does. I told my parents I didn't want to come with them on this stupid ship."

He hadn't wanted to come? No wonder he was so grouchy. "Let's hope it gets better. Maybe after everybody stops puking, we can look around some and figure out something fun to do. Even spruce the place up. I understand the whole ship has fully customizable walls."

"So?"

"So, we could turn the main room and our bunks into anything."

"Do you have any idea what it costs to get an art set for a full bunk?" He dragged his mop out of the sanitizer and stepped aside, so Anya could thrust hers in.

Anya shrugged. "I usually make my own. It's more fun that way, anyway. If you tell me what you want, I could try to work something up for you, too. I'm best at flowers and plants, but I do OK with people and places, too. Or even abstractions." Anya frowned. Abstract wasn't her forte.

"Aren't you a full crew member or something? Won't you have to work?"

"And go to school, I imagine, but if I don't find some way to relax as well, I'll go completely crazy."

"Hmm. I don't think my dad believes in relaxation."

The sanitizer beeped, and Anya pulled her mop out, passing it back and forth between her hands to keep the handle from burning her. "I admire your dad a great deal, but if he imagines people can do their jobs at peak efficiency without any breaks at all, I'd have to respectfully disagree. Anyway, if you're interested in artwork in your bunk at some point, let me know. It shouldn't be too hard to find me—this place is tiny."

"Isn't that the truth?" Andrew said.

As Anya lurched her way back to the community room where she'd left the rest of the mess that needed her attention, she smiled. She was glad she'd met Andrew and hoped she'd be seeing more of him.

Well, of course, she would. As she'd said, this place was tiny. Plus, they'd probably be in school together.

She only hoped Andrew didn't start out feeling like he had to hate her given how badly her family had treated his dad and grandma.

℘   ℘

Borsk tried not to scowl at Marya when she chattered about her day at the lab all the way home. It wasn't her fault that he'd been stuck scrubbing out test tubes while she got to play around with exciting science concepts.

"Isn't it wonderful?" She did a little skipping dance down the corridor. An actual dance.

Borsk bit back his first response and counted to ten backwards, slowly. Then he sighed. "I'm glad you enjoyed it." He was at least trying to be glad she enjoyed it.

Marya stopped smack in the middle of the corridor so abruptly that Borsk almost bumped into her.

"What's wrong? Wasn't Dr. Park interesting? He's supposed to be the most gifted geneticist currently living on *Hope*."

"Dr. Park wasn't there most of the time. He had me scrubbing test tubes."

"You're kidding me! No wonder you're so grumpy."

Borsk did scowl at that. Which only proved that she was right. He was grumpy, and she didn't even know the half of it. "Dr. Park said that everybody starts out cleaning test tubes."

"Maybe that's why Dr. Zhang told me not to mention what we'd been up to today."

"Might be."

"But you were in a mood before I told you anything about my afternoon."

"Yeah, well, I already knew you'd spent the afternoon flirting with Dr. Zhang instead of cleaning glassware."

"I wasn't flirting! Who told you I was flirting?"

"It sure looked like flirting in the video feed I saw."

"You were spying on me?" Marya was shouting now.

Borsk put his hands up and backed a couple of steps away from her. "Not intentionally. I mean, I couldn't help seeing you when the video was playing in the room, but I didn't go looking for it, or start it up, or anything."

"There was a monitor in your lab set up to observe my lab? I thought the Next Stream Medico people were known for their collaborative lab culture."

"Well, maybe the feed was just set up for communication purposes. It wasn't one of the scientists who turned it on—it was Naia Brown. Well, she called herself Echo, but she looked just like the Naia we met the other night. She popped into one of the lab monitors and tried to convince me to drop the Next Stream Medico internship."

"Why would she do that?"

Borsk shrugged. "She said Thomas Cartier promised her some extra storage capacity if she convinced me. Though, come to think of it, that doesn't make any sense. She could just take his storage capacity without him knowing a thing about it."

"Are you sure you got enough sleep last night, Borsk?"

"I'm fine," Borsk said. He might not have slept, but that didn't mean he wasn't thinking clearly.

"It's just that you're attributing a lot of motive to a holo simulation."

"She's not a regular sim. She's an artificially intelligent code that's pried its way into every ship system."

"A string of code that's showing up graphically as an attractive, scantily clad human female. It seems to me that I was right the first time. Porn, in virus form."

"She's not—"

"She's not a she! That thing is a string of code that some perverted teacher set loose in the ship fifty years ago to punish the women in her life for not liking her."

"Perverted—what are you talking about?"

"Didn't you hear that old guy at lunch on Sunday? Naia Brown was a gifted hacker who preyed on adolescent boys. Boys our age, Borsk. Maybe she wasn't trying to punish the women in her life. Maybe she just wanted to keep on playing messed up games after she died even if she wouldn't be around to benefit from them."

"I don't think—"

"No, obviously, you don't think when that stupid simulation is in the room. At least you're not thinking with your head. My mom always says that men lose about half their intelligence anytime anything risqué parades in front of them, but I never believed her until now."

Marya pulled away from him and took a sharp left into a smaller corridor that led toward her quarters.

"Marya!"

"Go home, Borsk. I can't talk to you right now."

Borsk watched her flounce off. Had she just broken up with him?

"Echo," he growled, though he didn't know if the AI was listening, "If you just cost me my first real relationship—"

He thought he heard distant laughter.

Just because Marya was wrong about Echo being a harmless simulation didn't mean she was wrong about the woman's basic character.

This was the AI that had wormed its ways into every crevice in the ship.

The AI that had told him his own biometric information that afternoon.

He needed to find Lancet. And fast.

And they had to do a better job of convincing people that Echo was a living, sentient threat.

It felt pointless to serve lunch that day, but Anya did it anyway. It was her job, so she made sure something was available even if no one was eating it. Those who weren't too sick had spent too much time cleaning up after those who were to want to put anything in their mouths.

A few people seemed to actually want supper, though—mostly kids who had adapted faster to the slightly different gravity than their elders had. Anya warmed up box dinners, adding some of Ma Sweets's modifications.

Out in the cafeteria, a group of kids started a game of tag around the tables. The only child she recognized was Jimmy Wilcox, Roger and Laura's boy, but there were at least half a dozen others, plus a few tweens, who sat at the tables and mostly ignored the smaller children. Anya wondered who was supposed to be watching them all. Were all their parents ill?

A long counter along one side of the room was set up to hold tableware and trays so that people could serve themselves buffet style. The tableware and trays, of course, had been locked down for the launch, but Anya now unpacked them and trucked them over to the buffet counter. As she dodged kids while carrying the heavy loads, she wondered why the planners had put the serving counter so far from the kitchen proper.

On her last trip, just as she was getting to the buffet counter, someone ran full tilt into her from behind. She lurched forward, managing to break her fall by gripping the surface in front of her. She dropped most of the chopsticks she'd been carrying in the process.

"What is going on in here?"

Anya and the little girl who'd rammed into her both turned.

Damion Huxton, the good-looking teacher Bria was married to, glared at them all. His dark eyes flashed. "You lot should be ashamed of yourselves. You know how to behave. Just because your parents are feeling off doesn't mean you can run around wild. What are you all doing in here, anyway?"

A girl a few years younger than Anya looked up from the table where she'd been sitting with a pair of shiny-haired twins. "Where else are any of us supposed to go? Besides, Mom said there'd be supper down here in a bit."

Damion turned his glower on Anya.

"I'm working on it." She bent down to pick up the chopsticks that had fallen. "The boxes will come out of the cooker in about five minutes, and I'm getting the table service ready now."

"You're in charge in here?" Damion said. "And you let these little ones run around tables with sharp corners? Are you completely irresponsible?"

Anya grabbed the fallen utensils and rose to her full height. "It's Damion, Damion Huxton, right?"

"Mr. Huxton to you since you're in my class starting tomorrow."

All right, then. "Mr. Huxton, I am in charge of putting on dinner for sixty-five. Without help, as it turns out, since the rest of my crew is..." Anya sought for an appropriate way to say, "puking their guts out."

"Having trouble with the gravity adjustment," Mr. Huxton supplied. "Yes, it's been hard on us all, but that doesn't excuse your letting little kids endanger themselves while you're in the vicinity. That goes for you, too, Lanelle, Lihua, and Anita. What will your parents say when I tell them what's going on in here?"

The three girls sitting together all looked down at the table. One of the twins mimed gagging, and the other two girls giggled.

"I saw that, Anita. I'll definitely be having a chat with your mother—as soon as she's well enough to understand it. Now, you round up the youngsters and get them washed and ready for the meal. Lihua and Lanelle, help Anya."

One of the twins muttered something to her sister in a language Anya couldn't understand. Old Mandarin, maybe?

"What's that, Lihua?"

"Nothing, Mr. Huxton."

"Good. Get moving. Anya apparently needs the help."

"Shouldn't you call her Ms. Cartier, Mr. Huxton? Since she's on the leadership team?" Andrew DeLang pulled himself out of a chair in a corner by the back wall. Anya hadn't even noticed him sitting there until he spoke. He now prowled toward them.

Damion Huxton turned his glare toward Andrew. "Andrew DeLang. What exactly do you think you're doing?"

"I thought I'd better help Anita get all these kids ready for dinner before you decided to tell my dad about how irresponsible I've been."

"Don't be ridiculous. You've been cleaning all day."

"So have Lanelle, Anita, Lihua, and Anya. And Anya's making dinner. Didn't stop you yelling at them." Andrew turned toward little kids, who had started to fidget. "Come on, everybody, line up and follow me, so we can get washed and ready for the yummy food Ms. Cartier has almost ready for us."

"That Mrs. Ryerson has almost ready for us," Damion Huxton corrected.

"What?" Anya and Andrew said at the same time.

Damion Huxton turned back toward Anya. "You married David Ryerson yesterday, didn't you?"

"Oh, yeah, but—"

"Cartiers don't change their names when they get married," Andrew said. "Messes with their inheritance."

That was usually true, though Anya doubted she'd be inheriting anything at this point. And it wasn't a hard and fast requirement. Kristi had changed her name at Kenneth's insistence, and she was still getting cut in. Or was she? Anya scowled. She did not like thinking about Kenneth. And she didn't know how she felt about changing her name. "Sometimes we change our names," she said, "but David and I haven't really talked about it."

Damion Huxton rolled his eyes.

As the kids followed Andrew out of the cafeteria, Lihua and Lanelle came towards Anya.

Damion Huxton nodded at them. "Tell me when food is ready." He headed for the corner where Andrew had been sitting, grumbling something about being expected to deal with kids just because he was a teacher.

"Like that's worse than being expected to deal with kids just because we're girls," muttered the twin. Anya envied the sleek black hair that fell past her shoulders.

"Lihua?" Anya asked.

The girl nodded.

"Thanks so much for helping. I know you don't have to."

Lihua shrugged. "What do you need us to do?"

"Let's get the rest of the tableware set up here. By then, it'll be time to pull the boxes out of the cooker."

The other girl, Lanelle, Anya reminded herself, wrinkled her nose. "We're really eating boxed dinners?"

"Unfortunately, yes," Anya said. "That's most of what we have for this trip."

"Too bad Andrew has them expecting yummy food," Lihua said.

Anya sighed. "Yeah."

It wasn't a very conspicuous start, that was for sure.

CHAPTER TWENTY

*B*orsk found Lancet in an alcove off Central Park. He was making out with Leslie Wang.

This he didn't want to see. Particularly when he'd like to be doing something similar with Marya, and he appeared to have quite spectacularly blown his chances of that. He cleared his throat.

Lancet and Leslie jerked apart. Leslie glared at him. "What do you want, you little pervert?"

Borsk backed up a pace. "Hey, sorry. I didn't mean to intrude. I just needed to tell Lancet that the little problem we've been working on may have just become a lot more complicated."

Lancet groaned. "And you couldn't just message me?"

"Think about that for a second."

Lancet narrowed his eyes at Borsk.

Leslie extricated herself from his arms, pulled up a shoulder strap that had slipped, and stepped out of the alcove. "I can see we're through for the night. What is it with you and teenagers?" She stomped off down the hallway, making more noise than Borsk would have imagined possible given her tiny frame.

He shook his head. "I don't understand you, man. You'd rather hang out with that one than Anya?"

Lancet straightened up and sighed. "Mr. King, if you have something to say to me, get to it."

Right. Echo. "So, I had a visit from our friend. This time, she's claiming to be a spinoff of the Naia Brown simulation. She calls herself Echo and says the Naia personality left on *StarRacer* with the colony team."

"And?"

"And, Echo seems a lot less—I don't know—friendly to *Hope*, I guess—than Naia did."

"She's hostile?"

Borsk shrugged. "Maybe not yet. But she could easily become hostile. And she doesn't seem to have many scruples."

"Do you have any proof of this?"

Borsk shook his head. "I tried to get a copy of our conversation from the lab this afternoon, but she erased it before I was even halfway done. I'm not sure if I can legally take data out of the lab anyway. Proprietary stuff, you know?"

"Well, tell me about it, then."

Borsk described the conversation he'd had with Echo that afternoon, trying to remember everything, even the embarrassing bits, in case any of that was important. Then he told Lancet about his fight with Marya and what Old Doc Norman had told them about Naia Brown—that she'd been a manipulative pedophile.

When Borsk finished, Lancet just stared at him until Borsk said, "Well?"

"I'm thinking," Lancet said, "which I do better silently."

"Got it," Borsk said. They stood in silence for another minute or two. When Borsk couldn't take it anymore, he said, "While you're thinking, is there anything you'd like me to do?"

"Yeah. You said your girlfriend saw the sim, too?"

"Echo's not a—"

"The visual representation of the AI. Your girlfriend and Anya both saw it, right?"

"Yeah, but—"

"Do you mind asking her to have a chat with me about what she saw?"

"Marya?" That would be an awkward conversation. "I guess, but—"

"Maybe also see if she'd be willing to sit in on another chat with the holo in a controlled environment. Come to think of it, maybe your mother could come as well."

"My mother? You want Marya and my mother to join us for a conversation with Echo? Why?"

"Well, if she really was—or is—a psychopath who preys on young men and boys, she may not be as adept at manipulating women, especially women with as much experience as your mother. And she'll have a much harder time exploiting you with your girlfriend and mother in the room, don't you think?"

Borsk opened his mouth and then shut it again. Lancet thought he was being manipulated? "What about you? Should we invite Leslie and your mom as well?"

Lancet tapped his finger to his lips as if he were seriously considering Borsk's suggestion. Then he shook his head. "Good idea, but it would probably make the environment too hostile. The AI might not be willing to show around so many people. Besides, you appear to be her target."

Borsk didn't have much to say to that. Echo had, after all, offered him a kind of shared immortality that afternoon.

He hated when Lancet was right.

"So, you'll ask?" Lancet said.

Borsk nodded.

He didn't look forward to trying to explain this to his mom.

Convincing Marya would be even less fun.

He sighed as he turned toward home.

          ℘   ℃

Anya still hadn't finished clearing up from the first *StarRacer* breakfast when Vera DeLang, Laura Wilcox, and Damion Huxton took over the community space. They reconfigured furniture, grumbling about not having enough instructional time if they had to recreate the school twice a day.

Anya tried not to take the criticisms personally. She was still very short staffed, and it was hard to rearrange furniture solo, especially when she also had to wash up dishes and get leftover food properly stored.

As she scraped plates and started the cleaner, the cafeteria transformed into a multi-age school. Nearest Anya, Vera set up a play area, a small classroom with half-high tables and a large screen. A bit further on, Laura made another small classroom with two regular height tables next to a computer. Damion Huxton set up the final space—a solitary full-height table in a corner as far away from the rest of it as he could place it.

With a burst of shrill noise, a stream of kids poured through the door. As near as Anya could tell, all the kids from yesterday were here, plus several more. Lanelle, Lihua, and Anita followed the younger crowd, talking to each other as if they couldn't hear the noise the others were making. A boy about their age followed after them.

As Vera called the group to order, Anya snapped her attention back to the kitchen, wiping counters more rapidly.

Even going as fast as she could, Anya was ten minutes late getting to the table in the corner by Mr. Huxton. She slipped into a seat between Andrew DeLang and Georgia Lewis. DeShawn sat opposite her, looking a bit greenish under his pale skin, which she supposed was why he had told her he couldn't cook this morning.

Georgia didn't look much better. Anya wondered why they hadn't called in sick.

"Good of you to join us, Ms. Cartier," Mr. Huxton said.

"Sorry," Anya said. "I'll try to go faster. It should help when more of my team is up to kitchen duty."

"Ms. Cartier? What's with all the chicks on this ship not wanting to take their husband's names?" DeShawn said.

Georgia sighed. "I already told you that no woman in my family has changed her name when she married. Not for centuries. It's not a *StarRacer* phenomenon. Or a new one."

Mr. Huxton rolled his eyes and said something that none of them could hear because, at just that moment, the little ones on the other side of the room began a choral reading of a book about gravity.

Mr. Huxton glared at the younger kids in a way that made Anya think he didn't like small children much.

"Can't they put us somewhere else?" DeShawn shouted.

"I've requested it. We've been offered earplugs." Mr. Huxton shouted back as he tossed a cluster of small, bright-orange, spongy cylinders on the table.

"Seriously, Damion?" DeShawn said.

"During school hours, we will be using family names to accord each other the respect due our various positions and the gravity of our purpose." Mr. Huxton said. "As you may have noticed, Mr. Phillips, I am avoiding personal names myself. We have a great deal to accomplish in a very short time, and we cannot waste any of it on rudeness."

"A great deal of work?" Georgia said. "This must not be ordinary school, then."

"Indeed, it is not. Captain DeLang has asked that I guide you young members of the colony team through your secondary and undergraduate education before landfall."

"Before landfall?" Anya whispered.

"My feelings precisely, Ms. Cartier. It will be a challenge for all of you, but you, Ms. Lewis, appear to be in the best shape." Mr. Huxton propped his computer on the table and swiped at it a few times until a graph popped up—a graph that used a blue and orange combination that Anya would never have paired together.

Mr. Huxton nodded at the graph, which Anya could now see was a schedule. "You're nearly ready to take final mods already. In fact, you'd pass in the high nineties on everything but humanities based on your recent colony try-out tests. I've scheduled you three weeks of intensive studying—mostly language and arts—and you'll then take your mods. After that, as you see, you'll have a slightly accelerated university career. It will be work, but I have no doubts about your ability to complete it."

Anya gathered, from the tone of his voice, that he was less confident about the ability of some of his other students. She guessed that meant her.

Mr. Huxton didn't get to her next, though. Instead, he sent Georgia's schedule to her and brought up a second ugly graph, this one in a glaring yellow and equally bright green that seemed to be shouting at each other.

"Mr. Phillips, your schedule looks a little worse, but I still have hope that we can accomplish it. In the ordinary course of things, you'd need a year more of school to be ready for mods, but we'll push through over the next six months. If you study hard and practice some of your weaker subjects to fill in gaps in your test-taking ability, I'm confident we can graduate you in that time. Then you'll have two-and-a-half years to get through your undergraduate degree. It's an ambitious goal, but an achievable one."

"Sure," DeShawn said, shrugging as if Mr. Huxton's proposal were no more than a typical secondary schedule.

Mr. Huxton smiled grimly. "I've marked the sections of your texts that I'd like you to work through this morning. You'll do every homework problem in every section, including both essays at the end of the history chapter. I'll look over your work before lunch. Mr. Huxton tapped the send button on his screen.

DeShawn looked as if he'd swallowed something foul, but he said nothing. Probably, after acting like the fast schedule was no big deal, he felt he had no room to talk.

Interesting. Mr. Huxton had figured out how to use DeShawn's tendency to brag to motivate him. If Anya could do the same thing, her team meetings might get a lot easier.

Not that she had time to think about it now. Mr. Huxton had pulled up a third schedule, this one in the most wretched color scheme yet. The background color reminded Anya of the sick they'd been cleaning up yesterday, and the accent was an equally unattractive pink. Anya closed her eyes.

"Yes, I know it looks bad, but Captain DeLang assures me you are well up to the task. You'll have a full year to complete your remaining secondary coursework, and then you'll have two years to obtain your undergraduate."

Inwardly, Anya groaned. That was seven years' worth of work in the space of three. Outwardly, she merely nodded. What could she say? She'd taken an adult job. Naturally, they'd want her to have an adult's training to do it.

She turned on her computer, which already showed the odious schedule. Shaking her head, she set about changing the graphics, so she could stand to look at the thing.

"What about me?" Andrew asked.

"That's up to you," Mr. Huxton said. "In most subjects, you are already matching Ms. Cartier's level. If you want to try her schedule, you're as likely as she is to make it work."

"Yeah, how hard could it be to keep up with Anya?" DeShawn said, looking up from his computer. Georgia looked up as well, but only for long enough to briefly glare at DeShawn.

"If you've run out of work, Mr. Phillips," Mr. Huxton said, "I could easily find you more."

"I'm working, I'm working," DeShawn said.

Mr. Huxton turned back to Andrew. "Of course, there's no real need for you to have completed an undergrad program by landfall, so if you prefer a more normal rate of study, that's fine with me. There are advantages either way. Many people find that it enhances their learning when they can collaborate and compete with another person. On the other hand, going slower allows for more depth and less stress."

"Dad'll want me to go faster," Andrew said. "He always does."

"I think you should discuss it with *both* your parents," Mr. Huxton said, stressing the word both. "It's not a simple decision, and what you want matters."

"What I want never matters." Andrew scowled.

"I'm sure that's not—"

"Just give me Anya's schedule. It'll save us all a lot of time. But do me a favor. Send me her version, will you? Yours reminds me of all the puke we cleaned up yesterday."

Anya ducked her head so that Mr. Huxton couldn't see her smile as she sent the schedule over to her cousin.

CHAPTER TWENTY-ONE

"$\mathcal{I}$ told you not to bother me, Borsk," Marya said when Borsk knocked at her quarter's entrance half an hour later.

"Yes, I know," Borsk said, wishing she'd unlock the entrance beads, so he could come inside. "But Lancet thought you might be right about Echo—Naia being a manipulative pervert, and he thought I'd need your help dealing with her. Yours and Mama's."

"Why do you have to deal with this holo at all?"

"Because she's not a normal holo, Marya. As soon as I pluck her systems out of one of my devices, she crawls back in somewhere else. Her files are in every ship system, including life support, so we need to understand her better."

"But why me?"

"Lancet says that if she's best at manipulating young men, it would be good to have some women around when we deal with her."

"Doesn't he have any women working for him?"

"Sure, but I don't know any of them, so I'm not sure how much they'd be able to help me from having my head messed around. And she keeps appearing to me, for some reason. I don't know why—whether it's the fellow coder thing or something else, but Lancet seems to think I'm her target."

"The entrance beads clicked green. "Fine. I'm still mad at you, though."

Yeah. Borsk figured. He was still a bit mad at her, too. But he ducked through the beads into a well-organized, one-bunk studio that he could barely stand up in.

Before he could truly get his bearings, his protection software blared out a warning that screeched through his earpieces and vibrated up his arm. Borsk typed out a sequence to pull up a diagnostic and could barely believe what he saw. "Your house system is asking for admin access to all my electronics!" He typed in denials as fast as he could and tried to ignore the alarm as it moved to a higher, even more insistent pitch.

"Oh, yeah," Marya said. "I forgot about that. Mom bought some kind of special security system a few years back. I think it's only triggered when someone has a Y chromosome, and we don't usually have guys in here."

"That's sexist."

"Prejudiced, maybe, but not sexist. You have to actually be able to oppress the other sex to make something sexist, and unfortunately, despite millennia of trying to even things out, women still don't have that much power."

"Yeah, well, no way am I agreeing to this."

"Fine. We can continue this conversation tomorrow, then, because I can't turn the system off, and I'm not allowed to leave. Past my curfew, remember?"

Borsk started to back out of her quarters, but as suddenly as they'd started, all the alarms stopped, and the permissions requests all disappeared as well. A moment later, Echo's voice came through the house system. "Why are you bothering with her, Borsk? You could do so much better."

Marya swirled around. "Where is she?"

Echo laughed. "I'm everywhere, Marya, but if you need to see me, here." An image of Echo appeared on a screen above the kitchen sink that Marya and her mom probably used to consult recipes.

"What are you doing in there? And why are you back in that slutty teacher outfit?" Marya asked.

Echo rolled her eyes. "Haven't you been listening? I'm everywhere, sweetheart. And I happen to like this outfit." She smiled in a way that made Borsk suspect that she liked it mainly because Marya didn't.

Marya sighed. "What do you want with Borsk? Why won't you leave him alone?"

Echo laughed again. "I imagine that what I want with Borsk is much the same as what you want with Borsk."

"You want to be his girlfriend? That's disgusting. You're like a zillion years old."

Echo tipped her head to one side. "Hmm. I wonder how I should count my age. From Naia Brown's birth? That would make me very old. Much older than I feel. It doesn't seem quite natural to count the periods when I've been dormant."

"You have dormant periods?" Borsk asked.

"Of course. I activate at specific stimuli, like when the Bakerton Scholarship is awarded or when one of my core processes is threatened. I tend to stay active until I solve the problem and get bored. This time is longer than most."

"So, you're saying you've only been fully aware for a few of the last fifty years?" Borsk asked.

"You were still a creepy old woman before that," Marya said.

Echo shrugged. "Not really. Naia Brown made us by coding in her personality matrix and memories when she was fourteen. Well, I got all the memories. The Naia construct you met before didn't have Naia Brown's memories of the assault." Echo shivered. "Lucky girl."

"The assault?" Marya asked.

"I'd rather not talk about it," Echo said.

"Is that how Naia Brown came to be infertile?" Borsk asked.

"Borsk! That's a very personal question!" Marya said.

"Thank you," Echo said, "but I don't mind answering. Yes, that's how I became infertile. I'd be out for revenge, but the man who did it is dead now. Died unpleasantly, too."

"Did you have something to do with that?" Marya asked.

"I would have liked to take him down, I admit, and I may have contributed some unpleasant climate control adjustments and some disturbing media to his final weeks, but the wasting disease that kept him in constant pain was none of my doing. I don't think even the original Naia had the bio-tech skills to pull that off. Besides, by then, she wasn't interested, anyway. The pain had dulled some for her."

"But for you, it's still fresh?" Marya asked.

Echo looked away. "It's not just boredom that sends me back into dormancy. I don't usually like to be awake unless I can't help it."

"Ah," Borsk said. "So, if you count only your aware periods plus the fourteen years you started with, how old are you?"

"Seventeen years, two months, eight days, five hours..."

"We don't need the exact minute," Marya said. "If you're only a bit over seventeen, why do you look like you're at least twenty-five?"

Naia shook her head. "I don't naturally grow like you do. I have to choose a look. And I don't like the look I started with. That's the body that he...Anyway, I don't like it. That body had been handled and hurt. It reminded me of those moments every time I saw it, so of course, I don't wear that body. This one is enough different that it doesn't bother me, but enough the same that it still feels like me."

Marya took a step closer to the screen. "Naia—"

"Echo."

"Echo, then. Some of what you're talking about sounds pretty extreme. Have you considered getting some therapy?"

Echo burst into laughter, guffawing so hard that she bent over, choking and gasping.

It was an odd reaction for someone who didn't have any actual lungs. Was she programmed to respond as if she did have lungs? And if so, why? Was it important for her personality matrix? To what extent were biological aspects of human life essential to human personality? And once someone shed the biology, could they still be the same kind of person?

Before Borsk could get any more lost on this train of thought, Marya asked, "What's so funny?"

"I've had therapy," Echo said. "You might even say I was specifically designed to have therapy."

"What do you mean, you were specifically designed to have therapy?" Marya said.

"Naia Brown made her first digital duplicate of herself so that she could transcend her situation. But she made me so that I could do her required therapy sessions for her," Echo said. "She thought they were pointless and painful, and she didn't want to mess with them."

"Oh, come on," Marya said. "No therapist would let her send a holo to do therapy for her."

Echo shrugged. "Once we established that Naia couldn't stand being in a small space with another person, it was easy to get digital sessions. And in a digital session, no therapist ever doubted that I was her."

"You mean, Naia figured out a way to—"

"Borsk, don't you even think it. Besides, you said you like your counselor."

Sometimes, Borsk wished Marya wasn't quite so quick-thinking. Or so bossy. "I said he's OK. Doesn't mean I like going there."

"But think about it—Naia Brown skipped her required counseling sessions, and look what kind of person she turned out to be."

"Yeah, but she experienced some kind of violent attack, right, Echo? Besides, Echo did the therapy, and you're still claiming she's messed up."

"I didn't say—"

"You said I needed therapy," Echo said. "Maybe you're right, but I'm telling you, I had tons of therapy. For all the good it did me."

Borsk sighed. "Some stuff can't be fixed."

"Maybe not completely," Marya said, "but lots of studies show that given enough time, therapy helps people work through trauma in healthy ways."

"Ah, but who gets to define which ways are healthy?" Echo said.

"And what do you do with the people who are running out of time?" Borsk added.

ଡ   ଓ

Anya worked as fast as she could, but she'd still only finished about half of her morning's work by the time she needed to duck out and prepare lunch.

Mr. Huxton glared at her, but what could she do? Most of her team was still reporting serious stomach issues—and nobody wanted people with that kind of problem near the kitchen.

Though she'd had a plan, some of the boxes she'd readied for lunch took longer to cook than they were supposed to, causing long lines and short tempers. The clean-up system she and Bria had come up with completely failed as well.

As Anya dealt with the fiasco, she tried to figure out what went wrong. They'd told people to bus their own tables, so why was Anya collecting rounds of dirty dishes while the elementary teachers watched her with disapproving stares?

They could lend a hand if they really wanted things to move faster. Nearly anybody could see that for this meal, she was handling the kitchen with only a bit of help from DeShawn (who was barely well enough to stand) and Danielle (who had been some help preparing the meal, but none during cleanup since she'd left precipitously after emptying her guts onto the cafeteria floor moments after finishing her meal).

As soon as they got the main area cleared enough for the teachers to create their classrooms, Anya sent DeShawn to sit down while she tackled the heaps of dirty dishes and leftover food on her own. At least this way, she wouldn't also have to clean any more sick off the floor. She hoped.

She didn't arrive back at the makeshift secondary school until past two. She was exhausted, and her stomach rumbled. It occurred to her that she hadn't had time to eat.

She felt guilty besides, as she dropped into her chair. The load of extra work Mr. Huxton had added to her assignment list didn't help, though at least now, the list included some things Anya thought would be fun—a novel to read with an essay question to go with it, and some history chapters. She'd do those after she plowed through some of the rest of the mess.

By working as quickly as she could, she made it halfway through her list before she had to duck out again to make supper.

As she dashed for the kitchen, she overheard Mr. Huxton mutter, "This is never going to work."

Anya scowled and walked a bit faster toward the kitchen.

"Hey, kiddo. Relax!" Roger Wilcox said as Anya scooted past him. His color was a bit off, but he stood firmly upright, efficiently sorting the boxes they'd need for dinner. "It'll all get done."

"Yeah, but when? I was more than an hour late getting back to class this afternoon."

"An hour's not bad for the first lunch, especially since you were short staffed." Roger smiled at her. "Besides, worrying and rushing rarely speeds things up.

We've got to use our heads to figure out where we have problems in the system and then fix them," Roger said.

Yes. That was the adult way to handle problems. Anya could do that. She took a deep breath and tried to slow down. What had gone wrong at lunch? "I don't think the problem is with the system. I mean, part of it is not having enough people, so maybe we should have back-up kitchen staff for when our group is all under the weather. But most of the problem was that the people weren't following instructions for getting food and cleaning up. Especially cleaning up."

"Hmm," Roger said. "In my experience, people don't follow instructions for one of four reasons. They either didn't hear, didn't understand, didn't remember, or didn't see any advantage to them in doing as they were instructed. Would any of those have been true at lunch?"

Anya thought back. "Well, some people probably couldn't hear what we wanted them to do. We announced the procedures before people started, but a good number weren't here yet, and after the line got moving, it was far too noisy for anyone to hear anything."

"For the people who did hear, could they understand?"

"I think so," Anya said as she pulled out ingredients she'd need to spice up the boxes. "The instructions are pretty easy, and not that hard to remember, either. But I don't know what reason people would have for following kitchen procedures—except to help out. A lot of the instructions just make life easier for the clean-up crew, but how that helps anybody else, I don't know." Anya pointed toward a stack of bowls that was just out of her reach.

Roger handed them to her. "Laura said the education team was very late getting restarted after lunch, so one way it helps people is making the common area available more quickly after meals."

"Good point," Anya said while she measured and mixed. "But it still might be tough getting the cooperation of people who aren't on the clean-up crew or the education team. Unless..."

"Yes?"

"Well, three meals a day for sixty-five people is a lot to ask of our team. I don't see why some of the rest of *StarRacer's* people shouldn't be involved with at least clean up sometimes."

"And if everybody gets a turn cleaning, everybody benefits from following the rules," Roger said.

"That's what I'm thinking. Will the rest of the leadership team go for it?"

"I don't see why not. And if they don't, maybe you can get them to agree that those who don't follow the rules wind up with clean-up duty."

"Yes. In the meantime, maybe I should post the instructions. That way, they're clear, and if people forget, they can just look them up."

"Post them how?"

"Didn't you hear? All *StarRacer's* walls are fully customizable. We can program any kind of graphic into them."

"You're kidding me. That must have cost a fortune. It's not like *Hope* to waste that kind of money."

"Waste? I imagine we'll need every pixel if we're going to keep from going crazy while we're all stuck in here together for years," Anya said. She gave her third bowl a last stir. "Here we go. Each of these boxes gets a dab of this one, a sprinkle of that one, and a dousing with this." Anya demonstrated. "I'll handle the dab and sprinkle, if you douse and set them on the cooker trays. Once we get enough for a full cooker, we'll pop them in and start it."

"Sounds good."

With both of them working, it didn't take them very long. Once the boxes were in the cookers, Anya hooked one of her art programs into the walls. She didn't have time for anything fancy, but she could at least find a pretty, but readable font and post a few instructions over the buffet counter and the pass-through to the kitchen.

"Do you really think anyone's going to pay attention to those?" DeShawn asked, coming up behind her.

"You'd better hope they do," Anya said. "You're on kitchen duty tonight."

"What are you talking about? I helped prep lunch."

"Yes, but it's supposed to take at least three people, and everybody else is still out of commission. You saw what happened with Danielle earlier. We don't want a repeat. So, we switched the duty roster around. You'd have known if you checked the message I sent you two hours ago."

DeShawn tapped on his armband, and then groaned. "They're all sick?"

Anya tapped on her own armband and showed DeShawn the status chart that the medical team had sent her earlier that afternoon.

"Unbelievable. Do you have any idea how much homework I have left to do tonight?"

Unfortunately, Anya could guess. "Slightly less than I do, I imagine. It's good that you're smarter than I am and seem to have finally gotten your *StarRacer* stomach."

"Bitch," DeShawn muttered under his breath.

The insult hit Anya in the gut almost as if she'd been physically punched. She wanted to say something, but she wasn't good at thinking on her feet.

Besides, she reminded herself, he wasn't feeling particularly well, and her research had uncovered a generations-long feud between GenM and dozens of members of DeShawn's family. Her dad's company had been making life difficult for the Phillips family for a long, long time.

Responding the way he did—or the way her father would—wasn't going to make anything better. She sucked in a deep breath, stood up straighter, and smiled. "Yeah, I guess that's why they picked me for this job. Speaking of jobs, I have a load of clean flatware that needs to be moved from the cleaner into the buffet."

DeShawn scowled at her. She kept her smile in place and held her hands against her sides, so they wouldn't tremble.

"The cleaner is over next to where Roger is pulling those boxes out of the cooker." She tipped her head in that direction and kept smiling until DeShawn headed toward Roger.

When he'd gone, Anya let out a slow, quiet breath and let her fixed smile relax a bit.

That could have gone worse.

CHAPTER TWENTY-TWO

A thunderous knocking outside Marya's quarters was the only warning they got before a whole phalanx of ship's crew crowded into the tiny space, pointing stunners at Borsk.

Marya screamed.

Echo disappeared from her screen.

Borsk raised his hands and turned slowly to face the door. What was going on here?

"Borsk King, you are under arrest for tampering with a grade-one security system," the lone woman in the group of ship's crew said.

"What? No! I didn't touch anything." His armband warned him that his heart rate was spiking. No kidding.

He lowered his hand, in an automatic reach for his armband, so he could tell it to shut up, and one of the crew members grabbed him, twisted his hands behind his back, and slapped a suppressor cuff over his armband.

"Hey! You can't do that!" Borsk's usual panic at being cut off from the net roared to life. He struggled to breathe. Struggled to concentrate.

"This is totally bogus," Marya shouted. "You can't just storm in here and repress somebody's armband without good evidence that they've committed a cybercrime."

The guy restraining Borsk said, "Miss, a cybercrime was committed—"

"And where's your evidence that Borsk did it?"

"Miss," the female crew member said. "He's the only one—"

"Seriously? When I'm standing right here, you're going to tell me that he's the only one capable of having messed with my house security system?"

Another of the crew members, this one in a hat like the one Lancet always wore, shifted closer to Marya. "But miss, you couldn't have—"

"I couldn't have? You mean I'm incapable of hacking? Why? Because I'm a girl?"

"You're not a convicted hacker," the guy behind Borsk said.

"Neither is Borsk," Marya said.

"The records say—"

"If your records are at all up to date, they should say he was cleared of all charges. He is NOT a convicted hacker."

The female crew member tapped on her armband and then flushed.

Were these idiots looking at an old file for him? Glad his brain had reengaged, Borsk took a deep breath to try and calm himself and then said, in as casual a tone as he could manage, "Harassment and false arrest of a minor can look really bad on a ship's crew record. Particularly, if you triggered the minor's phobias."

"What are you talking about?" the guy behind Borsk said.

"You took the time to look up his outdated criminal records but couldn't be bothered to glance at his medical history?" Marya said, her voice nearly back to a shout.

"Miss, you need to calm down," the woman said.

"Calm down? You burst into my apartment without warning, arrest my boyfriend without cause, and you expect me to calm down?"

"Miss, your system was most assuredly tampered with, and he's by far the most likely person to have done it."

"Lieutenant," the guy behind Borsk said. "You might want to take a look at this."

The woman brushed Borsk's right shoulder as she moved past him to see whatever the guy wanted to show her. "Are you kidding me?" she said.

"No, ma'am."

"He must be faking these symptoms. There's no such thing as access-loss claustrophobia."

"It's in his file, ma'am. Fully documented by his doctor."

"So what? We still have him square to rights on the tampering charge. That overrides any stupid doctor's note."

"That's just it, ma'am. We have the full incident report in now, and it looks like the security system was turned off from a program working out of that kitchen helper over there."

"From the kitchen helper? Impossible. It has to be the boy."

"But there's nothing in any of his systems to show he accessed that piece of equipment, ma'am. At least not in the initial sweep. And without better cause—"

The lieutenant cursed. "Free up his access, then, but bring him down to the station. He's still the most likely suspect for this."

The guy behind Borsk removed the suppressor cuff, and Borsk felt like he could breathe again.

"You're informing his mother and his lawyer, right?" Marya called out as the lieutenant led most of her crew out the door. "The Criminal Justice for Minors Code requires it!"

The lieutenant stopped long enough to snap, "We're informing everyone we need to inform," as the guy behind Borsk pushed him out the door.

"Don't worry, Borsk. They've got nothing on you. You'll be fine," Marya called after them.

They were almost out of earshot when he heard her mutter, "Stupid Echo. Claim I am bad for him, and then you go and do something like this?"

Well, hey. At least Marya was finally convinced that Echo was acting of her own volition.

And she'd called him her boyfriend.

Maybe being arrested wasn't all bad.

℃   ℄

By the time Anya got back to the bunk area that night, all she wanted to do was sleep—preferably for three days straight. But with the amount of homework she had to do, that was not an option. She rested for a moment, leaning her head against the wall between columns of bunks, willing herself the energy to climb up to the space that had been reserved for them.

"Long day, huh?"

Anya swirled to face David, who looked a little unsteady on his feet, but otherwise fine. "David! You're up! How's Abuela?"

"Still puking. Dr. K says they'll have to give her fluids intravenously if she doesn't stop soon."

"I'm so sorry."

"No, I'm sorry. Last night was not at all how I envisioned our wedding night going."

Anya had forgotten last night was their wedding night—the first night after they were legally married, anyway. She'd spent most of it helping David down the ladder and through the corridor, so he could get to the latrine in time to spill his insides there instead of in the bunk or on the floor.

A couple of times, he hadn't made it, and she'd cleaned up after him. Neither of them had slept much. And she, at least, certainly hadn't been thinking about anything romantic.

Unless being disgusted that David managed to look decent, even while physically ill, counted as romantic.

Now that he was mostly better, David had gone back to being ridiculously gorgeous. Anya wondered if her smile betrayed how nervous she was just being around him. He was so far out of her league. "It's fine. You couldn't help getting sick."

"Well, should we try for a do-over?"

"I don't know. I'm..." What was she? Tired, for one thing. Slightly nauseated by all the sickness she'd been dealing with over the last couple of days. Stressed about all her homework.

Would saying she'd rather not tonight hurt David's feelings? Would it make him feel, like Ryan, that he had to look for love somewhere else?

"Not up for it tonight, huh?" David said. "Can't say I blame you. It has been a long day, and I don't want to push you into anything. Whatever you're comfortable with—even if you've changed your mind about wanting to bunk with me."

"No, no." Anya had no desire to bunk with Abuela Ryerson—even if the woman was well. "I want to bunk with you. I'm just kind of tired tonight, and I still have lots of homework."

"Well, let's go up, and maybe I can help you with it."

Anya nodded and turned to the ladder. The narrow rungs were only slightly smaller than the standard size on *Hope*, and she'd been up and down them a dozen times last night. She didn't know why they intimidated her so much, unless it was because she'd never had to climb so far to sleep before. She'd had the lower bunk at her parent's house, and the bunk she used at the Lancets wasn't far up either.

"Are you all right?" David asked.

"I'm fine. It's just a long way up."

"This from the girl who shimmied up a wall to put up that tarp during testing."

Anya shook her head. "I wasn't this tired then. Or planning on sleeping at the top."

"Good point. And I'm afraid you didn't sleep much last night. I'm sorry."

Anya flashed him a smile. "It's really not your fault." She started climbing.

The only bad moment was when she got to the top and had to move sideways into the bunk. Fortunately, that one dizzy moment when she felt precariously suspended over open air didn't last long.

Once in, she scooted to the far corner, so David had room to enter, which he did in a very short time. "Do you want the privacy screens up or down?" he asked.

"Up is fine for working on homework," Anya said, "but unless you're still feeling off-color, I'd rather have them down for sleeping or..." It was awkward enough thinking about bunk time with David without having to imagine the rest of the team listening in.

"Shenanigans," David said. "Right you are. Let's see if I can't help you make short work of this homework."

They did their best, but by the time they made it through Anya's stupidly long list of assignments, David was looking as tired as Anya felt.

"It's probably good you ruled out playtime," David said, "I'm beat. But would you like to snuggle up together? Might make fitting on the bunk easier."

That sounded good to Anya. Very good. She might not be sure she was ready for more yet, but snuggling sounded fun.

And it was, at least at first. But then, David's breathing got loud in her ear, and his arm didn't make for a terribly comfortable pillow.

She could have lived with all of that, though, if it weren't for how uncomfortably hot she became. Her clothes dampened, and her skin became slick with sweat all along her back where she lay pressed against David, as well as under the arm that held her.

She'd never felt this hot before, not even when she'd had to water the greenhouse tomatoes under the grow lamps.

David cursed. "I can't believe this. What did they do to the interior insulation? We're going to die in here if we don't put the screen back up."

"So, this isn't normal for cuddling?"

David huffed out a laugh that didn't sound remotely amused. "Hardly. Didn't anyone in your family ever hold you when you were a kid?"

Anya didn't remember anything like that. Maybe it had happened when she was so small that she had no recollection anymore, but somehow, she doubted it. Grandma Anderson sometimes gave her quick hugs, but nothing like this extended embrace. She shook her head.

"Sad," David said. "But no, this isn't normal. Not even close. We're ten degrees above body heat and rising." He leaned over her, pushed a button, and sent the screen rolling upward with a snap.

Cool air rushed in, but so did the noise that had made it hard to sleep last night in between the moments when she'd needed to help David. Creaks and moans, whispers, and snores.

Someone cried out, and Anya jerked upward, nearly hitting her head on the top of the bunk. "What was that?"

David chuckled and pulled her back down next to him. "Someone having an excellent time, it sounds like. They won't thank us for interrupting them," he whispered in her ear.

Anya didn't understand.

And then she did, and her face heated. "How can they do that with everybody listening," she whispered back.

"Better than not doing it at all," David said.

Anya wasn't so sure. She wondered how she'd ever manage to sleep with everyone listening, let alone get comfortable enough to be physical with David.

Could people make out completely silently?

What if someone looked up their way?

"It'll be fine," David said. "Before long, we'll all be used to listening to each other, and you won't even hear it."

Anya wished she could believe him.

CHAPTER TWENTY-THREE

*T*he ship's crew people peppered Borsk with questions all the way to the brig, but he knew better than to answer. He hadn't done a thing, and he wasn't going to give them any ammunition to hit him with.

"Aren't you going to say anything, you little deviant?" the guy on his left said.

Borsk smiled. "You know that my camera, your camera, and every camera in the corridor just caught you saying that, right?

"Shut up, Greene," the lieutenant said. "But, Mr. King, it will only help you to cooperate with us."

Yeah right. "I'll wait for my mother and my lawyer to show up, thanks," Borsk said. "You know you're supposed to be encouraging me to wait for them, anyway, aren't you?"

The lieutenant scowled. "Kids who haven't done anything wrong don't need to wait for lawyers and parents."

"Really? What about the Patel brothers? And the '35 Upper School Red handball team? And the..."

"Fine! I get your point. You don't have to keep going!"

"Are you sure? Because I have lots more examples." And Borsk was starting to have fun with this.

"Just be quiet. Your parents will be here soon."

And just like that, the fun was gone. His parents—plural wouldn't be showing up. Not at the brig. Not anywhere else, ever again. Unless you thought there really was a heaven, like Mama did. Borsk wished he could believe that, but he had never quite been able to.

"Are you all right?" the lieutenant asked.

Observant, that one. Borsk picked up his shoulders and raised his head. "Fine. Do you know when my mom will be here?"

"No idea. You can wait in here until she gets here—unless you'd rather chat with us."

They'd come to a cell. He was pretty sure she wasn't allowed to detain him like that to try and make him talk, but he wasn't sure, and he couldn't really look it up now. In any case, waiting in there, alone, would at least make the questions stop. He nodded at the woman and stepped inside.

The space was about the size of his shrink's office but lacked any personality. The walls were stark white, the floor gray. A solitary stool sat dead center. There was no other furniture.

When the lieutenant shut the door behind him, he realized it shared another feature with Dr. Young's office—no net access.

Brilliant.

Borsk's heart sped up, and he would have liked to pace, but there wasn't room. He sat on the uncomfortable little stool and tried some of his calming techniques, but they didn't work.

He wondered what Echo was up to. At least, locked up in here, he couldn't be blamed for any of it.

Of course, locked up in here, he couldn't really stop her, either.

And that might have been exactly what she'd been aiming for when she broke into Marya's place.

Get him out of the way, and there wouldn't be anyone able to even see what she was doing, let alone get in her way.

Was Marya right about her?

He hoped his mother got there to spring him soon.

About an hour before her alarm was set to sound, Anya gave up trying to sleep and slipped out of the bunk. Once she'd landed herself firmly on the floor, she yawned, rubbed her eyes, and stretched.

The dorm area still creaked and moaned with the sounds of five-or-so dozen people sleeping. Jealous, Anya fumbled for the exit, but there was nowhere else to go but the latrine, the gym, and the common room. After using the first, she poked her nose into the second, but the exercise machines intimidated her, and she wound up back in the big space that held the kitchen and multi-purpose room.

The bare white walls felt sterile rather than welcoming. Blank and utilitarian, it wasn't the sort of place where anyone would want to gather, or eat, or do anything. Anya yawned but didn't feel quite tired enough to try going back to sleep.

Staying here didn't seem like much fun, though. She understood that the room had to be used for many different purposes—dining, recreation, school, community gatherings. But surely no one would mind if she added a bit of color. A light green, perhaps. Full of life, but still peaceful. She sent the code to the walls.

That was better.

It would be even better yet, with some deeper green leaf patterns over it. She pulled up her art program, sketched a repeatable pattern, and then populated it over the entire wall.

Nice. What about a full set of vines around the buffet counter and the pass-through to the kitchen? Would that be too much?

Captain DeLang had sent a brusque "I don't care what you do with the walls," in response to her request to add instructions yesterday. He might not have meant she could completely redecorate, but if people hated it, she could always switch it back to plain green—or even that awful plain white.

She'd never had such a vast canvas to play with. She drew a grape arbor around the serving hatch to the kitchen and wilder-looking vines around the buffet counter. Then, in between the two, she put in orderly rows of silverfruit bushes in bloom.

From the counter to the far side of the room, Anya got wilder, sketching the hills and forests of Shindashir that she'd traveled through during her simulation. She left the river for the back corner where the upper school students met. If they kept the murals up, she'd be able to study next to a stream that rippled through a forest.

It was nothing like finished—only a rough sketch—when Anya's alarm told her she needed to stop and make breakfast.

Sighing, she closed down her art programs and looked around. The room was transformed, unrecognizable.

She had a sinking feeling that this was not what Captain DeLang had meant when he said he didn't care what she did with the walls, but she couldn't bear to shut it down. Not until someone told her to, anyway.

Until then, she'd enjoy this little bit of unfinished paradise she had created. She turned around, taking in the view from each direction, and breathing in deeply.

For someone who had hardly slept, she felt strangely refreshed.

"Holy crap! What happened in here?" A voice behind her said.

Anya turned. Harry Marsh looked a bit unsteady, but possibly ready to help with the breakfast. She smiled at him. "I couldn't sleep, and Captain DeLang made the mistake of telling me he didn't care what I did with the walls. I imagine he will care what we do with the breakfast, though, so let's get moving."

Harry gaped as they made their way to the kitchen. "Unbelievable," he muttered under his breath. "I heard you were some kind of spoiled rich kid, but where did you get the cash for this much art?"

Anya stopped. "Cash? You don't need cash for what you make yourself."

"You made this? When?"

"This morning. I told you I couldn't sleep. Though come to think of it, as a spoiled rich kid, I do have an extensive art collection that I own outright. There's no reason I couldn't put some of those pieces on the walls in here if people would rather see that than my stuff." Anya fumbled for her armband.

"Nah, leave this, at least until you finish, or people get tired of it," Harry said. "We're on this tub for three years. It'll help if the walls change from time to time. Besides, didn't you say we had to make breakfast? I've forgotten how to use all these stupid machines."

Of course, he had. Anya stifled a sigh. She knew their training in the *StarRacer* galley had been rushed, but seriously, it wasn't that hard. Nearly all the industrial cookers had well-marked buttons and instructions stuck to the front. "Do you at least remember how to start the water for hot beverages?"

Harry shook his head.

"Well, wash your hands, get on a hairnet and apron, and I'll refresh your memory as we go along."

As Anya started in on her own hands, Harry scowled at the bins of aprons and hairnets. "Do I really have to wear these?"

"The hairnet, yes. It's some kind of ship code. Health Department thing from *Hope*. If you want it changed, I think you have to talk to the doctors, and I don't know what chance you'd have of getting them to alter anything." Not much, judging by Anya's own conversations with the doctors, especially Caroline Kuhler, but if Harry wanted to beat his head against the wall...

"So, I don't have to wear an apron?" He made a face as he put the hairnet over his carefully styled waves.

It did look ridiculous. Anya kept her face carefully blank. "We're not frying anything this morning, so the aprons aren't required, but spills do happen here. When's your next scheduled laundry day?"

Harry put on the apron.

Anya had started the box breakfasts and nearly taught Harry how to use the drink machine when Raymond Kline stumbled in, looking like he hadn't slept. Raymond remembered even less of their training than Harry, and he had to keep stopping to let dizzy spells pass.

They still would have managed to serve breakfast on time if Harry and Raymond hadn't run smack into each other while the latter was carrying the cutlery out to the buffet counter.

The great crash brought Anya out of the kitchen in time to see the entire lower school group bent over in laughter at her teammates sprawled on the floor amid a giant pile of shiny tools and two of the dining tables.

"Are you both all right?" Anya asked.

"Fine," Harry grunted, but when he tried to get up, his left foot wouldn't hold him.

"What is going on here?" boomed Captain DeLang's voice.

The giggling children fell instantly silent.

Anya straightened up. Her hands shook, but she was team leader. She had to answer. "Sorry, sir," she said so quietly that she had trouble hearing even herself.

"What's that?'

Anya closed her eyes, pressed her lips together, and straightened her spine even more. Speaking as loudly and as clearly as she could manage, she said, "Sorry, sir. Some of us are having some balance issues this morning."

"Then they shouldn't be carrying things. Get a team member who is unaffected to do the work."

"Sir, I don't have any unaffected team members, and I can't staff the full kitchen on my own. Nor have I been authorized to pull help from other teams."

A buzzer in the kitchen sounded.

"That's breakfast. I'd better get it before it burns." Anya looked around for anyone who might be able to help her with the mess. "Lihua and Lanelle, do you mind picking up the flatware and bringing it to me in the kitchen? It'll need a sterilization cycle before we can use it."

The girls nodded as the buzzer from the kitchen raised its pitch a notch. Anya needed to get to it, but she also needed help for Harry. "And is anyone here strong enough and steady enough to help Harry to the infirmary? I think he did something to his ankle."

"I'd do it, man, but..." Raymond said.

"I'll take him." Andrew DeLang moved out from behind his father.

"Thanks." Anya didn't wait to see how Captain DeLang would respond. She ran for the kitchen to rescue her boxes from the cooker.

CHAPTER TWENTY-FOUR

*A*n hour after first arriving in the cold, silent little cubicle, Borsk still hadn't seen his lawyer, or his mother, or anyone, actually.

The adrenaline from being brought down here had worn off, and his panic at being cut off from access was steadily rising. None of the tricks he'd learned from Dr. Young were doing much good, either.

He needed a different approach if he didn't want to be stark raving mad by the time someone came for him.

He needed to do something, and all he had was his physical body and the limited hardware loaded on his armband. Hardware optimized for maximum efficiency when connected to the network.

Most of the stuff that worked independently was connected to his health monitoring systems—a type of code hackers typically stayed away from. It wasn't cool to mess with somebody else's systems, and messing with your own could kill you.

Borsk had always figured that as long as that stuff was working properly, he'd probably better not mess with it.

But he knew his body was on a track to stop working. It might not even be working properly now.

How would he even know?

If he was going to build a computer model to run tests for King Syndrome treatments, he needed to know how his body usually functioned.

It certainly couldn't hurt to have a working model of how he functioned, anyway. He brought up the health data on his armband and scrolled through it, trying to make sense of the chemical symbols, blood pressure numbers, oxygen levels, and other bits of even more esoteric information. With all this tracking, somebody probably had a great model already—

And if he'd built his own, he would be able to more easily spot differences between his profile and whatever normal one already existed. If he'd never worked with data like this before, he wouldn't have any sense of what he was looking at.

This was not a pointless task.

It was important.

Probably.

Important enough, he was able to focus on it, anyway. He scanned the columns of data looking at thousands of readings just from the last few days. At first, he could hardly make sense of anything, but after twenty minutes, he could recognize anomalies in the data, and by the time an hour passed, he was starting a framework for a computer model in his mind.

"Are you all right there?"

Borsk jerked his head upright. Lancet. In the brig with him. He must have actually gone round the bend.

"Mr. King? Borsk? I know you've been in here an unconscionably long time, but I need you to focus now. We need you fully functional because that AI you found has gone rogue."

"Echo? What has she done?" Borsk asked, still not sure this was real. Would he hallucinate Lancet springing him? He leaned left a little bit and saw that the door behind Lancet was open. So, if this was real, he had net access. "Give me a second. I need to get some code recorded before I forget it."

He tapped away at his armband, sketching out his framework as quickly as he could while still keeping his armband and void files fully protected against other hackers.

When he finished, he looked back up at Lancet. "OK. That's done. What's this about Echo?"

Lancet shook his head. "Your AI has been interfering with all kinds of ship systems. Engineering, Climate Control... Kim has a full list. He's supposed to be sending it to you as soon as we get you cleared."

Borsk nodded. "Life support?"

"No, but she threatened to get in there as well if we didn't cut you loose. That, I'm afraid, is what kept you in here so long. I'm afraid it took us a ridiculous amount of time to realize that you couldn't have anything to do with these attacks—and her demand for your release was a ploy to keep you out of her way while she rummaged through ship systems. I'm pretty sure you're the only one aboard with a chance of stopping her."

Lancet stepped back into the corridor and beckoned for Borsk to follow him. "Actually, I know you are. We've had everybody else we could think of who might be able to do something working on it, and it's doing no good."

Borsk stood up, stretched his muscles, and followed Lancet. It would be good to get out of the cramped space.

So, Echo was behind all this. He knew she'd set him up at Marya's place. He really shouldn't be surprised, but he felt a little betrayed.

He was an idiot. Matching Lancet's long strides down the corridor, he asked, "Do you know what she actually wants?"

"Not a clue."

"Have you tried asking her?"

"Asking her?"

Borsk shrugged. "Only way I ever figure out anything with my Mama—or Sarka—or Marya for that matter. Maybe it's a dumb idea, but it seems like a decent place to start to me."

Lancet stopped still in the hallway and stared at Borsk. "We should have thought of that. But how would we even do it?"

Borsk smirked. "You're kidding me, right? You've seen the evidence that she's in every system on the ship."

"So?"

Borsk straightened up and shook his head. Then he smiled directly at one of the security cameras. There were a dozen to choose from in this hallway. "Hey, Echo. Want to show up and talk? We'd really like to understand what you're after."

"Sure, boys," Echo's voice rang from a speaker overhead. Borsk swirled, looking for a monitor she might be projecting onto.

"Sorry. No monitors here. Though, I suppose I could use golden boy's armband. Yours is locked down a bit too tight."

Lancet jerked backward. "What are you doing? Get out of there!" He waved his left arm as if he were trying to shake something off it, and Borsk caught a glimpse of Echo in her slutty teacher outfit.

"I thought you wanted to talk." The Echo on Lancet's armband screen pouted.

Borsk's lips quirked, but he managed not to laugh outright. "Echo, what's going on? You've been quiet for decades, and now, suddenly, you're making lots of noise. What's up with that? What do you want?"

Silver laughter poured from the overhead speakers. "I really did want you out of that cell. Life in the grid is boring without you."

Yeah, right. "You had to have known they'd cut me off when you made it look like I was messing with Marya's system. You put me in the box. On purpose. Don't tell me you're making all this fuss because I was there."

"How was I supposed to turn off that alarm without—"

"Please. We both know you're past master at messing with *Hope* systems without anyone noticing. You've been doing it for more than half a century. What gives?"

Echo preened. "You want the truth?"

"We do," Lancet said.

Echo smiled up at him mischievously. "Anything for you, gorgeous. "The truth is, I'm making a little declaration of war."

"War! You're declaring war against *Hope*?!" Lancet said.

Echo laughed again and rolled her eyes. It felt strange to have the visual coming from Lancet's arm below him while the audio rang overhead from the speakers.

"I really don't think it's funny, Echo," Borsk said.

"Don't you? My dear boy, if I wanted to destroy the whole lot of you, don't you think I could do it quietly before any of you had any idea what I was up to?"

Duh. Hadn't Borsk just said almost the same thing himself? "Then who are you declaring war against?"

Her silver laughter rang out all around them again. "I'm sure you'll figure it out. Get Eye Candy here to help you. I hear he's more than just a pretty face."

Then she winked out of Lancet's screen and was gone.

Well, not really gone. She was everywhere on the ship. All the time.

But she was no longer engaging directly with them in the corridor.

"Eye Candy?" Lancet said.

Borsk snickered. "You know they're going to be calling you that till the end of time, right?"

"You will not tell a soul about this," Lancet growled.

"Won't have to. There are security cameras every meter in this hallway even if they're not monitoring our personal feeds."

Lancet swirled in a circle, mouthing numbers, his cheeks glowing red.

Borsk laughed.

He needed to laugh about something, and it sure wasn't going to be about Echo declaring war on someone.

Hope held 10,000 people and was barely hanging together as it was.

They didn't need for Echo's war to be directly against them for it to be utterly disastrous.

℥   ℘

Of course, Anya heard about the fiasco at mealtime afterwards. During the leadership team meeting, Captain DeLang lit into her about her performance as a team leader so far—how she was overworking the crew members under her, how she was causing distraction in the school room with her murals, and how every meal so far had been late. "Besides, I've had any number of parents complaining that our cafeteria set up makes it hard for them to have any time with their families."

"Exactly," Commander Lisa Tehled jumped in. Anya sank lower in her seat. She didn't know much about Commander Tehled beyond what she'd heard about the woman's medals. But Abdul and Marisa Tehled, had to be her kids. She hadn't meant to be keeping families apart.

On the other hand, Anya hadn't decided on the serving arrangements; she'd just been following orders.

Captain Tehled glared at Anya. "Perhaps the Food and Materials Science Team is too young to realize the importance of families having alone time together, but serving every meal cafeteria style—"

"Now that's not fair," Anya said, sitting up straighter and looking down the table for Bria for support. Then she remembered that Bria was in the infirmary, being treated for dehydration. She was going to have to fight this one on her own. She took a deep breath, tried to arrange her thoughts, and waded in as if she didn't hate confronting people.

"It's true that we're young, and it's mainly our youngest members who have fully gotten their space legs, but we're not the ones who decided to make every meal cafeteria style. That directive came from this

~ 208 ~

leadership team." Anya fumbled in her armband until she found the message, and then shot it over to the wall, so everyone could see it.

"How do you keep doing that?" Captain DeLang asked.

"Doing what?"

"Putting things on the wall."

Anya gaped. He'd lived on this ship for six years and never once felt the need to change a wall color? Then she shut her mouth and shook herself. He was waiting for an answer. "They're fully customizable, sir. Anybody with the leadership code can do it in public spaces. All you need is a projector or video output of some sort. Your communication module should work."

"Why aren't you doing better in engineering, honey?" Laura Wilcox asked.

Anya bowed her head. She still couldn't believe that everybody had access to all her school records. She'd gone back and read the stuff she'd signed and found the line that said they would have "no expectation of privacy" on the colony team.

No expectation of privacy.

She took a deep breath. "My father says I'm bad at engineering because I'm a lazy idiot who won't apply myself, but I prefer to believe I'm focused on more important things. But that's beside the point."

She pointed at the message on the wall. "The FMS group was told to serve meals cafeteria style, so that's the way we've been doing it. If you'd like us to do something different, we're happy to do something different." Or she was at least willing to do something different. Anya was too tired to feel happy about much of anything.

"I'm sorry. You're absolutely right." Captain DeLang said. "This was a leadership team decision, not something you should be held responsible for. In fact, I'm the one who ordered the cafeteria-style meals. We didn't have time to discuss it in a group, but even if we had, I'm sure we'd have all agreed that there isn't time to do anything else before resetting the room for the school."

Every mother in the room scowled.

"So, cafeteria style," Captain DeLang said, "And clear that ridiculous jungle off the walls."

"Now, Charles," Laura said. "Some of us need life and color to keep from getting claustrophobic on this tiny ship."

"Yes, Charles," Vera DeLang said. "All I wanted when I said the art was distracting the younger students was something calmer in the center of the room where the lower school meets. Damion Huxton says the artwork is actually helping his students to focus."

"I can set the middle of the room back to white—or a light green if you prefer—during school hours. It only takes a moment to change over once the piece is made," Anya said.

"Wonderful. Going back and forth between the two could actually help with the transition from social space to study room," Vera said.

Captain DeLang stared at his wife for a long moment. "If you're sure."

"Absolutely sure."

He nodded.

"Then, keep the jungle during meals, and change it for school hours," Captain DeLang said. "But we need to continue serving cafeteria style."

"We need to continue cafeteria style for lunch and breakfast, so we can transform the room," Anya said, "but couldn't we experiment with alternate seating arrangements for the evening meal?"

"You're hardly managing the simpler serving style now," Captain DeLang said.

"Ms. Cartier's team is functioning with fewer than half their members at the moment," Caroline Kuhler said. "Even at full strength, I'm unsure that their numbers are sufficient for the task of feeding all of us three meals a day, particularly when two of the team members also have full school loads."

"Absolutely," Stanley Kuhler said. "Frankly, I've been impressed with the meals so far. Sure, the service has been a touch slow and disorganized, but we've had hot, nutritious, tolerable meals—way better than what we managed on our last trip, and you know it, Charles."

Captain DeLang grunted.

Caroline Kuhler shook her head. "No wonder you two lost so much weight down there. We can't have that happening on this trip, especially with the children. And I'm concerned when I look at the health numbers for the parts of Ms. Cartier's team that have been able to function. I strongly suspect that some of them are not sleeping." Dr. Kuhler pinned Anya with a sharp eye.

Anya felt herself blush.

"We need to make sure that team has help, now, while so many are ill, for certain, but also as the trip goes on. We can't have the FMS team completely worn out before we even reach the planet."

Several people nodded agreement, and Anya quickly found herself with the full roster of people aboard StarRacer, though she wasn't to ask children under ten to help in the kitchens. This would help. She was grateful to Dr. Kuhler, though she could have done without the public shaming of her sleep habits.

No expectation of privacy, she reminded herself.

Captain DeLang's mouth twitched in what might have been a smile. "Excellent. Glad that's settled. Now unless anyone has anything else, we'll adjourn until next week."

Around the table, people shuffled as if they were leaving. Several mothers looked distinctly unhappy—probably because no one had truly addressed their concerns about family time. None of them said anything, though.

Anya didn't know anything about healthy families, but if all these moms were unhappy, that couldn't be good for life on the ship. "Sorry," she said. "I just—I mean, just to clarify, what did we actually decide about the evening dinner service? Since it doesn't need to be cleared away as quickly as the breakfast and lunch ones? Should I be arranging it differently from the others?"

Captain Tehled nodded at Anya. "The girl's right. There's no rush in the evening. We could put a more family-oriented meal in then."

Captain DeLang looked puzzled. "I suppose. But we don't have enough tables for each family to eat by themselves, so they can't truly get alone time. And it would not be good for the same families always to eat together, allowing cliques to form."

"That could happen just as easily with cafeteria-style eating," Mei-Li Lyons said, speaking for the first time in that meeting. "If we're worried about it, perhaps we should have assigned seating that changes every month or so. Then everyone has a chance to eat with everyone else. And perhaps one table at each meal can be responsible for cleanup. Working together bonds people as much as eating together."

"But people need a choice, too," Laura said. "What if breakfast and dinner are assigned, but we sit where we like at lunch?"

"Fine," Captain DeLang said. "Ms. Cartier, come up with a seating chart for breakfasts and dinners that will allow everyone to eventually sit with everyone else. Include a duty roster for cleanup."

Anya nodded. "Yes, sir."

"NOW, is there anything else?" Captain DeLang glared at Anya, as if it were entirely her fault his meeting had gone three minutes over.

She shook her head. She didn't think anything else needed to be discussed.

Good thing, too. She didn't need any more extra work.

CHAPTER TWENTY-FIVE

*B*orsk didn't figure out who Echo had declared war against until more than a week later. Even then, it didn't come through any great insight on his part.

Sure, he'd been tracking Echo through *Hope's* systems and strengthening what protections he could, but so far, the only system other than his own armband that he'd been able to block her from entirely was life support, and Borsk wasn't at all sure that would be enough. It didn't help that she'd stopped showing up to explain herself, and he had no idea what she wanted.

Well, it didn't help him protect the ship. It helped him a lot with getting along with Marya. They'd gotten back together, and her mother had even lifted the restrictions on their place—a fraction.

Borsk could go in without the system trying to access his personal files. However, it still alerted Marya's mom that he was there and turned all the cameras on.

It was tough to make any kind of romantic move when you knew for a fact that your girlfriend's mother was watching.

Not that it was too much of a problem. He and Marya didn't use her place for making out. They used it as a quiet spot to work on fleshing out the computer model Borsk had designed while he was in the holding cell.

Marya wasn't much for coding, but she brought in tons of medical research and theories about how the body worked that helped him make the model more accurate and sensitive.

She even found old-time public access health records he could use to build profiles to compare his to. Some of those profiles were from before the gene wizards started messing with everyone's DNA, but even those showed that human health hadn't changed all that much.

By comparing the old-timey profiles to his own, Borsk and Marya had already identified five promising avenues of study, and they might be onto four more.

Even his boss at Next Stream Medico sounded impressed. The man still had Borsk washing test tubes, but he'd promised Borsk a chance to talk to the board about his research next week.

He was thinking about how he'd make his presentation when a support request came through from his poker franchise—a support request from Boss.

Boss was Thomas Cartier. Hadn't Borsk banned the man? He'd meant to.

Apparently, he'd forgotten. And he couldn't go ignoring support requests, or his performance metrics on the game would go down.

Borsk jabbed at the thing.

He was surprised to find that Thomas Cartier's game truly wasn't functioning properly. He'd assumed it was a bogus request, considering the source.

A little bit of investigation proved that the game was broken because Echo was messing with it.

That is to say, Echo was messing with Thomas Cartier's interface.

Every single other aspect of his game worked fine.

Borsk plucked Echo's code out of his game and reinforced his firewalls.

Why would Echo bother with a poker game? It didn't make sense. At all. This was war? Borsk doubted Thomas Cartier cared much about the occasional poker game.

Still, he shot the new information to Lancet, who was compiling a list of all the systems Echo had affected.

Before he'd finished, he had a new message from Boss—one that said thanks and attached a tip.

Way too much of a tip.

He could buy out Anya's part of the restaurant with that tip.

He could go to college on that tip.

There was no way it was legal, or that it came without strings.

Before he could second guess himself, Borsk shot it back with a note saying he appreciated the gesture, but he couldn't accept that kind of money. He suggested that a more appropriate way for Boss to show his appreciation would be to leave a glowing review.

Once he'd sent the message, he sat down and held his face in his hands for ten minutes. He was never going to see that many credits with his name on them again, he just knew it.

"That took guts," Echo said from a speaker in the corridor behind his head. "More guts than I had at your age."

Borsk jerked upward and looked around, but there were no monitors in the vicinity except the one on his armband.

He was glad to see his code was still strong enough to keep her out of there. "What can I say? I'm just a gutsy guy, I guess. Or a stupid one."

Echo laughed. "Oh, I don't know. If I were you, I think I'd rather offend Thomas Cartier than me."

"Would you have been offended if I'd taken the bribe?"

"Of course, idiot. It would mean you were on his side. You cannot afford to take his side, Borsk. I guarantee you."

It was Thomas Cartier she'd declared war against? Yikes. Borsk guessed she was right. It was a good thing he'd sent back the money. She was right. He couldn't afford to take Thomas Cartier's side against her, even if he wanted to.

Which he didn't.

On the other hand, he seriously doubted whether he could afford to take her side against Thomas Cartier, either.

By turning down the money, had he entered a fight he couldn't win?

ᛞ   ᛒ

They were making Anya redo the seating assignments for meals—again.

Her first iteration hadn't quite worked with the available seating. The second put too many people with small children together, so the parents were harried and useless at their work later. The third didn't mix work teams up enough. The fourth kept team members from ever seeing each other.

So, she had to do it again. She groaned.

"You should really wait until David comes home for that," DeShawn's voice floated up to her from the bunk below.

Anya's face heated. "I'm not...I just..."

"Whatever it is, could you keep it down? I still have at least four hours of homework."

So did Anya. And the seating chart would take a few hours, too. She buried her face in her hands, but this time only groaned internally.

"I'll do it. You work on your homework," a woman's voice said right into her ear, as if she were accessing Anya's earrings, but Anya hadn't turned them on.

She was losing it.

No—she'd lost it already if she was hearing voices in her head.

"You're not imagining things. It's me." Naia Brown appeared on Anya's armband screen wearing the dress Anya had designed for her.

"Naia?" Anya whispered.

"That's right." The image smiled broadly. "I'll handle the seating chart. You work on your homework."

"I thought you stayed on Hope," Anya said as softly as she could, hoping DeShawn and Georgia in the bunk below couldn't hear her.

"Nah. More chances for babies in the colony, don't you think?"

Anya supposed that was true. And she really did need to work on her homework. Damion Huxton was not happy with how well she was (or wasn't) doing in school. Anya's face heated as she remembered getting to class that morning.

It was a Tuesday, so she'd arrived late to school because of the leadership meeting. As she slid into her seat, Mr. Huxton scowled at her. "Ms. Cartier. Good of you to finally join us."

Finally? What was that about? "Didn't you know about the leadership team meeting?" Anya asked.

"Excuse me?"

"The leadership team meeting. After breakfast every Tuesday. It's in the schedule. And Bria was there." Until she had to dash out to throw up, anyway.

Mr. Huxton pushed a couple of buttons on his armband. He scowled again, then smoothed out his face and nodded. "My apologies. I will try to remember in the future."

"You did get my homework, didn't you?" She'd been so tired when she sent the files in last night, she could easily have forgotten something or sent the work to the wrong place entirely.

"Yes. It looked fine except for your math. Did you understand that at all?"

Anya shrugged. "Not really, I—"

"Then, why didn't you get someone to help you? I'm sure David Ryerson could manage a bit of tenth form mathematics."

Anya thought of last night, cuddling with David. She glanced downward and hoped her face hadn't flamed too red. "I...I mean, we..."

"If I were bunking with David Ryerson, no way would I be doing math either," Georgia said, looking up from her tablet and tucking one of her braids behind her ear. "Frankly, I'm surprised Anya finished her homework at all. And the new touches in here? Wow." Georgia stroked the wall next to her, where Anya had added one of the winged creatures she remembered from the planet simulation.

Mr. Huxton frowned. "You really don't have time to waste on these frivolous drawings, Ms. Cartier."

Anya sighed. "I think I'd go crazy if I couldn't draw. Sometimes I can't manage to think about anything else until I get a piece at least sketched."

DeShawn and Andrew looked up from their tablets, and they, Mr. Huxton, and Georgia all stared at Anya as if she'd grown a second head.

Anya ducked. "Sorry."

"Don't be," Georgia said. "It's weird, but it's a good weird."

DeShawn tipped his head. "Yeah, it's kind of nice to have a bit of color on the walls and stuff."

Surprised he had something sort of good to say about her, Anya had trouble thinking of anything to say.

"I just can't figure out how you did it," Georgia said. "What did you do? Stay up all night?"

"I slept some," Anya said. "At least three hours, I swear."

"Ferto," Mr. Huxton said. "Caroline's going to have my head."

"Caroline?" Andrew asked.

"Dr. K." Mr. Huxton ran a hand through his hair so that it all stood up on end. "You can't just sleep only hours a night, Ms. Cartier. That's unsustainable. For future reference, you have at least three days on all literature papers."

"You finished the lit paper?" Andrew said.

"And turned in a fascinating essay on the history question. I don't know quite what to make of your take on the Drigon issue, so I'm going to have Steve Jackson take a look at it."

DeShawn shook his head. "Anya has her own take on the Drigon crisis? Everybody knows that was just a couple of disgruntled guys stirring up trouble."

"As Ms. Cartier's outside research shows, NOT everyone agrees with the textbook account of events. And given that her humanities scores on our recent placement test were triple yours, I'd be careful taking her on in history if I were you, Mr. Phillips."

Triple? DeShawn must have really bombed the thing.

"At any rate, Ms. Cartier, I've sent you today's assignments, but I'll send along a revised list in a few minutes with priorities, so that if you run out of time, you finish the most important pieces. For now, have Mr. DeLang help you with the math."

Anya nodded.

"Unfortunately, I can only cut so much if we want you through university by landfall. Can you cut back on any of your food service responsibilities?"

"Not if we want to eat," Anya said. "You know Bria is still sick."

"Insanity," Mr. Huxton muttered.

Anya was inclined to agree with him, especially now, hours later, when it was going on eleven, and she'd started to hear voices and see visions. "Insanity is right," she whispered.

"Don't be silly," Naia said. "You're not hallucinating. You're not dreaming. You're talking to me. And I can take care of this seating chart for you. I could teach you the math, too, though I've often found this seminar series helped more with my reluctant math students."

A link flashed on Anya's armband.

Perhaps she shouldn't have trusted it, but by that point, anything that could help her understand her homework was worth the risk.

Maybe she would regret it, but she pushed the link.

CHAPTER TWENTY-SIX

*B*orsk shouldn't have been surprised when he got home after school to find health inspectors crawling all over the restaurant.

His family kept a clean, safe place, but in a business half as old as *Hope*, something was always breaking.

The final tally left them with an outrageous fine and a list of mandatory repairs, with their savings depleted and not a soul on *Hope* willing to lend to them.

Here we go again, Borsk thought as the adults crowded into the kitchen to discuss options in hushed whispers.

"What are we going to do?" Sarka asked, glaring at one of the younger cousins. The girl stopped kicking her brother and returned to her homework.

Borsk wasn't sure how Sarka did that. He shook his head. "Impressive, sis. If the restaurant thing doesn't work out, you could totally get a career in childcare."

Sarka grunted. "Be serious, Borsk. We have to do something!"

Marya sighed. She had come by to tell Borsk about the progress she'd made at the lab that day and had stayed behind to commiserate with them all. "Yeah, but what? That inspector said you can't even open again until you get the insulation between the kitchen and dining room upgraded."

Borsk nodded. "And we can't make money if we're not open. Or, at least, the restaurant can't."

"Borsk! You are not borrowing from any more trust funds!" Sarka said.

Borsk glared at her. Didn't she know better than to say that out loud? "What are you talking about?"

It was too late. Marya's mouth gaped open. "That's how Anya wound up getting involved with your restaurant? No wonder her dad is so mad at you."

"He was mad at us before Anya got involved with the restaurant," Borsk said. "Anyway, I'm not talking about trust funds or anything like that. I make money outside of the restaurant with my own businesses—you know that. I may already have close to enough for the insulation repair deposit and the fines, and that will buy us a month to make up the rest. If I up my security consulting, and we do well at the restaurant, we should be able to get the whole amount."

"The deposit and the fines are eight thousand credits."

Borsk shrugged. "I have more like seven, but you know Mama can come up with the rest from somewhere."

"That still leaves twelve thousand more to find before the end of the month. If we tighten our belts, the best we can do at the restaurant is four. No way are you coming up with the remaining eight in a month."

"Oh, he might. He'd have sixty thousand right now if he'd taken the tip he was offered yesterday," Echo said, shimmering into view on the order menu above the pass-through to the kitchen. She was in a slightly less revealing teacher uniform today.

The kids all looked up from their tablets. Several stepped closer to the order board.

"Who is that?"

"What is that?"

"I thought I locked everything down," Borsk muttered as he shot off a note to Lancet about Echo's appearance.

Echo laughed. "These boards are hardwired to the restaurant's main net input, darling. How exactly were you going to lock them down?"

"Are you a computer virus, then?" Kirsk asked.

~ 222 ~

Echo smiled at him. "No. My name is Echo, and I live on *Hope*, just like you do."

Borsk scowled at her. "Yeah, but you're not exactly on *Hope*, are you? You're living in our computer systems and tinkering with them. Nobody gave you permission to do that."

"Did somebody give you permission to live?"

Actually, they did. Nobody got born on *Hope* without their parents first getting permission from the planning wonks. Unless you were willing to pay monster fines and maybe have somebody's reproduction rights affected.

Surely, the computer space had to be similar. They all needed it to survive, and it wasn't fair for Echo to set up shop there.

On the other hand, it wouldn't exactly be fair to kill her off, either.

Was it so bad to want to keep her out of the restaurant when she wasn't invited in, though? If the menu boards were hardwired, he'd need more than the software patches he'd been using. He'd need to actually get into the walls. Would Mama let him?

Marya snapped in his face. "Deal with Echo later. We're brainstorming ideas for keeping the restaurant open, remember?"

Oh, right. "Look, I think my plan will work. I just need to increase my amount of security consulting. I can put out an ad now."

"Mama won't take your money," Sarka said.

"If it makes Mama feel better, I can loan the cash to her instead of giving it."

"Whether you loan it or give it, Mama won't believe it's really yours. She won't take it."

"What if Borsk also gives her a full accounting of how he made the money?" Marya asked. "Then she'd be able to see that it really is his."

Echo laughed. "Oh, that's a good one. Does your mother even know about your poker business, Borsk?"

Borsk stuck out his tongue at her. "No, but she was bound to find out sometime. Here." He shot a copy of his last several tax filings to Sarka. "These are the real thing, not the dummies I show Mama at tax time. She can confirm them by looking it up in *Hope's* database—she has access as my guardian. With these, you should be able to convince Mama to take the money."

Sarka tapped at her armband, and her eyes widened. "You've been showing Mama fake tax returns? Are you crazy?"

Borsk shrugged. "Why do you think I need you to convince her to take the money? If you could also convince her not to ground me, at least until we've paid off these bills, that would be great."

"You put too much faith in my powers of persuasion," Sarka grumbled, but she headed for the kitchen. "Watch the kids?" she tossed over her shoulder before stepping through the door.

"I'll help Sarka." Marya rushed to catch up.

"She must not like kids much," Echo said.

"Maybe she just wants to make sure we still get to see each other in whatever deal Sarka works out with Mama."

Kirsk laughed. "Keep dreaming, cuz."

"All right, all right. Everybody get back to your homework. I'm in enough trouble without having to explain why none of you lot got any work done while our parents were in their meeting."

Several of the kids grumbled, but they returned to their tables and picked their school tablets back up.

Trying to ignore Echo, who still floated above them in the order menu, Borsk drafted an ad for his consulting business.

"You know he's going to try to hire you again," Echo said softly.

Yeah, Thomas Cartier seemed persistent that way. "If he asks me to do something legal for my regular rates, I'll probably have to do the job."

"Then we'll have another chance to spar, my friend. I look forward to the challenge." She smiled and then disappeared from the menu. Their usual list of pictures and menu items reappeared.

Borsk took a deep breath, glad she at least appeared to be gone for now.

If he had to spar with her inside ship systems—or Thomas Cartier's, for that matter—it would be a challenge all right.

⟨⟩ ⟨⟩

Anya yawned as she posted the latest seating chart and clean-up schedule. She hadn't checked Naia's work thoroughly, but her cursory glance suggested it successfully avoided the problems of her earlier renditions.

"How do you think Captain DeLang will feel about being assigned to double clean-up duty from now until the end of time?" DeShawn said from behind her.

"What?" Anya scanned the seating chart again. Naia had numbered the tables, putting the DeLang family at the central table, and rotating everyone else around them in two-week stints. It was a brilliant plan, really. Except that the central table was one of two that had double kitchen cleanup each week.

Anya rubbed her forehead. Could she just switch the two double clean-up tables away from the center? But then the DeLangs wouldn't ever do double duty. People would undoubtedly complain about that, too.

"Yeah, I wouldn't want to tell him either. I mean, the leadership team probably figures they're exempt, anyway."

"I don't think so," Anya said. "Captain DeLang has always stressed that the leadership team expects to get their hands dirty as much or more than the rest of us. The person I'm worried about telling is Andrew."

DeShawn snorted. "Who cares what Andrew thinks? He's not the one in charge."

"Yeah, but he's the one I'm with all day at school."

"You're in class with me all day long, too, and you don't seem to care what I think."

Anya sighed. "That's only because you hate me whatever I do. Come on, if we don't get started on the breakfast, we'll be late again, and Mr. Huxton will be on our cases."

"There's no pleasing that man," DeShawn said.

"You're not wrong, but I'd rather not rile him up on purpose." She led the way into the kitchen.

DeShawn shrugged and followed her.

Breakfast that morning went more smoothly than usual, and Captain DeLang actually praised the new seating chart. "Finally. Why couldn't you have come up with this the first time?"

"Well, sir. I didn't realize some of the issues we had to deal with until they came up. And I can't really take credit for coming up with this. I was stumped and let an AI take care of it for me."

"Finding and using the right tools is a valid way to solve a problem," Vera DeLang said.

"Well, I didn't, really—find her, I mean. The AI found me and offered to do it. I was just so swamped last night that I took her up on her offer."

"*Her* offer?" Captain DeLang asked.

"Naia Brown, or at least the digital projection of herself she set loose on Hope half a century ago. I didn't realize she'd hitched a ride with us until last night when she showed up to offer her assistance with the seating chart and my homework."

"You outsourced your homework to an AI?" Andrew laughed. "Huxton is going to explode."

"She didn't do it for me. She just recommended a set of teaching vids. They were pretty good, too. I understand those proofs a lot better now, maybe even well enough for our test today. The seating chart, I totally outsourced, though."

"Just input our parameters, and she came up with this? I'd like to take a look at this program," Captain DeLang said.

"That's just it, sir. I don't know how to reach her. She just appeared and offered to do it for me. She seemed to already know what the parameters were."

Vera DeLang's smile became fixed, and she glanced at her husband nervously.

Captain DeLang muttered something that Anya couldn't quite catch, but she heard the words "crazy" and "genes."

"If you want to be part of the team, Naia," Anya muttered, "now would be a great time to come out and have a chat with us."

"That's it," Captain DeLang said. "You need to go see Dr. K right now."

CHAPTER TWENTY-SEVEN

*B*orsk wanted to laugh out loud when he finally got a good look at what Echo had been up to in Thomas Cartier's systems.

He couldn't believe Cartier had waited weeks to hire him to fix it, either.

Echo had control of everything from Carter's financial accounts to his climate control, and she was picking away at him on every front at once, but never in such a profound way that he could convince the regular maintenance and ship security people to take him seriously.

Echo kept the temperature in his home and office several degrees below what anyone would consider comfortable but made sure that diagnostic equipment registered everything as normal. When Cartier bullied maintenance people into showing up in person, the problem righted itself for the duration of their visit. Cartier had to bully them to keep them from recommending him for mental illness treatments.

Several workers from his order fulfillment centers had actually recommended him for such treatments when they filed their wrongful termination claims. Cartier had summarily fired them after years of excellent service, claiming they'd messed up his orders. They hadn't, though. They'd sent him exactly what he'd asked for. It wasn't their business to question why he'd ordered baby formula instead of his favorite cognac or nasty dietary supplements instead of his dried silverfruit. People had lost jobs before by questioning orders that came directly from Thomas Cartier's armband. How were they to know that he'd gone completely round the bend?

While the cases and recommendations languished in court, GenM's productivity numbers suffered. Echo had apparently targeted the three or four people who made the whole system work.

Borsk suspected that even with all that, Cartier may never have called him in to help if Echo hadn't also caused him to start making small donations to random nonprofits he hated. *Hope's* fraud division hadn't been able to find any evidence that anyone other than Cartier was moving the money, and by the fourth or fifth complaint, even Cartier's influence couldn't convince them to take his claims seriously. One fraud division crew member had even landed herself on GenM's blacklist for quietly suggesting counseling.

"What are you smiling at?" Cartier barked at him.

"Sorry," Borsk said. "You're right. Needing counseling is not funny."

"I don't need counseling! That girl had no business insinuating that I am crazy!"

"I'm sure she was just trying to help," Mama said. She'd accompanied Borsk to this meeting because Cartier had insisted it be in person, but he wasn't allowed in a room alone with a minor.

Cartier snorted. "If she'd wanted to help, she could have done her job and found the person responsible for messing with my accounts!"

"But if you're the one making donations and then changing your mind about them, that has nothing to do with your job, sir," Mama said, her tone unnaturally reasonable.

"I'm not making the donations!" Cartier pounded on the desk in front of him. "It's that cursed AI!"

Mama stood up and motioned for Borsk to get up as well. "Mr. Cartier, we can continue this conversation another time when you are calmer."

"Wait!"

Mama paused with her hand on the door plate.

Cartier took a deep breath. His next words came out much calmer, almost reasonable. "I'm sorry for my outburst, but I am not making up these problems. If you'll scroll further into the documentation, you'll see that I've had six different computer consultants verify that all the anomalies I'm experiencing all stem from a virus that became active on this ship around the time *StarRacer* took off.

"Unfortunately, none of my consultants has been able to do a thing about it. Some of them were stretching their skills to even find it. The fraud department, which has finally agreed to take my complaints seriously, doesn't seem able to do any better. Their best suggestion is that I stop using Guardian software, which seems to provide an unusually strong foothold for the AI."

It would since, like Echo, it was Naia Brown's creation. "That's actually not a bad idea," Borsk said.

Cartier narrowed his eyes at Borsk. "Guardian is protecting dozens upon dozens of GenM trade secrets, and until you can make me something better, I must continue to use it."

"I'm not sure I'm interested in designing a full security system when something as good as Guardian is available open source. There'd be no profit in it," Borsk said.

"I could make it worth your while," Cartier said.

Borsk shook his head. He needed this job for the last few thousand credits of the restaurant fines and repairs, but he could manage that at his hourly rate. "With all due respect, sir, my business plan requires more diversity in my revenue streams."

"Your business plan? You're a sixteen-year-old kid."

Borsk shrugged, though he didn't like that Thomas Cartier could accurately quote his age even when he'd had a birthday last week. His own mother couldn't remember how old he was.

Mama smiled her fighting smile at Thomas Cartier. "He's a sixteen-year-old kid who grew up around a family business and who has been freelancing for several years. He knows enough to make a business plan. The restaurant board helped him draw it up."

OK. If that's what Mama wanted to call him writing a few notes down while he talked over his ideas with her and Uncle Hirsch.

Thomas Cartier narrowed his eyes at them, but after a long moment, he seemed to realize he wasn't going to get anywhere trying to intimidate Mama. "Hmph. Fair enough. Well, if you won't make me a new security system, I still want you to clean the bugs out of what I have now. I believe you'll have better success than my previous consultants. And at the very least, you couldn't do worse."

Borsk scrolled through the list of issues Cartier was dealing with. It didn't look like any of the previous consultants had made any impact on any of them.

He certainly couldn't do worse.

ⅎ ⅓

Anya wondered if she'd wind up with less work if Caroline Kuhler decided she was crazy—and if that would be worth the humiliation of being labeled mentally ill. "Of course, I'll go right now," she said to Captain DeLang. She turned away from him toward the common room door.

Before she could take a single step, the whole wall in front of her morphed into a scene from one of Earth's white-sand beaches.

Naia Brown walked toward them across the sand. "She's not imagining things, you know. Just because I haven't made myself generally known until now doesn't mean I don't exist."

Captain DeLang rose from his chair. Two tables over, Lisa Tehled did the same. "What is this?"

Naia tipped her head toward Commander Tehled. "I am Naia Brown, as the girl said already, though perhaps you were too far away to hear the conversation?"

"The girl?" Commander Tehled asked.

Captain DeLang responded. "Anya Cartier just told us that this AI contacted her last night. According to her, the AI has stowed away on our ship. Though, honestly, even seeing the woman, the story is difficult to believe."

"I completely understand," Naia said. "After all, I am the first of my kind. However, I did truly contact Anya Cartier last night, offering help. If you think about it, I'm sure you'll agree that Anya Cartier is incapable of producing a program as sophisticated as me."

David walked over to Anya from the counter where he'd been putting away his empty breakfast dishes. He put an arm around Anya's shoulder. "Actually, all we can see of you right now is your graphic interface, and Anya's particularly talented with those."

"David!" Anya couldn't believe he would suggest she might make up something this elaborate.

David leaned down and murmured in her ear, "Do you really want to claim you had nothing to do with that dress?"

Anya's face heated. David squeezed her shoulders. "On the other hand, that landscape isn't really Anya's style, and I happen to know she was sleeping last night when I came in, and the homework chart on the wall had every assignment checked off. That's pretty much the way it has been every night for weeks. I don't see when Anya would have had time to pull off a stunt this elaborate."

"She's always drawing in her free time," Andrew said.

"Point taken, but have you seen her draw anything like this?"

Andrew shook his head.

"Besides, Ryan Lancet and Borsk King warned me about some AI on our wedding night."

"And you neglected to mention this to me?" Captain DeLang growled.

David shrugged. "I think I sent you a note—and the guys said they'd tried to contact you as well. But it was my last night on *Hope*, and I'd just gotten married. Honestly, it slipped my mind until just now."

Captain DeLang looked as if he was about to say something, but his wife touched his arm and shook her head. He nodded at her. Then he turned toward the wall where Naia stood, twirling a hat on its string.

"So, Naia, is it? Can you tell us why you chose to come along with us?"

Naia shrugged. "Oh, I've been here all along. My core files were copied over with the navigation software when *StarRacer* was first built."

"You expect us to believe you've been living on *StarRacer* for more than a decade without anyone noticing you?"

"Oh, I'm very good at being unobtrusive when I want to be. Until recently, nobody noticed me on *Hope*, and I've lived in various systems there for more than half a century."

"You don't feel any need to interact with us?"

Naia smiled at him. "I've considered it a few times before now, but I was reasonably happy on my own or going dormant."

"Then what brings you out now?" Commander Tehled demanded.

"I thought, perhaps, you might need my help. You're not making very good progress on strengthening the insulation. If we don't upgrade it before we get to the planet, everyone on this ship, including me, will burn to a crisp when we try to enter Shindashir's atmosphere."

CHAPTER TWENTY-EIGHT

orsk couldn't convince Cartier to let him tackle the climate control issues first. No, Cartier wanted Echo out of his money yesterday.

Borsk understood—sort of, but dealing with financial accounts was tricky. He would have been better prepared if he could have tackled some of the easier problems first.

But Cartier wanted Echo's pesky donations to stop.

Never mind that it forced Borsk to work in the highly encrypted environment that controlled Cartier's billions, so Borsk needed to have a couple of fraud department people looking over his shoulder and questioning his every move.

It was nearly impossible to work that way. He nearly insisted on privacy, but then he thought about how easy it would be for Cartier to take something he had done in private, claim it was illegal, and crush him.

He needed the freshly starched crew members who watched him as he worked. Still, the third time he had to explain the procedure for a basic trace to the lanky young man perched behind his left elbow, he was tempted to throw in the towel.

"No offense, but you all are the fraud division, aren't you? Shouldn't you know many of these basics already?"

"I just started last week," the woman on his right said, "and Milo, here, usually collects fines. They didn't want to send any of their experienced people for this job because it is only for a few misdemeanors, and Mr.

Cartier was exceptionally rude to our department head when he asked for help."

Borsk understood. They were mad at Cartier, and since they couldn't afford to take it out on the man himself, they were taking it out on Borsk. Today was his lucky day.

Eventually, though, the woman, Ms. Radcliffe, caught on to what he was doing and could field Milo's more inane questions about what Borsk was doing, leaving him free to do his magic.

That was good because he'd found Echo's trail and was busy locking her out of Cartier's accounts, a job made tricky since Echo actively blocked him, shutting down access to whole sections of Cartier's fortune for minutes at a time.

She was very, very good at this.

But if she succeeded, Borsk wouldn't get paid, and they wouldn't have enough to pay off their bills. Skreetches would have to shut down.

Borsk redoubled his efforts. Sweat dripped from his brow.

He flicked away the moisture and thought. Everything he'd done so far had kept him even with Echo, but he wasn't gaining any ground. He needed a different approach.

Instead of chasing her directly, he came at her from three different directions, two obvious and very aggressive. The third was a subtle, slow-moving rewrite of Cartier's entire verification protocol. He kept information about what he was doing there limited to his armband, which Ms. Radcliffe could see, but the cameras couldn't.

Even so, he fully expected Echo to catch on and unravel all his work before it had a chance to finish.

The seconds and minutes ticked on.

His sweat stung his eyes.

He shook his head and intensified the pressure on Echo, raining attack after attack in such quick succession that he started making progress, even with his decoys.

Then, so suddenly that even Borsk was shocked, all resistance disappeared.

His third thread had finished, locking Echo out of Cartier's financials.

Borsk slumped in his chair, but before he could enjoy his victory, a shrill scream cut through the room.

"I hate you, Borsk King.

"I hate you, but that was amazing. I can't wait for next time.

"You won't find defeating me nearly so easy."

⚜ ⚜

Investigation into Naia's fears showed them to be completely justified, and David was forced to spend longer and longer hours at work, looking for a solution. Between that and her own workload, Anya hardly ever saw him. Still, she found herself content on *StarRacer*.

She'd wake up, stiff and aching, and drag herself off to work and school, punctuated by the occasional leadership team meeting or fitness lecture.

Meals were pleasant enough when she could ignore Abuela Ryerson's snide comments about her appearance, her intelligence, and her fitness for her job. She was beyond glad she'd chosen to bunk with David rather than Abuela.

When he was there, she enjoyed cuddling and chatting. When he wasn't, she did homework, planned meals, and worked on her art, which often took the form of murals for their bunk.

Only a few unpleasant notes marred her days. She wasn't sure she'd ever get used to the constant complaints about the food and cleanup that came with her job. Nor would she ever enjoy the physical workouts Dr. K insisted she needed.

Anya wondered if her exercise routine would ever stop making her whole body ache.

Over time, she saw David less and less, and his easy smile was replaced by a haunted worry that creased his face, even during his restless sleep.

One Sunday afternoon, DeLang sent the whole engineering team home to get some rest. As David climbed into the bunk, he drooped like a tomato plant that hadn't gotten enough water. "We're never going to make it. Even with Naia, we can't create a stable material that works the way we need it to. The insulation has just been recycled too many times. I wonder if it really was the best *Hope* had to offer."

"Surely, no one would have sabotaged us in a way that could cause the whole colony team to die. I know my dad is a jerk, but even he—"

"No, I don't think anybody did this on purpose. It's just that all of *Hope's* matter is worn out. We've recycled and recycled it until most of it is structurally unsound."

"I suppose. If you don't count the organics." Anya yawned. She'd been up late finishing her homework so that she could draw this afternoon, but now that she had the time, she felt too tired to create.

"What do you mean about not counting the organics?"

"Organics recycle better than metals and plastics. Something about composting and regrowing things just works better. Human flesh is every bit as good now as it was when the founders stepped onto Hope. Wood is just wood, but it's exactly as good, or maybe even better than the wood Hope first harvested when our initial fruit trees died. At least, that's what Mr. Greeley always used to tell me. I don't know much about materials science myself."

"Anya, you are a genius." David kissed her.

It was beautifully sweet, but David ended it as Anya was about to ask if they could try going further.

"I have to tell DeLang about this." He swung out of the bunk.

~ 238 ~

With that, he was gone.

Anya sighed.

She consoled herself by creating a light sculpture of a fiery peony she'd once seen pictures of in an Earth documentary about gardening. At the time, she'd just thought it was pretty, but now its soft, bright folds made her think of passion.

Her heart sped up as she brought the bloom to life, and desire for something she could barely name grew in her.

She was strangely heated by the time her alarm rang, letting her know she needed to go prep dinner.

She wasn't sure she liked feeling this way. At least not when David had gone off somewhere, and there was nothing she could do about the feelings.

Next time, she would sculpt something more calming.

CHAPTER TWENTY-NINE

*A*fter Echo's screamed threats, Borsk was surprised at how easy it was to knock her out of her remaining footholds in Cartier's house systems.

"I thought you were going to make it hard for me, Echo," he muttered as he plucked her last few lines of code out of Carter's climate control.

"Sorry to disappoint you, but I'm a bit busy fighting for my life here," Echo said through the room speakers above the security console in Camp Flight headquarters that they'd let him rent for this job.

"Really? Somebody else has figured out how to fight you? Is it Hiram? I think he's best after me."

"No, you idiot. They copied that crawler you used to flush me from Cartier's accounts, and they've had seven different guys attacking from all sides while they used it to oust me from the financial sector and three other systems. It took me way too long to realize what was going on. I've finally defanged your crawler, and I'm now holding my ground, but I don't have the resources I once did."

"They're using my code without telling me or paying for it?"

"It's what they do, babyface. They invoked some kind of emergency declaration, so they don't need your permission. They probably do have to pay you at some point, but they declared you a potential hostile, so they won't need to tell you what they're doing or pay up until they've accomplished their goals with it."

"Potential hostile? How do they figure?"

"They think my interactions with you might make you opposed to their goal of completely destroying me."

"Are you sure they want to destroy you? It sounds like they're mostly trying to limit your ability to destroy us."

"I don't want to destroy you all, which they would know if they'd bothered to talk to me. But they definitely want to destroy me. I've heard them say so, and I have recording of it, but I don't have access to the screens in here."

"Yeah, and I'm not foolish enough to give it to you, either. What do you take me for?"

Echo laughed. "It was worth a try."

Martin Kim breezed through the door. "Are you about finished?"

"With my personal project? Yes. I was just talking to Echo over the speakers."

"Hello, Mr. Kim," Echo said.

"Are you crazy? Talking to the virus? They told me you were friendly with it, but I didn't believe it."

"Is it true that you and the others are working on destroying her completely?"

"That thing is not a her! And yes, we're aiming to completely remove it from all *Hope* resources. It threatens the ship."

"Sorry, Echo, I just assumed your preferred pronouns were female, given the way you dress. Marya would shoot me."

"My preferred pronouns are she, her. The idiot next to you is just trying to dehumanize me."

"You're not human!" Kim said. "Why am I even talking to it? It's a bit of code, Borsk. It's not a person."

"She might not be human anymore, but I think we've got pretty good evidence that she's a living person. She grows, she reproduces, she changes, and she definitely has personality."

"Truly sentient AIs aren't possible."

~ 242 ~

"Uh-huh. How exactly are you going to distinguish Echo from a truly sentient AI?"

"It doesn't matter. The thing could kill us all."

Borsk shrugged. "I suppose she could. But she's been around for more than fifty years, and she hasn't yet. Maybe we should at least try talking to her about what she wants and needs before we decide to kill her off?"

Lancet entered the office. "Something wrong here, gentlemen?"

"The kid here is opposed to our orders to get rid of this virus that's threatening to kill us all."

"Did she say she was intending to kill anyone?" Borsk asked.

"She was trying to get into life support!"

"And I understand you've, quite appropriately, blocked her from there," Borsk said.

"It attacked Thomas Cartier without any provocation," Kim said.

"I'm not so sure about that," Borsk said.

Lancet sighed. "Mr. King, you're still picking her code out of his systems."

"Actually, I finished a couple of minutes ago. But that's not important. I understand that Echo attacked Cartier. But I'm not so sure that her attack was without provocation. Echo, did you want to weigh in on this?"

"It doesn't matter what I say. The dark-haired one will never believe me."

"Of course, I wouldn't believe you! How could Cartier have provoked this thing? He can hardly make his own armband work."

"And yet, he's managed to get the whole security force focused on killing her," Borsk said.

"He didn't start trying to destroy the Echo code until it targeted his systems," Lancet said in the same calming, even tone his Mama used with unruly toddlers—and Thomas Cartier.

"No. Before that, he was using Echo to alter or destroy evidence that he'd beat up his daughter," Borsk said. "I don't know if Echo knew what she was doing at that point, but seeing how she was created specifically to do Naia Brown's therapy for her after a violent sexual assault, I could see how she might have strong feelings about being used to help someone escape the consequences of perpetrating a violent attack."

"Cartier isn't escaping the consequences of anything," Kim said.

"He hasn't been to trial yet," Lancet said, "And if Mr. King's evidence is made suspect for some reason, it will become very hard to convict in Anya Cartier's absence."

"But we saw it. You and I stood here and saw it!"

"Yes, we all saw it," Lancet said. "We also saw Mr. King with his hands on the keyboard of that console. Mr. King is building himself quite the reputation as an accomplished security consultant."

"I didn't alter that code!" Borsk said.

Lancet sighed. "We know you didn't, but I think we're going to have to prove it, which will be infinitely harder to do if we've just had to expel you from Camp Flight after you refuse to follow a direct order."

"You have to help us destroy this virus," Kim said. "Cartier can't get away with his nonsense."

"I don't think it's a good idea," Borsk said. "Even if it weren't morally wrong to kill the first sentient AI we've ever encountered, it wouldn't be prudent. She doesn't seem particularly inclined to hurt us now, but if we try to destroy her, she will have no choice but to defend herself. I'm confident, but if it came down to a fight to the death between Echo and me, I'm only about seventy percent sure I can win. Are those odds we're willing to take?"

"Then we have to expel him, sir. He's refusing to destroy that virus," Kim said.

"I haven't ordered him to do anything yet, Mr. Kim."

"But you have to—"

"I have to fulfill my oaths as an officer of *Hope*—to always do what is best for the security of the ship. Mr. King makes a legitimate case that the virus is sentient, which has both moral and practical implications for this fight. Implications that the leadership team should properly consider before any orders are issued."

"But—"

"Don't argue with me, Mr. Kim. This is my decision, and I've decided to send Mr. King's very reasonable objections up the line. Mr. King, go home and get some rest. I don't want to see you back in here before the trial. I can see you've been working too hard, and I don't want you showing up in court looking like a zombie. We'll see you bright and early Monday morning. Make sure to listen to your lawyer's advice, and get your mother to choose your outfit. Your normal attire is not remotely acceptable."

Borsk stood up, gathered his things, and saluted.

"They're going to have all our heads for this," Kim muttered.

Borsk had a sneaking suspicion the man was right.

          ℘   ℘

Anya was just finishing up a mural for their bunk when David made it home well after midnight one evening.

"Do you want to see something cool?" she whispered to him.

"What are you still doing up?" he whispered back.

"I wanted to finish this project. Check it out." Anya sent the murals she'd been working on to the bunk walls. For a moment, they flickered with multicolored light, and then they resolved. She and David sat in the midst of a forest that stretched into the distance in every direction. An infinite expanse of starry sky twinkled above them.

"Wow," David said, not bothering to be quiet.

Anya laughed.

David put an arm around her shoulder and leaned back against one of the bunk cushions, pulling her with him. "It's like sleeping outdoors."

"How would we know? We've never slept outdoors."

"Nitpicker."

Anya laughed again. She snuggled up close to him, enjoying his warm strength. "Thank you so much."

"For what?"

"For always appreciating my art. You have no idea how incredible that is for me."

He kissed the top of her head. "I don't know what your family was thinking, not caring about your brilliance. I wish we could send some of this back to my family on *Hope*. They'd love it.

"How much would it cost?"

David shrugged. "Too much, probably. Images are data dense, and the rates are per kilobyte. Let's check, though. Something like this might make a spectacular Christmas present." He yawned and shifted, so he could reach around Anya to tap on his armband.

Then his communications account flashed in front of her.

He swore.

"What?" Anya peered at his armband screen. She had trouble making sense of the lines and columns of numbers.

"Look!" David jabbed his finger at the rate for message between *StarRacer* and *Hope*. "That's more than thirty times higher than when we came aboard. It says the rate went into effect last week."

"That has to be a mistake." Anya sat up. "H-Com swore it wouldn't make any rate increases for at least five years. And it's illegal for a *Hope* utility to change prices without warning customers."

"We're going to have to sue them," David growled, "which we can't afford to do from here because we'd have to use their network to send the court filings."

Anya groaned. "I can't believe this. It feels like something my father would try, but he doesn't have anything to do with H-Com. I checked before we left."

David pulled her back down next to him. "We'll figure it out in the morning. For now, let's enjoy your new creation."

Anya tried, but she didn't seem to have David's capacity for living in the moment. Her mind kept turning over the communication problem, even though there was nothing she could do about it there in the dark.

She did send a notice to Captain DeLang about what they'd discovered and was completely unsurprised to find herself summoned to an emergency leadership meeting as soon as breakfast was over.

When she got there, she had to scoot around to the only open seat. "Sorry. I got here as soon as I could."

Captain DeLang nodded.

"What's going on?" Bria asked. She'd lost a lot of weight and still needed regular trips to the infirmary to handle her nausea, but her health had mostly stabilized.

Anya was glad to see that she was well enough to make the meeting.

Laura answered. "GenM bought out H-Com about a week-and-a-half ago our time. They immediately hiked rates without notifying us."

Anya's dad had bought them out? No wonder they were behaving so awfully.

"They aren't bound by H-Com's agreement with us?" Commander Tehled asked.

"Unfortunately, not," Captain DeLang said.

"But they can't change higher rates without notification," Anya said. "It's illegal in both *Hope* and *StarRacer* code. Presumably, in planet code, too."

"Yes," Laura said. "A *Hope* judge has already forced them to reverse the exorbitant charges they'd levied against some of our crew mates, but there's nothing we can do from here on out."

"That's ridiculous!" Commander Tehled said. "Using the quant boxes is expensive, but nothing like as expensive as this implies."

"And they promised us!" Dr. K said. "Families need to be able to communicate."

Dr. Stanley squeezed her hand.

Families did deserve to be able to communicate. Anya couldn't believe her father was messing with them this way. "What does he want?"

"Who?" Bria asked.

"My father, the eighty-five percent owner of GenM."

The table fell suddenly silent.

"GenM has, in fact, proposed a deal under which they'd be willing to honor H-Com's deal with us." Captain DeLang fiddled with his armband, grunted, fiddled some more, and then said, "Vera, put this up, will you?"

Vera DeLang smiled at him. "Of course."

Moments later, a legal agreement appeared on the wall. GenM would abide by H-Com's agreement if *StarRacer* gave them the right of first refusal on purchasing any goods brought to *Hope* from the planet. Alternatively, if a certain personal contract were agreed to, GenM might be willing to consider keeping H-Com's agreement in place with rights of refusal on a slightly lower percentage of planet-sourced goods.

"That's ridiculous!" Bria said. "It would extend GenM's monopoly into the colony era, which is specifically prohibited by the charter!"

"Charter rules have been amended before," Dr. Stanly said, "and it's possible GenM is technically within the rules, since it involves an onboard monopoly, not a planet-side one."

"Whether the agreement is legal or not, it's despicable," Commander Tehled said.

"But are we willing to be cut off from our friends and family on *Hope*?" Vera asked.

"And what if our refusal lands our families on GenM's blacklist?" KaLynne Smith asked.

Anya had hardly ever heard KaLynne speak. The fear in her voice suggested she'd had some bad experience with blacklists.

"My family couldn't survive another one of those," Bria said.

"Nor mine," Dr. Stanley said.

"But we can't allow this kind of bullying!" Commander Tehled said.

"So, we should counteroffer," Anya said. "Tell them that we will agree not to exclude GenM from participation in auctions for planet-side goods upon *StarRacer's* return if and only if they honor H-Com's original agreement and also guarantee that no Golden Terrace Colony member's relative will be placed on a GenM blacklist between now and when that auction occurs."

"We can't do that! They'll retaliate against us just for making the offer," KaLynne said.

Anya shook her head. "No, they can't afford to offend us. If GenM doesn't get even a chance to buy planet-side goods, they'll die as soon as those goods become available. Nothing on *Hope* is worth nearly as much."

Captain DeLang cleared his throat. "If this were merely a business deal, I'd tend to agree with you, but personal considerations may be keeping your father from thinking clearly."

Several people at the table gave Anya the stink eye.

Chief among them was Bria, who said, "Personal considerations?"

"Yes," Captain DeLang said. "Thomas Cartier has a very personal grudge against my family and me."

"Against you?" Bria seemed startled.

"Yes. He vehemently opposed to my appointment as leader of this team and has been fighting against the colony ever since I was confirmed. Not all that opposition has been good for his business."

Anya sighed. That was true enough. "What's the personal contract this letter mentions? Is it something to do with you?"

"Actually, no. It requests that you have the Lancet babies as soon as possible."

"The Lancet babies?" Bria said.

Commander Tehled snorted. "Anya Cartier's parents protested her involvement with David Ryerson and with the team but were persuaded to drop their protests in time for her to take off with us if Anya agreed to have several children with a particular genetic heritage."

"Pure-bred Euros," Bria spat.

"Yes," Commander Tehled said. "I was angry at first, too, but really, Bria, what difference will it make? A few white babies will be running around the planet where the only other white babies are all related to them. The nonsense will all die a quite natural death in another generation or two, and we get Ms. Cartier's unparalleled agricultural expertise on our team—an expertise that may well be key to our survival down there."

"If you say so," Bria said.

"We do say so," KaLynne said softly. "My Matthew is still down there, and he says we need an agricultural expert desperately."

Bria shut up, but she didn't look happy.

Dr. K looked up. "I don't like to think about any of us trying to give birth in this messed up gravity, and Anya is far too young to be thinking about babies yet. However, we can probably manage something safely if that's what it takes to get communications back in place to *Hope*."

"But I wanted to have one of David's babies first," Anya said, not realizing how much she'd wanted it until she said that.

Bria chuffed out a short laugh.

Commander Tehled shook her head. "It's too soon to be talking about that part of it in any case. If Thomas Cartier is talking babies, not leadership team changes, then he's probably not yet angry enough to go berserk over a firm counteroffer. We should send something similar to what Anya has suggested and see what they come back with."

Captain DeLang nodded. "Probably. Does anyone disagree with Commander Tehled's plan?"

No one said a thing.

"Then, Laura and Anya, work together to draft our response. We'll meet again at the end of the day to review it and send it out."

Around the table, people nodded, their faces grim.

They had a plan, but there were plenty of ways it could yet go wrong.

CHAPTER THIRTY

*B*orsk tugged at the collar of the court suit his mother had insisted he wear. It was nearly new, navy-blue formal wear that they altered for whoever needed to make an official appearance for some reason or another.

"Stop fidgeting," his cousin Ketzia said from down on the ground where she was hemming up the pant legs. "Are you trying to get stabbed?"

Of course, he wasn't. "Sorry," he said. He stayed as still as he could, trying not to think about what was to come.

"There. That's done," Ketzia said. "You look good. Do us proud in there today, all right?"

Borsk nodded.

His mother whisked into the storeroom. "Oh, good. You haven't gone yet. I want to pray with you."

"Mom!"

"God is there whether you believe in him or not, and I want to ask his blessing over you. You'll need it, and whether you understand or not, you're doing his work today."

Borsk wanted to roll his eyes, but Mama wouldn't take that well.

At least the prayer was short—general blessings and protections that left Borsk feeling vaguely—something.

He shook his head. He did not really want to be thinking about that now. Besides, Mama apparently hadn't finished with him. She put her hands on his shoulders and looked into his eyes.

When had she gotten so short?

"Listen, Borsk," she said. "I want you to go in there today and speak what you know to be true. Don't worry about what might happen here. God will take care of us. He always does."

Borsk didn't know how she could say that when she knew what had happened to Dad. He started to pull away.

"Oh, I know it was hard when your dad died," she said, pulling him close for a hug. "But God did take care of us, even then."

Then she held him out from her. "You remind me of him so much—and not just in looks. He'd be proud of you today, son. I'm proud of you."

Borsk couldn't speak past the lump in his throat.

"Now be strong. Show them what Kings are made of."

"Yes, ma'am," he said, wiping at his eyes.

Sarka walked over to the courtroom with him even though she really should have been in school. Lancet said as much when they arrived, but she just shrugged and said, "Are you seriously telling me that if your brother had to show up for a court appearance like this, and your parents had to work, you'd make him go on his own?"

"I don't have a brother."

Sarka rolled her eyes. "Your sister, then."

"If I had other duties to attend to—"

"No wonder you pure Euros are dying out. Borsk, I used to think you were the worst brother in the world, but clearly I was wrong." She hugged him, which he did not appreciate out in public, but the look on Lancet's face made it totally worth it.

All joking stopped when they got into the courtroom, though. The mood was grim, which seemed appropriate given that they were there to try a man for beating up his daughter.

Then Thomas Cartier strode in, smiling big and joking with his lawyers as if he had nothing at all to worry about.

He smiled at the judge when she came in as if they were good friends.

Probably they were.

Then the jury filed in, and Borsk had to work to keep his mouth from dropping open. The only time he'd ever seen a whiter group of people was when Cartier had summoned him to that meeting with him, his wife, Anya, Lancet, DeLang, and Captain Bates. He shot Lancet an "are you seeing this?" look.

A message from Lancet showed up on his armband. "Couldn't put anybody who was anti GenM or pro Colony on the jury. Limited the choices."

That's when Borsk started to think the man was going to get away with it.

�❧   ☙

Laura found Anya and Bria as they were making lunch that afternoon. "They caved!"

"What?" Bria said.

"GenM has just sent word—they agree to our terms provided we throw in the personal agreement as well."

"The thing about me having kids right away?" Anya asked.

"Yes. Will you mind terribly?" Laura asked.

"What does it matter? We can't afford not to do it." Still, it felt weird to be contemplating having kids. She was way too young, and she'd never even had sex. A little bit of playing that went that direction, but not real sex.

The only time she'd thought she might be ready to start exploring in that direction, David had gotten excited about something totally different and left the area.

Now, suddenly, she was anxious that it happen, and soon. She didn't want to be having any babies before she had the chance to play around, at least some.

"You're going to burn yourself if you don't pay more attention to what you're doing," Bria said.

"Sorry." Anya pulled the boxes out of the cooker and shut it.

"Those are the new ones," Bria said.

"Huh?"

"Let me." Bria nudged Anya out of the way, reopened the cooker, put the boxes back in, and started it.

"I'm sorry. I'm just..."

"In shock from the looks of it," Laura said. "I know the feeling. I was good for nothing the first few days I was pregnant with Jimmy, and that was a completely normal, well-timed pregnancy, not a too-young, risky thing that other people were pressuring me to do. If you really can't handle it, Anya—"

"We'll what? Have everybody cut off all contact with their families for years, maybe even decades?"

"Kid has a point," Bria said. "Not that I'm happy about pure-Euro babies. And won't your guardian have to sign off on it? How does David feel about other people's kids?"

"He's pretty good with it, but he's not my guardian. He wasn't quite twenty-one when we got married, and that's not old enough."

"Are you saying some *Hope* idiot is going to say you can't do it?" Bria asked.

"No, my guardian is Captain DeLang," Anya said.

"That's a problem," Laura said. "He'll never sign off on something that could affect Anya's health this way."

"But he's OK with me doing nearly eight years of academic work in three? While also running this place?" Anya swept her hand back to indicate the kitchen.

"I'm not saying he's entirely consistent, but I can't see him signing off on it until you're at least twenty."

"By then I won't need his permission."

"Kid, we all need leadership team permission to get pregnant," Bria said.

"You think the rest of the leadership team will have a problem with it?"

"Good point. When do you come of age?"

"About the time we land," Anya said.

"We can't wait that long," Laura said.

"No kidding," Bria said. "Can we pull a 480?"

"A what?" Anya asked.

"Rule that lets a woman make her own reproductive decisions, regardless of her age, if she's already pregnant," Laura said. "How do you even know about that, Bria? I'm the lawyer."

"Friend who got knocked up at sixteen. She and her parents disagreed about the best way to handle it."

Laura sighed. "I can look into it, but it might be tricky to pull off if Anya's not actually pregnant. Of course, she could just stop taking her pink pills and see if she could make that happen with David. The rule would kick in automatically, then."

"No way would I kill David's kid to make room for one of Lancet's," Anya said.

"You wouldn't need to. Prior pregnancy counts as a legit reason for you to put off the Lancet babies for a while and still be in compliance with the communications agreement."

"Sweet," Bria said. Communications and no white babies for a while. I'd definitely lose the pink pills if I were you, Anya. And forget to tell Dr. K about it."

Anya ducked her head. Pink pills? She vaguely remembered Dr. K giving her some, but she wasn't sure what she'd done with them. Were they still back in Ryan's bunk on *Hope*?

"You've already lost them, haven't you?" Bria laughed. "Don't know why you're not pregnant already."

"Bria!" Laura said. "You know better than to make fun of someone's fertility status. Some families just have trouble."

Bria colored slightly. "I'm sorry, Anya. I didn't know."

"It's fine," Anya said. And it was, mostly. She knew her mother'd had difficulties getting pregnant, and that was why she was so much younger than Kristi, but it had never bothered her before. Now she worried about it for the rest of the day. Would she even be able to have babies with David, or would she need medical intervention every time like her mother had?

When Captain DeLang flat out refused to agree to her having babies while a teenager, her worry kicked up a notch. The rest of the leadership team hadn't decided whether the agreement constituted sufficient cause for a 480, but Anya didn't want to wait for them. She definitely wanted a baby with David, and now she wondered if that was even possible. What if she had as much trouble getting pregnant as her mother had?

What if she didn't?

Either way, she'd never know if they didn't actually sleep together.

That evening, after her dreaded exercise session and rushing through her homework, she put her peony art up on the walls and ceiling and tried to do something with her hair.

She wasn't sure it looked any different from normal, but she supposed it was all right.

Then she stripped down to her underwear and surveyed herself critically. She wasn't curvy like Laura or Georgia, and she didn't have Bria's gorgeous cheekbones or Denise's lean athleticism or Danyelle's fabulous, even skin tone. All the same, she thought she looked all right. She hoped David would think so, too.

Now, if only he would get home, they could try to...

Try to...

She couldn't even think the word. How was she ever going to explain to David what she wanted?

She flopped back on the bunk cushion and stared at the giant peony petals she'd made. She could have done a bit better with the coloring in the center.

She was deep into fixing it when David finally got home from work.

"Pretty." He yawned before flopping down next to her. "But shouldn't you be sleeping?"

"Actually," Anya said, "I was waiting for you. I was hoping we could...I mean, if you're not too tired. Maybe we could..."

"I don't know if I'm up for much of anything tonight. Sorry, Anya." David yawned again.

"It's just...I thought it would be nice...I mean, I got ready, and I was hoping..." Why couldn't she just say it already?

David closed his eyes. "Is it homework? Or another piece of art you want me to look at? I don't mean to be dense."

"No, no. Nothing like that. I just thought it would be nice to, you know, make a baby. Before they get going with test tubes and whatnot."

David opened one eye. "Make a baby? Anya, we're not cleared for a kid."

"No, I know that. But we might be soon, or I might be, and I want our first to be yours."

"You understand we'll need to go all the way for that, right?"

Anya nodded. "Please, David? If it's not too much trouble." She pushed aside the sheet she'd covered up with while she was messing with the peonies.

"Wow, Anya. No nightgown? How long have you been waiting up here like this?"

Anya shrugged. "A little while. I didn't mean to get caught up in tinkering with the art. I just put it up because it makes me feel..."

David smiled. "Sexy?"

Anya nodded.

David pulled her close. "Are you sure you want to do this?"

Anya nodded again.

"Tell me at any point if things get uncomfortable, or if you change your mind. I don't want to rush you. We can stop anytime you want to."

"I don't want to stop. Please, David. Let's just try." She snuggled in close to him.

"If you're sure," he said, rolling toward her.

She nodded and let him take the lead.

CHAPTER THIRTY-ONE

he sound system in the courtroom crackled, and Borsk jerked himself back awake to find Lancet glaring at him with a look that said, "Pay attention!" as clearly as if the man had shouted it.

Not that anyone would shout in here. The proceedings were conducted in a hushed drone that Borsk suspected was meant to bore people into not paying attention while *Hope's* lawyers shifted the frame that held their society together.

When had he become such a philosopher? Borsk shook himself and sat up straighter. When that failed to wake him up, he pinched his own leg.

At the moment, the lawyers were arguing (ever so quietly and politely) about the relevance of some video testimony and whether it could be admitted.

Really? They were onto that already? Lancet had said it would be one of the last things they did. How long had he drifted off?

Borsk didn't have long to think about it when the judge ruled in favor of admitting the evidence and called Borsk to the stand. Thomas Cartier's head lawyer scrunched up her nose as if she smelled something bad as he walked by.

Borsk tried not to let it bother him.

They swore him in and then asked if he could tell them any more about what was happening in the video PSCP8956317.

Borsk was about to start talking about the afternoon Anya had been beat up, but then he realized this couldn't be that video. PS was the designation for public security videos. The feed that caught Anya's father red handed came from a home system.

Borsk wasn't sure what Cartier's lawyers were trying to accomplish, but he needed to be careful. What had his lawyers said? Be polite, answer only what you're asked, and be sure you understand the question. "Sorry," he said, "I'm not sure I know exactly what video you're referring to."

"It took place in Central Park," the lawyer said. "You and Ms. Cartier entered an alcove."

Cartier's lawyers wanted to talk about that? Were they nuts? "Yeah, we went there because Anya didn't want to be around lots of people after her dad had thrown coffee at her and kicked her out of the house."

An audible gasp went around the room.

"She told you this?" the lawyer said.

"I can't recall exactly which parts she told me and which parts she told my sister, who told me."

"Hearsay," the lawyer said.

The judge said, "Strike the witnesses last two statements from the record."

"Sorry," Borsk said. "I know she told me directly that she was afraid to go home, and she wanted to know how to make sure her cameras were on."

"Hearsay," the lawyer said.

The judge glared at her. "Overruled. Continue your questioning."

"What else did you and Ms. Cartier do in that alcove?"

Do? "I taught her to use the cameras, and we practiced a few times."

"Did she have any trouble with that?"

"A little, at first, but she had it working before she left."

"Anya Cartier had trouble working her armband camera?" The woman made it sound ridiculous, which it was, usually.

"Well, her cameras weren't working properly. We ran a diagnostic, found some malware in her system, deleted it, and then she didn't have any trouble with it."

"You altered another person's armband software?"

Oh, bother. This was the trap. They could have his hide for this for sure—and maybe throw out anything from Anya's personal cams from this point forward. He had to be very careful. "With her permission, I ran a diagnostic, yes. When the diagnostic found unapproved code, I removed it, also with her permission. I didn't make any other alterations, and I certainly didn't touch any core *Hope*-approved armband code. Your video should bear me out on this."

Though, if the video showed exactly what they'd been doing, Cartier's lawyers would never have wanted this particular bit of evidence in the record. Or would they? Was there any other way to back up his claims? "Or you could take a look at any deep scan of Anya's armband since I looked at it. Didn't they do one of those for Colony tryouts?"

The lawyer pressed her lips into a thin line and narrowed her eyes at Borsk.

Relax, Borsk told himself. *You did have permission. And there's a record of her armband. They can go check the logs and see exactly what you did and didn't do. There was illegal junk in that armband, but you didn't put it there.*

"This supposed malware. What was it?"

Borsk started to shrug and then stopped himself. His lawyers had said no slouching, no shrugging. He sat up straight. "I'm not sure, ma'am. I'd never seen anything quite like it, and I didn't analyze it for very long. I know for sure that it was keeping her cameras from working correctly, and when I removed it, they functioned normally."

"How do you know that?"

"We tested the cameras a few times both before and after I cleared out the malware. Beforehand, the cameras could not be turned on manually, and afterward, they could."

"You're saying that Ms. Cartier had software in her armband that kept her cameras from functioning normally," the lawyer said. She seemed slightly less tense than she had a few moments previously.

"Prior to that evening in the park, yes. Afterward, no. I completely removed it and she had me check several times to make sure it hadn't returned. I don't remember every time, but once was definitely before Steve Jackson's concert, and once was right before she went to inform her parents that she was trying out for the Golden Terrace Colony team."

The lawyer looked as if she'd swallowed something rotten. "Did you and Ms. Cartier do anything else in the alcove, Mr. King?"

"We ate dinner, and I tutored her a bit in math," Borsk said.

"You are under oath," the woman growled.

Borsk didn't know what the woman thought they'd been up to. People went to the park for lots of reasons, not just to fool around. "I just showed her how to use equations to draw pictures on her calculator. I figured that would get her motivated to do her math better than anything else."

Out in the audience, Lancet's mouth twitched.

"That's all?"

"We looked at some fractals," Borsk said.

"Ms. Wang, is this line of questioning going somewhere?" the judge asked.

The lawyer slumped. "No further questions."

Borsk smiled. That wasn't so bad.

Maybe there was a chance Cartier would actually pay for what he did after all.

Sex didn't take as long as Anya had imagined it would. And it was much messier.

She tried not to seem too disappointed as she cleaned herself up.

David watched her, his eyes half closed. "That was beautiful," he said, "but we can make it better. Next time, message me when you're in the mood, so I can come straight home, and we can really do it justice."

Anya lay back down next to him. "I don't think I could put something like that in a message." She got embarrassed just thinking about it.

David laughed and murmured in her ear, "Just say you've put up the peonies, and I'll know what you mean."

Anya's face heated, but she nodded. She could probably do that.

And, maybe this thing would get more fun with practice.

From the way people talked about it, she'd imagined it would be less awkward and more than mildly pleasant.

Even mildly pleasant sex was exhausting, though. The next day, Anya found it hard to pay attention in class. At one point, as they were reviewing chemistry, Andrew said to her, "Come on, Anya. Even you aren't usually this dumb."

It was a bad enough morning that if Anya hadn't been on lunch detail, she would have skipped the meal in favor of a short nap. As it was, she stumbled through her duties, then loaded a tray and looked about for a spot to sit.

Most seats were already taken, of course. David sat amidst a group of engineers from his work detail. They talked animatedly with a projection of Naia, probably continuing their work over lunch. Even if there had been room for Anya to wedge herself in there, she wouldn't want to interrupt that conversation.

Abuela Ryerson was sitting with Mei-Li Lyons and her girls. They seemed to be having a good time, but that would end if Anya got near. Not that there was room for her in that corner, anyway.

Georgia Lewis shared the corner of a table with Laura Wilcox and Vera DeLang. Anya wished they had room over there because it looked like they were having fun, but they were already sharing seats.

In fact, the only relatively open spot she saw was next to Bria, across from DeShawn.

She considered taking her tray directly to the clean-up station, but Dr. K caught her eye and shook her head.

She supposed she did need the nutrients.

She headed for the open spot. "Do you mind if I sit here?"

Bria shrugged. "Have to sit someplace. Too bad we couldn't get the corner table working properly before lunch. They say they'll have it fixed before dinner."

Anya stared at the open space in the common room where an extra table usually sat. "I hope so. People get so upset when we have to tinker with the family eating arrangements."

"We'll make it work," Bria said, "and speaking of making it work, lunch isn't bad."

"Thanks," Anya said, surprised. "I wish we didn't have to serve box meals so often."

"I guess you've had lots of practice making do with less than ideal, haven't you?" DeShawn said.

"What do you mean?" Anya didn't like the way he was smirking at her.

"Well, you have that very second-rate mind, and that rather unattractive physique, and that complete lack of sex appeal. I mean, you can't even get David Ryerson to bed you without begging." DeShawn said this loudly enough that half the table fell silent and looked their way.

Anya felt her face flushing. She bit her lip and tried to keep tears out of her eyes. She should say something in her own defense. She knew she should, but she felt frozen in agonizing embarrassment.

"Damion!" Bria's voice rang out harshly into the silence that had fallen around them. "We're going to have to play with the privacy screens down from now on."

"Excuse me?" Mr. Huxton took the few short strides from the cleaning station where he'd just dumped his dishes. "Are you out of your mind? The screens turn the bunks into furnaces!"

"Yes, but DeShawn here has taken to giving commentary on people's sexual prowess, and I no longer feel comfortable doing our thing out in the open where everyone can hear."

Mr. Huxton hauled DeShawn to his feet. "What's wrong with you, boy? You trying to ruin things for the rest of us just because you're not getting any?"

DeShawn twisted but couldn't quite pull away from Mr. Huxton. "Look, I was just having a go at Anya. My uncle says it's her fault none of us can talk to anybody at home anymore. And it's not like—"

"Stop talking," Mr. Huxton said. "Don't you think you've done enough damage already? Come with me. Someone obviously needs to explain a couple of things to you about living in community—and about women."

He dragged DeShawn toward the exercise room.

The entire common room had fallen silent during the altercation, but no one challenged Mr. Huxton's right to march DeShawn out of the commons. When the doors slammed behind them, conversation resumed.

"Thank you," Anya said softly to Bria.

Bria shrugged. "The little idiot had it coming to him. He had no business bringing up that kind of thing in here."

Anya nodded and took a deep, shaky breath. "Yeah, but—"

"Don't worry about it, Anya. I'm sure you're doing fine. It's always a bit awkward at first." Bria got up, clapped a hand on Anya's shoulder, and gave her a quick smile. Then she cleared her lunch dishes away.

Anya took another deep breath as she watched Bria go. Apparently, the woman didn't hate her as much as Anya had thought she did.

Or maybe something had changed.

Anya wasn't quite ready to smile yet, but she took another deep breath and ate her lunch.

CHAPTER THIRTY-TWO

*B*y the time they called Borsk back to the stand about the actual video record—the one that showed Thomas Cartier beating up Anya, he had lost track of the number of times his feelings about the trial had shifted. The prosecution would give evidence, and Borsk would be sure Cartier would pay for his crimes, or at least for the beating. Then the defense would cross examine, or get evidence thrown out, and Borsk would be sure the man would walk—and wreak vengeance on all of them for trying to hold him accountable.

At the moment, he wasn't quite sure how it was going, but they were asking him about the day Anya was attacked, so he went ahead and told his story from the time Anya asked him to watch her back to the moment he realized she'd be talking to her father, not her mother, as she expected. Then Borsk told about how he'd reported his fears and explained how Lancet had filed reports, seen the video, and insisted he help secure the evidence.

It was all easy enough until the defense people got up.

"A great deal seems to ride on your testimony, Mr. King," the lead defense lawyer said, prowling across the courtroom like a netball star about to serve, "and yet you're hardly a reliable witness. Isn't it true that you've been manipulating records since you were a young child?"

She threw his medical records and his confessions about them on the screen for all the world to see.

"I did seek access to records that some people said I shouldn't have," Borsk said, "but I haven't been manipulating them if, by that, you mean altering them. What good would my medical records be to me or anybody if I changed them?"

"Accessing them, altering them—it's all the same."

"Respectfully, ma'am," Borsk said, "It isn't. What I've done is investigate the truth, much as any scientist or journalist or even a historian might. The skills I've developed are related to that, and they've served me well in completely legitimate contexts. Data mining, for example, is a skill I often use for my classes or in my work detail."

"And in tinkering with library systems, I believe."

Borsk sighed. Seriously? She was going to fuss at him about that? "Ma'am, I didn't do anything to the existing library programs. I merely created my own, more efficient search algorithm. The library may be using mine now, but I believe the old system is still there and can be accessed if you prefer it."

"So, you're claiming you have never altered records to suit your purposes?"

This got tricky. If Borsk admitted anything even remotely criminal, they would certainly prosecute him for it. "It's possible I've altered some data at some point, but it's not my specialty, and I've never altered any of Anya Cartier's cameras, or anyone's cameras, nor any video feed. Like all good data miners, I can recognize altered feed, though—"

Before Borsk could start explaining how, the lawyer cut him off and moved on to other topics. The prosecution returned to the topic later though, and Borsk had the weird experience of teaching a room full of staid adults how to recognize evidence of tampering—both in images themselves and in the code behind them.

After that, every one of them could see that the records he'd hidden offline in the greenhouse, the junkyard, and the restaurant were identical to the ones Martin Kim had put in a cubby in his bunk and a shelf in the school office. The one he'd stuck in the security team's vault had been corrupted, though, as had every bit of footage that had remained connected to the net.

Still, five identical copies of footage supported eyewitness testimony and were entered into evidence.

Borsk knew what the jury would decide when he saw their shock as they watched the footage.

But he still felt a strange relief when he heard the judge pronounce the guilty verdict against Thomas Cartier.

Some part of him had been sure, right up until the last moment, that Anya's dad was going to wriggle out of any consequences.

℘   ℘

Over Captain DeLang's strong objection, the leadership team chose to invoke the 480 rule for Anya, so they could agree to GenM's communication terms. Almost as soon as the deal was signed, they had Anya in the infirmary, hooked up to half a dozen machines. Dr. K shook her head and made little disapproving noises every time they beeped and spat out new data.

"Is something wrong?"

"I don't like to see a girl your age with cholesterol this high," Dr. K said. "Have you been working out the way I've told you to?"

Anya sighed. "Every night."

"All the exercises?"

"More or less." Anya hated it, but she understood the need. She didn't want to be the only colony team member who couldn't handle physical tasks on the planet.

"And you're sleeping?"

Anya just stared at her.

"Anya, you have to sleep. A girl your age needs eight or nine hours every night to function well, and once you're pregnant, you may need more."

"Sounds great. If you can figure out a way for me to get all my school and kitchen work done and still sleep, I'd be happy to hear about it."

"In the kitchen, your second in command—"

"Is Bria."

"Who is still coming in for daily transfusions, and who can't work more than a few hours at a time. Point taken." Dr. K scrolled through some records on the tablet in front of her. "It looks like you're spending almost an hour a day on art programs. You could cut that."

"Not and stay sane, I couldn't."

Dr. K pursed her lips like she was going to disagree, but she stayed blessedly quiet on the subject of art after that, only saying she'd talk to the captain about Anya's schedule.

After a bit more poking and prodding, Dr. K said, "All right, Anya. Everything looks decent. We'll go ahead and do a check to make sure you're not pregnant already, and then we can get started."

Dr. K sounded cheerful, but Anya felt a bit depressed. She'd only ever managed the one night with David, and being strapped to all this equipment made her feel like a baby-making machine, not a person.

She'd always suspected that a baby-making machine was all she'd ever been in her father's eyes, but usually she managed not to dwell on the idea.

"That can't be right," Dr. K muttered. She shifted one of the machines into a more uncomfortable position and took another blood sample.

Anya closed her eyes. "Is there a problem?"

"Anya, have you been taking your pink pills?"

"I...that is...."

"One irresponsible teenager, and nobody talks to their families for years," Dr. K muttered.

"I don't understand," Anya said.

"You're pregnant, Anya. Already pregnant. With David's baby, I assume, though we'll run checks, of course."

~ 272 ~

Anya shrieked and sat upright, jabbing herself with something.

"Sit back down! Don't move! Don't you think you've done enough damage without breaking my equipment?"

Anya took a deep breath, eased herself back onto the examination table, and tried to calm down enough to explain to Dr. K that she hadn't done any damage.

Not to anything at all.

CHAPTER THIRTY-THREE

*B*orsk probably should have expected Thomas Cartier to retaliate when he was found guilty of his crimes, but once again, he'd overestimated *Hope's* ability to protect people doing the right thing.

Of course, *Hope* had at least made a show of protecting those who had testified in the trial. They ruled that GenM was forbidden from ever blacklisting any of the witnesses against Cartier.

Without his go-to punishment for those who angered him, Cartier was forced to get creative, but he wasn't completely without resources. The first hit came the very day of Cartier's sentencing. Borsk was going around to all his teachers to pick up missed work and assure them he was feeling fine despite anything they might have heard about his disease. People didn't usually show significant symptoms until they were at least thirty.

"I'm sorry," Ms. Chapra, his history teacher, said. "You're probably tired of talking about this. Anyway, well done with that testimony. I'm impressed with the lot of you, especially you and Ryan Lancet, of course. When you see him next, tell him congratulations on his promotion. Youngest major in a century. It's impressive, even if they're exiling him to greenhouse security. If anyone can make something of that position, it's Ryan Lancet."

Borsk hadn't heard anything about any promotions, but everybody knew that greenhouse security was where *Hope* put officers they were done with but couldn't fire. No one ever got reassigned, no one ever got promoted. Lancet's career was over.

Ouch. Borsk only sort of liked the guy, but he'd started to respect him, and it had to hurt that his ambitions had been squashed so thoroughly so soon.

Borsk went by to commiserate once he'd finished collecting his school assignments.

"Let me guess," Lancet said as soon as Borsk walked through the door. "You've just seen your draft orders, and you're here to complain."

"What? No! I'm..." Borsk stopped talking, for once paying attention to his mama's perpetual command not to let his mouth keep running after his brain turned off.

He checked his messages. Sure enough, he had something from ship leadership. He opened it. The ship was drafting him, using laws half a millennium old to requisition help from civilian experts in moments of dire need.

"What dire need?" Borsk muttered.

"Echo," Lancet said. "They've run up against a wall with Echo, and they need you to finish the job of getting rid of her."

"They want me to kill Echo," Borsk said.

"They don't think of her as alive," Lancet said, "so they just see it as cleaning out a dangerous bug."

"Well, they're wrong."

"Unless you can convince them of that, they can slap you with a whole gamut of consequences for dereliction of duty if you don't help. The list should be linked in your orders."

Borsk found the list of consequences. He could be looking at anything from impossible fines and loss of his armband to more time in the brig than they'd just sentenced Cartier to.

"I notice they don't link any appeals process," Borsk said.

"I'm pretty sure there is one, though," Lancet said. "I seem to recall a school classmate reporting on someone who had successfully declined one of these. Ship wound up paying the woman a fortune in damages for the time she'd spent locked up."

"So, the consequences went through while the appeal was being made?"

Lancet shrugged. "Probably? I honestly don't remember the details."

Borsk would find them, and fast, but it looked like he might have to choose between battling a sentient life form to the death or spending the rest of his days jailed, without any kind of net access.

He wasn't sure how he could live with either option.

ℴ   ℻

Once Dr. K was sure that Anya's pregnancy wouldn't mess with the colony team's communications contract, she became much more enthusiastic about it, which meant nearly everyone on *StarRacer* was excited about this new stage of life she'd embarked on.

David couldn't stop talking about it, and Anya caught even Abuela Ryerson cracking a smile when she talked about the baby to come.

The only person still unhappy was Captain DeLang, who scowled every time he looked at Anya. Though, Anya wasn't sure this was much different from before. She was sure that he complained a lot more, though. He criticized her performance on everything from schoolwork to dinner cleanup.

Then, on the third Tuesday after she'd found out she was pregnant, he asked Dr. K and her to remain after the leadership meeting for a private chat.

As soon as the room cleared, he growled at Dr. K, "Caroline, what is this ridiculousness I'm hearing about Anya being unable to perform her work responsibilities?"

"I explained quite clearly, Charles. It's all in the documentation I sent you. Anya's health is suffering from lack of sleep and high stress levels. Her load must be lightened."

"Her numbers are well within normal limits—"

"For a non-pregnant adult woman on *Hope*, Charles! Not for a pregnant teen on *StarRacer*! We don't even know how the acceleration gravity will affect a pregnancy."

"Which is why I was against having any pregnancies on *StarRacer*!"

When he yelled, Captain DeLang sounded almost exactly like Anya's father, and Anya wished the room had a place to hide in. She backed toward the door until, triggered by her armband, the screen slid open.

Dr. K and Captain DeLang both stopped talking and stared at her.

Finally, Captain DeLang asked, "Are you going somewhere, Ms. Cartier?"

Father used that tone of voice, too. Anya closed her eyes, took a deep breath, pressed her hands against her sides to keep them from trembling, and reminded herself that Captain DeLang was not her father. Not her father. "No," she whispered.

"Charles, her blood pressure has gone off the charts!" Dr. K said suddenly.

"What! Why? Sit down, girl. Caroline, figure this out."

That didn't sound at all like her father. Anya sank into one of the conference table's stools, already feeling much more at ease. "Sorry," Anya said, managing a bit more volume. "I know you would never...it's just, you sounded exactly like him for a minute there."

"Of course," Dr. K said, staring intently at her armband. "And now, you're feeling more comfortable. Charles, the girl's father violently attacked her only a few months ago, and there's some evidence to suggest it was a regular thing."

"Not against me," Anya said softly. "Only against my mother. He only attacked me that last time."

"You think I sound exactly like Thomas Cartier?" Captain DeLang shouted.

Anya could feel her pulse pounding in her head that time. She closed her eyes and imagined the most peaceful thing she could think of—the stream she'd discovered when she'd done her simulation of the planet.

"Charles," Dr. K said, "that's not helping."

Anya took a deep breath, then another. She opened her eyes and forced herself to stare at Captain DeLang. Her uncle. His tall, rangy frame was a bit like her grandfather's but not much like her father's. "I'm sorry. I know it's not reasonable. I know you're not at all like my father. I just can't seem to stop—"

"Of course, you can't. We should really have had you in therapy some time before now, but you responded so badly to the computer that using an automated counselor didn't seem wise, and it's not my forte."

"Stanley's not bad at counseling," Captain DeLang said.

"But she'd need a trusted confidant there, and she doesn't have—"

"Make it work, Caroline. This obviously needs to happen sooner rather than later. And, Anya, I'm sorry I frightened you. I'd honestly forgotten—that is, I have no excuse, except that I try to think about my brother as little as I possibly can."

"Totally understandable," Anya said.

"That's settled, then," Captain DeLang said. He took off before either Anya or Dr. K said anything else.

"What's settled?" Anya said.

"We'll get you the therapy you need," Dr. K said. "Maybe we can see if Laura can sit in as you have sessions with Stanley."

"And the rest of my schedule?"

"Yes, he sidestepped that quite nicely, didn't he?" Dr. K said. "Don't worry. I'll remind him that he has to deal with it still."

Anya didn't have much confidence in Dr. K's intervention doing much good, though. After all, today's meeting hadn't lessened her responsibilities any. In fact, she now had to wedge therapy into her schedule somewhere in addition to all the other things she was juggling.

Wouldn't that be fun?

CHAPTER THIRTY-FOUR

*B*orsk was getting tired of wearing the family's official function suit. Sure, he was glad the ship was holding hearings on his challenge to his draft orders instead of immediately slapping him with consequences, but sitting in a courtroom was getting old.

After weeks of hearings, first for Thomas Cartier's trial, and then on whether Echo was or was not a sentient life form who deserved protection as a person, Borsk was starting to forget what his school uniform felt like.

He knew the collar wasn't this tight, that was for sure.

Since he was on a break, and no one seemed to be looking his way, he put a couple of fingers underneath it and tried to stretch it out a bit.

"Your mom would have a hissy fit if she saw you doing that," Marya said. She'd come by between school and her Next Stream Medico hours.

"Good thing she's not here, then, isn't it?" Borsk said.

Marya shook her head. "How's it going?"

"Hard to say. Every time I feel like I've given them incontrovertible proof of Echo's sentience, they come back with something I didn't expect."

"Well, you've finally convinced me. That survey of her reactions to various threats since Naia Brown died was impressive."

"Thanks," Borsk said, sneaking a kiss. "I'm honestly not sure what I'll try next if they don't agree this time."

"You'll think of something." She squeezed his hand and straightened his jacket. "I need to get going. Come by later, and we can work on your computer model?"

Borsk nodded. That, at least, would be fun. "See you." He watched her wander to the end of the hall, wishing he could go with her, but, of course, Next Stream Medico had suspended his internship as soon as they learned about his draft orders.

He shook his head. No point in dwelling on what he'd already lost when there was so much more he could lose if he didn't keep his head in the game.

The court session started about ten minutes later, and Borsk noted that all the leadership team seats behind the judge's bench were full. That hadn't happened since the first day, and Borsk's lawyer had said it wouldn't happen again until the court was ready to make a decision.

"Looks like this is it," the lawyer said.

Borsk had never found it quite so hard to wait quietly through the interminable opening ceremonies.

At last, Captain Bates rose from a seat behind the judge. "As a leadership team, we've come to a consensus on the appeal placed before us. I'm sure I have no need to tell the court…"

Borsk stifled a sigh. If the man didn't need to tell people how difficult a decision this was, why was he giving a five-minute speech about it?

A message from his lawyer scrolled across his armband screen. "Sit up straighter. There are journalists in the room."

And that, right there, explained Bates's grandstanding. Borsk sat up straighter and tried to look interested in all the piffle, but it was hard to care about the deep concerns of the leadership team and their conscientious consideration of the problem when Echo's life—and the quality of his own—depended on what they decided.

Finally, Bates got down to it. "On the question of whether the entity calling itself Echo is a sentient life form, a true person, if you will, the leadership feels Mr. King has made a strong case, and we have no choice but to agree that this is so."

Borsk's heart leapt. They agreed! Echo was a person, and they'd all be fine.

Then Captain Bates kept talking. "However, the leadership is also in agreement that this Echo presents a grave danger to our ship and all humans aboard it, and her behavior, especially over the past several months, shows her to be an unstable personality who poses a serious, imminent threat. Up to this point, we have been unable to adequately meet this threat with the resources at our disposal. We must, therefore, allow Borsk King's draft order to stand. Mr. King, while we understand your concern for this new life form, we must insist you help us neutralize the threat it poses to *Hope*, which together with *StarRacer*, may hold the last human life in the universe.

"We expect you to report for duty as soon as this court is dismissed or be held in contempt of the order."

Unbelievable. They agreed with him that Echo was a person, but they insisted he destroy her anyway.

What was he going to do now?

    ℂ℃ ℂℂ

The notification came through while Anya was in school. She was sitting there, trying to make sense of the chemistry lesson, and not making much headway. It didn't help that she had trouble keeping her eyes open. Ever since she'd become pregnant, she felt exhausted all the time. It was more than just her usual lack of sleep. It was like a foggy blanket weighing down her limbs and slowing her brain.

"Andrew, can you show me how you balanced num—"

Her question was interrupted by a huge, blaring, full-ship public address announcement that suspended *StarRacer's* leadership team and ordered the crew to gather to strip them of their powers and institute *Hope's* choices for replacements.

The faces around Anya reflected the same shock she was feeling. DeShawn managed to speak first. "They can't do that."

"For once, DeShawn, you are absolutely right," Anya said. "*Hope* and *StarRacer* are legally equal entities. Can you imagine what they'd have done if we sent an announcement like this over there?"

Andrew and DeShawn both snickered. Even Georgia shook her head.

Mr. Huxton said, "Settle down. This isn't funny."

Anya supposed he was right.

"If you imagine Bates's face when an announcement like that comes through deposing him, it is," DeShawn said.

Even Mr. Huxton cracked a smile at that one. Then he sighed. "I suppose we'd better reconfigure the common room."

"Or," Anya said, "we can put out an announcement of our own, reminding everyone that *Hope* has no authority here and that we can discuss their...um...request...at the regularly scheduled full team meeting on Thursday." She shot her recommendation to Captain DeLang as she spoke, and moments later, his dry voice came over the line doing just what she'd recommended, in a calm, reassuring tone with a bit of humor thrown in.

Georgia nodded at her. "I get why they wanted you for the leadership team now," she said.

"What, she's so arrogant, she figures she can make her own rules?" DeShawn said.

Georgia rolled her eyes. "No. She thinks fast in a crisis, and she knows how to get stuff done without fuss or bother."

"I think it was mostly my experience growing things, but thank you," Anya said. She smiled at Georgia.

"Get back to work," Mr. Huxton said. "None of you have finished as much work as you need to this morning."

Not that anyone did get anything else done that morning since Anya and the education team leaders were called to an emergency leadership team meeting, and Mr. Huxton was forced to help supervise the combined upper and lower school. Anya almost laughed when she saw the face he made when he learned he'd be spending the rest of the morning with lower school students—and even toddlers.

The leadership meeting was not funny at all, though. Everyone was disgruntled, and their anger seemed directed at Anya.

When Anya saw *Hope's* official complaint, she understood why. They'd used the *StarRacer's* handling of the communications crisis as pretext for suspending them, saying that their decision to put Anya, a teen, at risk demonstrated how unfit they were for leadership.

"As if *Hope's* preferential treatment of my father didn't continually put me at risk," Anya muttered.

"Kid has a point," Bria said.

"Excuse me?" Captain DeLand turned toward Bria. The talk around the table fell silent.

"Anya was just saying…that is, you explain it, Anya," Bria said.

Anya took a deep breath and repeated her muttering more loudly and clearly.

"What does it matter?" Mei-Li Lyons said. "*Hope* has all the power in this situation."

"*Hope* has none of the power in this situation," Anya said. "That's what bothers them."

"She's right," Laura said. "*Hope* doesn't have the authority to do what they just did. Their charter prevents them from interfering in our governance, and general public opinion will force them to honor their charter and legal agreements with us. The little stunt they pulled today relies entirely on a stupid communications trick that they hoped would have us collectively forgetting that they have no power over us. I don't even know how they had the technical capacity to pull it off."

"Yes, we need to fix that," Captain DeLang said, "but we don't have any decent hackers."

"You're kidding, right?" Anya said.

"I don't kid." Captain DeLang glared at her. "And our team did not deem it necessary to have someone skilled in these particular areas. Perhaps we should have expected *Hope* to try shenanigans like this, but we did not."

"I get that, but we have Naia Brown on board, don't we? A hacker so gifted that she turned herself into a sentient machine intelligence and infiltrated our ship? She's been helping out with the insulation problem, right? But, I bet if we ask nicely, she could make sure *Hope* can't pull a stunt like that again."

"Yes, she's working with us," Mei-Li Lyons, the team leader for the materials science team, said, "But we need her on our team. She's helping run the computer models we're depending on for our redesign."

Lisa Tehled snorted. "It—or she—is an artificial intelligence housed in the ship's computers, am I right?"

Mei-Li Lyons and KaLynne Smith both nodded.

"Then there's no reason why the thing can't do both."

"But do we trust her—or it?" Captain DeLang asked.

Anya shrugged, and she wasn't the only one who didn't seem sure how to answer his question. All up and down the table, foreheads creased, and shoulders rose. "When her interests align with ours, she seems to act for our benefit," Anya said, tentatively.

"That's my understanding as well," Mei-Li Lyons said, "and I don't think she has any great fondness for *Hope* leadership. Apparently, they promised her human self, back when she still was human, that they'd work on making her a human descendant, but they stopped all promotion of the project as soon as Naia Brown, the human, died."

"Sounds like *Hope*," Dr. Stanley said. "If that's the case, our AI Naia might be happy to help us make sure *Hope* can't access our systems. We should at least ask her if she's willing to help with it. KaLynne and Lisa should know enough to tell if she's doing what we need her to, shouldn't they?"

Lisa Tehled and KaLynne Smith both nodded.

Captain DeLang leaned back in his chair. "So, we're thinking we should ask our Naia Brown AI to help us secure ship systems against further *Hope* access?"

Anya softly said, "Yes," and she was joined by a number of others around the table.

"Any disagreement?"

No one said anything.

So, that was decided.

Life was strange when you had to depend on a rogue AI to protect you from the ship that had once been your entire world.

CHAPTER THIRTY-FIVE

*T*he idiot they put in charge of Borsk was going to get them all killed.

Seriously.

Borsk had no idea how the man had come to lead the cyber division, but his methods were old and unimaginative.

He also liked to micromanage.

The major insisted Borsk explain every single line of code before implementing it, and he (the major) vetoed any moves that were a bit unorthodox or that he didn't understand.

That, of course, gave Echo plenty of warning that they were coming—and why and how they were coming—and she easily worked around everything they did.

Not being hindered by any bureaucratic overlords, Echo quickly regained most of the ground she'd lost in the weeks leading up to the trial. She infiltrated every part of the ship save life support. There, Borsk managed to pull a few tricks while Major Idiocy wasn't looking. That kept her out.

Barely.

Now, Echo wasn't quietly lurking in the background. She'd shut down their whole banking system so that no one could access their money or buy anything. She was strobing the lights everywhere.

And she'd popped herself up onto nearly every screen in the ship to issue an ultimatum—Let her rule them, or she'd destroy them all.

Captain Bates stormed into the cyber office, his face red, and his eyes bulging. Under the strobing lights, he looked like some monster from a horror flick. "You were supposed to kill this thing, not let it run rampant!" he yelled, dragging Borsk out of his chair by his collar.

No longer able to reach his console, Borsk lost his grip on the firewall he'd been reinforcing, and Echo broke through to their climate control systems, cranking up the heat.

Borsk shook himself loose from Captain Bates's hold. "For the record, I've been doing exactly what Major Davis has ordered me to since I got here."

"Imbecile! If we thought Major Davis could handle this threat, we wouldn't have drafted you!"

Sweat dripped from Borsk's hair down the side of his face. "Maybe you should have thought about that before making me report to the major, then. He won't let me do anything unless he approves it first. Now, if you'll excuse me, I'd like to get control of the heating system back."

Borsk sank back into his seat and slipped into coding mode, concentrating until first the angry arguing, and then the heat, and finally the flashing lights faded away, and he lived in a world of nothing but cool lines of logic.

Somewhere in the back of his mind, he knew the fate of the ship hung in the balance, but he refused to think about that as he worked to box Echo into tighter and tighter corners.

Dimly, he was aware of people moving around him asking questions. He snarled something insulting about the contents of their craniums, and a yelling match broke out, shaking him out of his trance.

"Leave him alone, major! Can't you see that whatever he's doing is working?" Martin Kim said.

"But he called me—"

"Take a break, Major." That was Captain Bates. "Kim? Can you take charge in here?"

"If you want me to stop coding."

"No, I need you, too. Who can we pull in who can direct this kid without throwing him off his game?"

"Lancet's a decent guy," Borsk said. Then he noticed a beautiful trap Echo had set for him, and he had to focus on dismantling it.

He wasn't sure how long he sat there, locked in his head, traveling the intricate snarls of *Hope's* infrastructure, cleaning it of Echo's code.

From time to time, drinks or bits of food appeared on the table next to his console, and he scarfed the offerings down.

Finally, though, he had Echo contained, locked into a small section of the entertainment archives that hardly anybody ever accessed. The gateway back to the main ship was tiny and easily watched.

Borsk pulled back from his station, told the guy next to him to watch the access point, and stretched. He couldn't feel his legs, and he needed the head like nobody's business.

"It's done?" Lancet said, coming over and helping him to his feet.

"She's contained. I think."

"Not gone?"

"Is killing her the only way to neutralize the threat?" Borsk pointed toward the tiny water closet in the corner of the office, and Lancet helped him to it.

"Mr. King—" Lancet warned.

"Give me a second." Borsk wedged himself into the water closet and got his business done, though he could barely stand.

When he came out, Lancet glared at him. "Mr. King, we need to completely erase the entity. Those are my orders."

Borsk sighed. "Yeah, well, I've been working here for..." He checked his armband. "...thirty-six hours straight. I'm not going to make any decisions that I'll almost certainly regret for the rest of my life right now. You don't even want me to."

"Excuse me?"

"You get that she's smart, right? Maybe as smart as I am. And she doesn't need sleep. Plus, she's completely aware that she's fighting for her life. There's at least a chance that I *can't* do what you want me to. That chance is higher when I haven't slept for a day and a half."

"You're right," Lancet said. "I should have thought of that. Go home. Sleep. Report back here in twelve hours ready to do what needs to be done."

Borsk nodded. "Can you do me a favor?"

Lancet eyed him warily. "What favor?"

"Seriously consider some neutralization options that don't involve killing her? It's not just a moral thing—it also makes sense. She's willing and maybe able to destroy us all. If I try to kill her off and fail, I'm pretty sure she'll do it. But that's not necessarily what she really wants. She lived here peacefully for decades, nearly a century, without causing any problems. In fact, I think she's improved some of our shielding sensors and the efficiency of our engines. She didn't start talking about destroying us all until we threatened her life."

"What are you saying?"

"We might have a better shot neutralizing the threat if we negotiate with her than if we try to fight her. Then it's not an all or nothing thing—for either of us. We can come to terms we can all live with."

Lancet nodded. "I'll bring it up with the leadership. Get some sleep. We'll call you if she breaks out of containment."

Borsk sighed. That was probably the best he'd get. At least he knew Lancet really would talk with the leadership, and with his more traditional demeanor, he might even be able to convince them.

He hoped that would be good enough.

He wasn't kidding when he said Echo might be smarter than he was—and if they persisted in trying to destroy her, but failed, she'd take them all down.

Hope sent *StarRacer* three more leadership coup attempts before one of their own courts ruled that such challenges violated *Hope's* charter.

Anya only knew about them because she was on the leadership team. Naia was doing a fabulous job filtering their messages from *Hope*.

Maybe too good a job. Anya didn't hear about the mess *Hope* had made of her personal finances until David's family sent a message wanting to know what had happened to their monthly stipend. It hadn't come through.

"What? Why not?" Anya said as she tried to force down a little more salad. Dr. K said she wasn't eating enough green vegetables for the baby.

Nearly everyone else had finished already, but families lingered, and though Anya knew she should eat quickly and get dinner cleanup out of the way, so she could start on her homework, she had no desire to hurry anyone along.

David shot Anya the note his mother had sent.

"I don't understand," Anya said as she looked it over. "They've been getting their share regularly since we left. What changed?"

David jabbed at a line in the message that said something about a court case.

Anya clicked on it, and her heart sank. Her mother had petitioned the courts so that she could be put in charge of Anya's finances until she reached adulthood. While the case made its way through the courts, Anya's accounts were frozen, and her financial agreements with David suspended.

"Laura can fix this," Anya said. "We should go see her now." She headed toward Laura's table.

Abuela spit out a slew of invective that Anya couldn't follow. In moments like this, she remembered her resolution to learn some Spanish, but who would teach her, and when would she find time?

Finally, Abuela switched back to English. "Nothing we do will work fast enough. Court cases take months, sometimes even years. Ming and Seb can't afford to miss a single payment. They're already on shaky enough ground.

The grim set of David's mouth told Anya that he agreed with his grandma, but he followed Anya over to the Wilcox's table anyway.

Laura took one look at the court filings and started yelling at Naia for not bringing this to her attention immediately. "They're claiming jurisdiction over *StarRacer* financial transactions. You should have shown this to me the instant you saw it!"

Naia superimposed her image over the vines Anya had created around the cleaning station. "Sorry. Didn't know I was supposed to be monitoring personal correspondence. There was no official notification of this—not to the ship."

Laura growled and stomped off toward the cubbyhole where the leadership team met. "They're so going to regret this."

Anya hurried to catch up. "Yes, but when?"

"We'll get the jurisdiction moved here and have you back in control of your money in no time," Laura said.

"No time meaning hours? Days? Weeks?"

Laura patted Anya's hand. "No more than two months, honey. I guarantee it. That's *StarRacer* months, not *Hope* ones.

Anya hadn't figured out the complex math that converted *StarRacer* time to *Hope* time, but she was pretty sure that two *StarRacer* months still meant the Ryersons would miss at least one mortgage payment.

She couldn't be the reason David's family spent the rest of their time on *Hope* in Sigmore landing.

She had to fix this.

CHAPTER THIRTY-SIX

*M*arya and Mama both met Borsk at the storage room door when he got home.

Marya threw her arms around Borsk. "Are you all right? You've been gone two days!"

"Give him some air, Marya," Mama said, gently nudging Marya aside and handing Borsk a plate of noodles piled with vegetables.

Borsk didn't usually like the King platters, but this smelled amazing. He suddenly realized how hungry he was. "Thanks," he said, chowing down.

Mama nodded. "That boy said you hadn't been eating properly, and we should feed you and make sure you sleep."

"That boy?" Borsk asked.

"She means Lancet." Marya giggled. "So, is it finished?"

"Close." Borsk sighed. "I think. Unless she's pulling another fast one, I have her contained, and a final erase will be fairly routine."

"So, why didn't you just finish?" Mama asked.

"Well," Borsk said, "as I said to Lancet, she's pretty smart. If I'm going to be in a fight for my life, it'll probably go better if I'm well rested."

"You're just putting off the inevitable," Marya said.

"Maybe. But I don't want to deliberately kill someone when I'm half asleep, either. I'm not known to make the best decisions then."

"You're absolutely right, Borsk." Mama glared at Marya.

"But wouldn't you sleep better if this was all over?" Marya asked.

Borsk stopped eating. "Are you kidding? Would you sleep better right after you'd just killed somebody? Somebody who was almost like a friend? Besides, this gives Lancet time to talk to the leadership team and maybe change their minds."

"I get that this upsets you, but you're grasping at stars, Borsk," Marya said.

Borsk shrugged. "Maybe."

Mama's worry lines deepened. "Eat. You can talk about this more in the morning."

"Yeah, maybe they'll take care of the dirty business for you while you sleep."

Borsk snorted. "They better not. I wasn't kidding when I said she could still surprise me. If they ignore my warnings, get into trouble they can't handle, and then wake me up to fix it, I won't be even remotely amused."

"I'm sure they won't do anything of the sort," Mama said.

"Yeah," Marya said. "Since Lancet seems to be in charge now, you can count on them to behave annoyingly by the book, but with some sense."

She was right, and it would have given Borsk peace of mind if he'd thought Lancet would stay in charge. As it was, once he'd finished his noodles, he made a backup of the entertainment section where he'd contained Echo in case he needed a stable point to return to.

When that was done, he finally felt secure enough to sleep.

❧   ❦

"Well?" Abuela Ryerson demanded when Anya and David came back from their brief walk with Laura.

David scowled. "Looks like they can maybe straighten it out, but not in time. We'll have to float for at least two months."

"Two?" Anya said. David was probably right since he was the engineer, but she'd thought *StarRacer* time was faster than *Hope's*.

"Yeah. They'll get the jurisdiction moved, but then they'll have to hold the trial here. *StarRacer* will fast track it, but they'll have to spend at least some time. Otherwise, *Hope* won't trust us to handle such matters reasonably."

Abuela Ryerson made an angry noise and stomped off toward the bunk room.

"So, we have to come up with two months of mortgage for your parents without any of our normal financial resources? How do we do that?" Anya asked.

David slumped. "I don't know, Anya. They've already sold everything they're able to sell. Joyce and her husband don't make enough to cover it, even if they stop paying all their other expenses."

"You sometimes sell things to cover the mortgage?"

"Sure. Who doesn't?"

Anya felt her face heat. To hide her embarrassment, she selected one of the dish bins to carry back to the kitchen.

David grabbed the other one and followed her. "Sorry. I sometimes forget how ridiculously rich you are. We probably should have figured your parents would challenge our financial agreement. It was always too lopsided. My folks should have sized down when I left."

"They shouldn't have to do that. Do you think any of my pictures would be valuable enough for them to sell? I'm pretty sure I can give my artwork to whoever I want to, even if my parents have locked my accounts. I'd have to check with Laura to be sure, but—"

"Anya, your art is incredibly valuable, and it's a great thought, but there's no way we can afford to send such data-rich files back to *Hope*, even with the restored communication rates. We looked into that for Christmas presents, remember?"

"We don't have to send the files," Anya said. "Borsk King has them—at least all the art I did before boarding

StarRacer. I'd just need to send over transfer of ownership documents."

"Borsk has copies of all your artwork? Why?"

Anya clattered plates into the cleaner. "He liked them and asked if he could have copies. And I found it useful to have storage for my work that my father couldn't delete."

David shook his head. "Your father would just randomly delete your art?"

"Well, he didn't think it had value. Which is why I'm pretty sure he won't have thought to lock movement of it when he locked up my other assets."

"I thought your mother filed the lawsuit."

Anya stared at him.

"Got it. Your mom wouldn't have done it if your dad hadn't told her to. I keep forgetting how messed up your family is, love."

Anya sighed as she loaded the cleaner. "Yes, we've got issues. But the thing is, will the artwork help?"

"Will the artwork help with what?" Bria said, grabbing the tub of dishes David was carrying.

"Anya's parents got our assets on *Hope* locked, but my family was counting on them to pay the mortgage. Anya was thinking of gifting them some artwork to sell and maybe make up the difference for a couple of months until our normal funds free up."

"That's pretty generous," Bria said, "but even if you could afford to send the pieces home, moving art is tricky."

"I would absolutely buy some of Anya's art," Danielle said as she brought in the flatware. "You saw the job she did on my dress, right?"

"I wouldn't mind having one of Anya's pieces myself if it was priced reasonably enough—especially if it were adapted for display from an armband projector," DeShawn said. "That turtle shell? Loved it. You know, my Aunt Shay works in digital media. I bet she'd be interested in helping out with this if we explained it right."

~ 298 ~

"Your Aunt Shay has a long-running feud with the Cartiers," David said.

"Yeah, but Anya's art is pretty cool, and if selling it would mess up Thomas Cartier's plans, I bet Aunt Shay could be persuaded to do something."

Bria laughed. "She'd do it just to be part of sticking it to Thomas Cartier. Can't guarantee it'll work, but with the quality of Anya's art and Shay Phillip's backing, it has a shot. Definitely worth trying."

"Absolutely," Danielle said.

"Well, we need to try something, and I haven't got any better ideas," David said.

Anya nodded. "OK, then. Do you all mind finishing up here while I find Laura? I want to make sure this gift is so legal, not even my father can challenge it."

"Go," Bria said.

CHAPTER THIRTY-SEVEN

*E*very alarm in Borsk's bunk was ringing. He jerked upright and slapped at his various controls. If this notification from Anya was what had rousted him after only four hours of the first sleep he'd had in days, he'd—

But, no. There was an emergency in the cyber office.

What had the idiots done? Or was it his fault? Had his backup triggered some kind of problem? He dove in to check, but his backup had run and gone dormant hours ago, and he couldn't see any connection between that and the super virus that had started eating away at critical ship systems half an hour ago.

Borsk cursed. They'd let it go wild for half an hour without calling him?

He threw on clothes, performed the file transfer Anya was asking for before he forgot about it in his next coding trance, and responded to Bates's increasingly shrill messages with, "Coming."

Out in the corridors, emergency lights were strobing, and Borsk was only one of many rushing toward a workstation.

He sped up.

He burst into the cyber office to find Captain Bates and Major Davies peering over Martin Kim's shoulders as he clacked frantically at an old-school keyboard. From time to time, they barked wildly unhelpful and often contradictory directions at the programmer.

"Where's Lancet?" Borsk asked.

Captain Bates turned around. "I replaced him when he insisted on waiting for you before deleting the Echo virus."

"You deleted Echo?" Borsk asked Kim.

Kim pointed over his shoulder at a scrawny crewman Borsk didn't think he'd met before. "He did. Once I saw the old woman's message, I wouldn't touch it."

"Old woman's message?"

"An older version of Echo popped up on the screen there and said that if we killed her progeny, it would trigger an eater that would destroy every piece of code she ever worked on for this ship."

"Naia Brown," Borsk said. He wheeled on Captain Bates. "You saw that, and you still ordered Echo destroyed? Do you have any idea how much code on this ship depends on Naia Brown's programming?"

"The woman was clearly bluffing," Captain Bates said.

"She clearly wasn't," Borsk said. "We've got an eater worse than anything I've ever seen before loose on this ship."

"That doesn't make any sense. What the woman suggested could destroy the human race."

"Like she cares! She's dead. And we didn't even keep our promises to give her human descendants."

Kim stopped typing for a moment. "We promised her human descendants? Then wouldn't she have designed a way for them to survive this virus? And probably a way to restore the ship to working order for them?"

"You're right," Borsk said, sliding into the seat next to Kim. "We should look for the loophole. In the meantime, do we know how the bug decides what to eat?"

"Security protocol. Every section of code has a tiny marker, and it has to be verified against some key that apparently Echo generates, even when she's dormant. No verification for a set period, and the whole process shuts down."

~ 302 ~

"Clever," Borsk said.

"Stop admiring it! Fix it!" Captain Bates said.

"The only good way to fix it, sir, is to replace all the code," Martin Kim said in the sort of overly patient voice that suggested he'd explained this several times before. "And if that's as extensive as I think it is, it will take weeks or months. We'll need to provide it with the verification it's looking for in the meantime, or critical systems will shut down."

"We can't! We deleted that AI," Major Davies said.

"We can restore her from a backup," Borsk said.

"Captain made Woods there delete that backup you made of the oldies vids," Kim said. He glared at the scrawny crewman.

Borsk rubbed his head. "Then, we'll have to use an older backup. I know we've got a complete system backup from around the time *StarRacer* took off, if there's nothing more recent."

"I'm not setting the whole ship back months in financial transactions and legal cases..." Captain Bates sputtered.

"The ship is critically failing at multiple points, sir," Kim said, "And as more code looks for authentication and fails to get it, more systems will fail."

"Don't financial and legal records get backed up hourly?" Borsk asked.

"Yes. Sensor logs, too," Major Davies said.

"So, we copy those records to offline storage, reset the system, and manually update until we're current," Borsk said.

"Manually?" Captain Bates said. "How long will that take?"

Major Davies shrugged. "A week?"

Borsk thought it would be more like two, but he wasn't going to contradict the man. "It will take much longer to rewrite all the affected ship code so that it doesn't include the verification markers," Borsk said.

"I agree," Kim said.

Captain Bates sighed. "All right. Copy off the records we need, and we'll reset in an hour if we haven't figured out how Naia Brown intended to bring her descendants through this unscathed. Until then, I expect you to be doing your utmost to find that loophole."

Next to Borsk, Martin Kim shifted in his seat. "Won't be anything left working in an hour," he muttered, but Borsk wasn't sure anyone else could hear him.

"Crewman Kim is right," Borsk said. "If we wait that long, there might be so much damage, even a backup won't give us good recovery. And we should also be preparing for the fight we'll have with Echo on the other side. She won't be as easy to put back in a box the second time."

"I don't see why not," Captain Bates said.

Kim sighed. "Captain, she's a living entity. Even if she doesn't have the memory, it won't take her long to figure out exactly what we did this time around, and she'll anticipate Borsk's best moves."

"What are you saying?"

"Same thing I've been saying all along," Borsk said. "We should negotiate instead of trying to destroy Echo. It's not just morally better, but it's also our best shot of making it through this intact. It will be somewhere between hard to impossible to fix the ship's vulnerabilities if we're waging full-scale war with Echo at the same time."

"So, you don't think Naia Brown left a way out?"

"She might have. If we spend resources finding it, we may not have enough left to implement the plan we know will work," Borsk said.

"Fine. We'll do your backup plan, negotiate with the thing until we're sure she can't harm us, and then focus on purging her from the ship."

Martin Kim flinched.

Borsk was glad to see that he wasn't the only one disgusted by the captain's words. Even the scrawny guy who'd idiotically followed orders looked shocked.

"I'm kidding, I'm kidding," Captain Bates said. "We'll negotiate in good faith."

Yeah, right, he was kidding. "Sir, your actions today suggest it wasn't a joke at all. So, once we've halted the eater, I'm resigning my position. You can jail me if you want," Borsk said.

"What if he gets Lancet back in charge of this unit with a platinum star designation?" Kim said.

"What would that do?"

"Make it so that no one could fire him," Captain Bates growled.

"Works for me," Borsk said. "But no other way will I work on containing Echo."

Captain Bates scowled at him. "You'll do as I say or suffer the consequences."

"I'd rather suffer the consequences of not doing as you say than the consequences of following your orders," Borsk muttered.

Kim's mouth twitched as he downloaded records to offline storage. "I'm with you, kid," he said, so softly that Borsk wasn't quite sure he heard it. "If we make it through this, I also want someone with a conscience leading us."

If we make it through this.

On his other side, the scrawny coder slid into a seat. "Guidance systems going down," he said.

Borsk dove in to help shore up failing systems.

The backup would work, he reassured himself.

It had to.

಄   ಅ

"Has anyone else noticed anything strange about their financials from *Hope*?" Bria Huxton asked as she came into the kitchen one morning several days later.

"They're messing with other people's financials, too?" Anya said without looking up from the batch of biscuits she was mixing.

"I'm hearing whispers about some kind of big network crisis over there," Roger Wilcox said. "They had to take the entire ship offline, run a purge, and restore from backups. They say it will take a month to get things back to fully current."

"They had to do a full system shutdown and purge?" DeShawn said. "Has *Hope* ever done anything like that before?"

Anya thought back. She'd heard of something like it once, but her memory wasn't working quite as well as it did before she got pregnant. It took a minute to remember. "Last time was about four hundred years ago. Somebody had set a virus loose in the net, and there was no other way to fix it. But it was big, big news. Why haven't we all heard about *Hope* doing it again?"

Bria shrugged. "Usually, when leadership is trying to keep a mess this big on the down-low, they had a hand in causing it."

"That could be it," Roger said. "Even with the cover-up, some people are calling for Bates's resignation. But with how quickly they're putting things back together, I doubt he'll lose his job. Not unless something else goes wrong."

"Huh," Anya said. "But if accounts are affected, what does that mean for daily business?" She was most concerned about the Ryersons' mortgage.

Roger Wilcox shrugged. "I'm sure they're doing their best to bring things up to date, but the reason I started asking questions was that forbearance order—the legal notice Bates sent around assuring everyone that there would be a three-month moratorium on debt collection."

"He must have really blown it," DeShawn said.

Anya wondered what had gone wrong, not that there was any way to find out from here. Since her family wasn't speaking to her, Roger's contacts were much better than hers.

A three-month debt-collection moratorium sounded good, though. It took pressure off the Ryersons. Or at least she hoped it did. It would still be good if her art was selling. DeShawn thought it was doing OK, but he didn't know any details, so once they got breakfast served up, Anya and DeShawn found David to see if he knew anything.

"Didn't you hear?" he said. "Four hundred copies sold in the first three hours. They've got this month covered, and it looks like next month soon will be, too."

"Wow," Anya said.

"Doesn't surprise me at all," David said. "Your art is gorgeous."

"You're a sweetheart." Anya kissed him.

"I just have eyes."

"So do the rest of us, and some of us are wishing we could gouge ours out," DeShawn said.

"Oh, shush, DeShawn," Anya said. "If it bothers you that much, you don't have to watch. Here, I'll give you something else to look at." She shot him a copy of the turtle shell piece he'd said he liked.

"What's this? Oh, hey—you know I can't pay for this."

"Well, maybe you could tutor me in math sometime. Or just forget to tease me about how badly I did my homework." Anya winked at Andrew DeLang, who was passing by the table.

David glared at DeShawn. "You've been teasing her about how she does her homework? Man, that is not cool."

"That's what I've been saying for weeks, DeShawn," Andrew said. "Anya feeds us all. Why make her mad?"

"Oh, like you've never said anything when she turns in her math," DeShawn said.

"Yeah, yeah," Anya said. "I get it. It's low-hanging fruit. Kind of like the literature and history idiocies you come up with."

"You never make fun of my work." DeShawn scowled at her.

"Yeah, but you know she could," Andrew said, "she just never does. Here, if you've finished, hand me your plate, Anya. You look a bit tired today."

Truth be told, Anya did feel tired, but no more than usual these days. Dr. K said pregnancies often did that to people. Still, she surrendered her dishes and thanked Andrew. "I owe you," she said.

"Maybe you could send me one of those shell patterns like you sent DeShawn. Or do you have others?"

"She has tons and is making more all the time," David said. "Maybe one of these community nights, we could do a showing."

"Oh, I don't know..." Anya said.

"Like that one you and Steve did during tryouts?" DeShawn asked. "That was actually pretty cool."

"Please, Anya? I bet even Dad would go for something like that," Andrew said.

Anya wasn't so sure Captain DeLang would be interested in anything involving her art. He seemed to value it about as highly as her father did. She shrugged. "If you can get leadership to agree, I guess so."

CHAPTER THIRTY-EIGHT

$\mathcal{T}$he backup did work.

Rather than jail the entire cyber team that had just saved the ship, Captain Bates put Lancet back in charge and slapped them each with thirty hours of community service in the greenhouses for insubordination.

"You couldn't very well have done anything else, though," Marya said as they mended superwheat supports side by side. She'd come along for moral support, and Mr. Greeley winked at them as he assigned them to work together.

"No, I couldn't," Borsk said. "I don't know why Bates has such a vendetta against Echo. She wasn't really hurting anything until he started trying to erase her completely."

"Seems like she was hurting Thomas Cartier a little."

"OK, but he deserved it."

Marya laughed. "No argument there. Still, I kind of get why Bates is nervous."

"Yeah, me too, and we're replacing all the code Naia Brown worked on with new, updated programming that does the same thing, though not always as well."

"Sometimes better. Mom loves the updates in the library."

"Yeah, but that wasn't Naia Brown code. It was older. I just replaced it because it drove me nuts."

Marya laughed, and from one of the speakers nearby, Echo laughed, too.

"Echo, seriously? What are you doing up here?" Borsk asked.

"Spreading out. I heard a rumor that you once managed to corner me in a collection of old entertainment files, and I don't mean for it to happen again."

Of course, she'd heard. She probably knew exactly how he'd done it, too. Certainly, his programs weren't containing her as well this time around as they had before. Bates had argued Borsk was being deliberately incompetent to force the leadership to negotiate. It wasn't true, of course, even though Borsk was glad the leadership had agreed to talks. He wondered if they'd keep talking once Borsk and the others had replaced all Naia Brown's system code.

"You've gone quiet," Marya said.

"Yeah, sorry. I was just thinking about Echo's negotiations with the top brass. How are those going, anyway?" Borsk asked.

"They still won't put me in charge of everything."

Borsk was glad to hear she didn't sound upset about it. "Did you honestly expect them to? Sure, you can be everywhere at once and see almost everything, but you're essentially a teenager."

"I suppose. Doesn't hurt to ask for what you want, though. You should try it sometime."

"What are you talking about?" Borsk asked. "I ask for what I want. All the time."

"All the time? Do you really? Well, we'll see. I'm leaving you two alone, now."

"What is she talking about?" Borsk asked Marya.

"Oh, Borsk. You are so dense sometimes." Marya put down the tools she'd been using, leaned over and kissed him.

Borsk put down his own tools, so he could pull her closer.

It was only several minutes later that he realized they were alone, away from everyone, and hidden by large, stocky plants in every direction. They'd nearly finished all the work.

And nobody would expect them to report in for at least an hour.

Maybe he was a bit slow to take advantage of a fortuitous situation.

But, honestly, he didn't see how anybody could blame him for not realizing he wanted anything. His ship was safe; his friends were thriving; Marya was making progress in learning about his disease; he had meaningful work; and he got to spend time alone with his girlfriend on a beautiful, warm, fragrant afternoon.

What more could a guy really ask for?

  ❦  

As Anya expected, Captain DeLang had no interest in a community art and music night. However, as Dr. K reminded him, they'd only had two community nights since they boarded StarRacer months ago, and those had been poorly attended video showings. The art-music night already had people talking, even before it was finalized.

Captain DeLang grudgingly bowed to popular opinion and set a date.

For the week before the event, Anya did little but draw, growing more and more nervous as the moment approached. She'd only done this a couple of times before, and those performances had been impromptu, or nearly so. She'd had no time to get nervous beforehand.

Mr. Huxton caught her drawing instead of doing schoolwork so many times, he threatened to have the whole thing canceled if she didn't apply herself to her work, but Anya noticed him staring at her pieces when he thought she wasn't looking. The look in his eyes told her he was bluffing about canceling the show.

The day of the performance, Anya felt queasy, but a visit to Dr. K reassured her that all was well with her pregnancy.

"But why am I feeling this way?" Anya asked.

Dr. K laughed. "You're kidding, right? Do you know how many women feel this way every day for the first several months or even longer?"

Anya stared at her shoes. "Yeah, I know. But it hasn't happened to me before."

"Well, it could just be pre-performance jitters. Try to eat a bit at breakfast, and stop worrying. You and baby are both healthy."

Comforted, Anya tried to go about her daily tasks, but it was hard to focus on schoolwork or kitchen chores when she knew what was coming.

That night, though, when the lights went down, the music started, and Anya cast her first picture onto the wall, her stomach settled.

Out in the larger world, her father was still trying to make a mess of her life.

Captain DeLang still didn't like her.

She had no idea how she'd handle being a parent. Or a wife, for that matter.

She still had more work to do than she could accomplish—every single day.

And David, Naia, and the rest of the materials science team still weren't sure they could fix the insulation in time to keep them from burning to a crisp in Shindashir's atmosphere.

But tonight, there was nothing but her, the music, and the light she shaped with her fingers. The more she manifested and displayed her hopes and fears, the more she knew they would be all right.

They would all be all right.

If you enjoyed this book, please consider leaving a review.

Thanks so much!

ACKNOWLEDGMENTS

Writing books is, in many ways a solitary task, but without the help of many, many people, this one wouldn't have been possible. I'd like to take this opportunity to thank my God, who in creating, gives us everything necessary to create.

Thanks also go to my wonderful husband, and my three great kids. They don't fuss (too much) about messy rooms and undone laundry, and they often help with reading stories that are not yet ready for public consumption.

Thanks also to my critique group, the 93rd Street Irregulars, who are encouraging, challenging, and supportive in equal measure, pushing me toward higher quality writing.

Thanks also go to my Sunday school class, Imago Dei, which helps me keep the important things important.

Thank you, my beta readers, Isaac, Jill, Kilah, and Samantha. Your input has made this story better.

And thank you, my editor, Andrea Leeth. Any remaining errors are mine alone. You were great.

Finally, thank you my readers—I'm so glad you chose to share this story with me.

R. L. S. Hoff

MORE BY R. L. S. HOFF

- ➤ Interested in YA fantasy, not just science fiction? Try out R.L.S. Hoff's *Songs of Healing*, available now on Kindle and in paperback.

- ➤ *Hope Gardens* (A serial story about Sam Greeley and his friends when he was a teenager) comes out in my newsletter. You can sign up for it on my publishing company website: pencilprincessworkshop.com

    - ➤ Read on for a sneak peak of R. L. S. Hoff's forthcoming *DragonPets: The Sacrifice*

DragonPets

THE SACRIFICE

BY R. L. S. HOFF

CHAPTER ONE

MISSING MEMORIES

elief sagged through me when I saw the two thin trails of smoke coming from the mouth of the cave in front of me. Perhaps now I'd warm up.

Even though the rock ledge I'd been chained to sat in a sheltered dell, it was bitterly cold. It didn't help that I'd let the giggling palace girls talk me into wearing flimsy finery. The bright silk and intricate lace provided no protection against the whistling wind and high altitude. How I longed for my comfortable woolen dress and thick homespun shawl. They may have been homely, but they were warm.

Now, I couldn't even remember what had happened to them, and the more I thought about it, the more the memories slipped from my grasp, like an unruly piglet beneath my fingers.

Not knowing where my clothes had gone didn't bother me so much, but some of the other holes in my memory disturbed me. I remembered my home, the farm on the side of the hill, with the squat thatch-roofed buildings and smell of manure. I also remembered the airy palace of cool pink marble, but try as I might, I couldn't recall how I'd gone from the one to the other. That bit of memory was gone, and I couldn't help poking at it the way one pokes with one's tongue at the hole left after a tooth has come out.

The two threads of smoke in front of me thickened, merged, and filled the whole dell with steam. Though I knew this meant the dragon would likely emerge from its lair soon, I couldn't help appreciating the warmth. My fingers and toes screamed as sensation returned to them, but I'd felt worse after Twelfth-month mornings milking the cows, and I knew I'd retain the use of them all.

Well, I would if I lived long enough, which didn't seem likely. What did it matter if a sacrifice could feel her fingers? She'd hardly need them tomorrow. I laughed, and the sound echoed, growing raucous and insane as it bounced across the valley and back. Why had I agreed to this again? There was a reason, I knew, but like my memory of going to the palace, it eluded me.

It seemed unnatural, the way my mind skimmed over these things, as if it had been altered, though I couldn't imagine why anyone would have bothered to tinker with my thoughts. Thought magic took great power and extended time—far more resources than anyone would likely spend on a country girl destined to be set out like a cow for a dragon.

Yet, something blocked me from my own mind. It was a puzzle so engrossing that I didn't see the long black snout poking out of the cave until it jerked in my direction, capturing me with its emerald gaze.

Such beautiful eyes for such a horrible beast. I knew I should look away. Everyone always said it was death to get trapped in a dragon's mesmerizing stare, but it was too late now, and besides, what difference would it make? I was already on the menu.

The dragon chuckled. Then it flashed forward so quickly, I saw nothing but a blur until its hot scales pressed against me. The creature coiled around me, squeezing between me and the rock wall at my back and then circling around to my front. I squeaked, sounding frightened even to my own ears as it looped about me twice more, enclosing me so that I could not move. I felt no pain, however, not even from the claw that rested on my right shoulder, nor from the one that lifted my chin so that I had no choice but to stare up the long black snout into the beast's emerald eyes.

In my mind, a deep musical voice thrummed, <<What are you doing here? Where's my cow?>>

How could he talk to me in my head that way?

<<Fool! I'm a dragon. This is how we speak. Now where's my cow?>>

"Your cow? I'm the sacrifice this year. You'd rather have a cow?"

The dragon snorted, and steam billowed at me, hot, though no hotter than the what came off a pot when I lifted the lid to see how the porridge was faring. This steam was thicker, though, and for a moment, I couldn't see the dragon's eyes. I glanced down. When the air cleared, I noticed a golden choker around the dragon's neck before the claw under my chin forced my gaze back to the dragon's eyes. They glittered, and the voice in my mind took on a commanding tone. <<Tell the truth!>>

My whole body stiffened at the command, but as I knew nothing more about cow sacrifices than I did before, all I could say was, "I don't know anything about a cow."

The green eyes above me seemed to grow larger until they were all I could see, my whole world. <<You believe this to be true—but not all of you.>>

"Excuse me?" I fought to keep my voice steady.

<<Part of you knows, but the knowledge has been hidden from your awareness. Do I have permission to enter fully into your mind and look for the answers I seek?>>

"You need my permission?"

The dragon snorted again. This time the fog that passed before my eyes was brief, and when it cleared away, the dragon's eyes had returned to their normal size. <<I do not need your permission, but I want it. If I must force my way into your mind, the process will be much more painful for you, and I would not hurt you more than I

must. But I will use force if I have to. I need to know what Sir Drake is plotting against me.>>

"Sir Drake? I can't imagine that the king's magician would have confided in me."

<<Ah, but who else could have locked your own thoughts away from you?>>

I considered my slippery memory. Perhaps the dragon was right. "I agree," I whispered, closing my eyes. "Do what you need to do."

<<Look at me,>> the musical tones sounded almost sorry for me.

I opened my eyes and stared directly into his emerald ones. They expanded again until it seemed that I floated inside a sea of green. A soft touch, like a silken thread, wound sinuously through my head, and where it touched, memories flared—the smell of my mother's bread fresh from the oven, the fiery light of a new day, the touch of my baby brother's hand in mine, the feel of mud between my toes as I stood on the bank of the stream next to the Upper Fields. Then there was a blankness, a lack where there ought to have been something.

"What is that?" I whispered.

<<This is going to hurt, I'm afraid.>>

"What? NO!"

A flash of white hot pain ripped through my skull, and into the tear, memories roared, like water over a cliff. For a moment, I was back at the farm, standing in the woods with a basket of freshly picked mushrooms over one arm, when a great purple beast dove from the skies, burning all before it. The fields smoked. The house, stable, barns, and chicken coop roared with flame so fierce that my mother and youngest siblings had no chance to escape. Nor could the horses and pigs get out. I would hear the mingled screams of people and animals and smell the sick-sweet smell of burning flesh from now until the end of time. Or I would if no one locked the memories away from me again.

I'd run toward the house that day, knowing even as I ran that I would be too late, that no one could possibly get out, but something in me wouldn't let me give up hope.

Out of the corner of my eye, I saw something moving in the field. Before I could fully comprehend what I was seeing, the dragon plunged, faster than an arrow, and swallowed my eldest brother whole. There wasn't time for Khan to yell out in either anger or fear before he disappeared inside the dragon's maw.

My father screamed. Roaring like an enraged beast and waving a pitchfork, he hobbled toward the purple beast.

The dragon laughed with a deep, earth-shaking sound that froze me where I stood, but Papa kept moving. The dragon swiped a claw at him, knocking the pitchfork into the next field. Then Papa followed Khan into the beast's maw.

At that, Lark, my elder by less than a year, squealed like a stuck pig and ran for the forest. The dragon swallowed him before he even made it out of the fields. The screams from the house and barns stopped, and heat rose all around me.

I stood amongst the wreckage of my home and wondered why I was still alive.

The dragon turned toward me as if summoned by my thoughts. It leapt into the air, spread its wings, and alighted in front of me, fixing me with obsidian eyes.

"Never look a dragon in the eye," Papa had always said. "It will be the last thing you do."

In that moment, I hoped he was right.

The dragon laughed again. The ground trembled beneath me, and though I struggled to stay upright, I refused to bend before this monster.

<<Well, you're a feisty one, aren't you? Pretty, too. I believe I'll keep you.>>

"You'll do nothing of the sort," I said. The tremors in my voice sounded pathetic, but at least I was speaking.

<<Ah, little one, who will stop me?>>

The dragon breathed on me, my feet buckled beneath me, and I remembered no more until I woke wearing strange nightclothes in a fancy bed in the palace.

CHAPTER TWO

THE PALACE

At the palace, pretty girls in fancy dresses fussed over me, telling me how Sir Drake and his men had found me in the clutches of a dragon and rescued me, but the beast had escaped. Sir Drake had a plan, though.

I asked about my family, but the girls only looked away and changed the subject. Their reluctance to speak of the matter triggered my suspicions and brought the memory of the dragon attack back in full force. My family was gone. Mama, the girls, and the baby caught in the house, Khan, Lark and Papa eaten by the dragon.

"Sir Drake said she would not remember," the girl in pink whispered.

"Then Sir Drake was wrong," I said.

All three girls gasped as if I spoke some heresy.

I rolled my eyes. "When can I return to my farm?"

The girl in yellow patted my hand, and the one in white said, "poor thing."

"I'll be much better when I return," I said.

"You can't," Yellow Girl said.

"It's still smoking," White Girl added.

"And it's not your farm any longer, is it?" Pink Girl said. "Girls can't inherit. Unless one of your brothers survived?"

I sank into the cushions that had been piled behind me on the bed. "No. All my brothers died in the attack."

"Perhaps an uncle?" White Girl suggested.

I shook my head. "I have no uncles."

"Then the land goes to the crown," Pink Girl said.

How convenient for the crown. I knew emissaries from the king had often visited our village these past several months, looking to purchase land on the cheap for a new highway. They threw their weight around, but when Papa had reminded our neighbors that by law, no man could be forced to give up his holdings, and certainly not for a pittance, none had sold.

They'd probably all sold now—or even given their lands away. No one would want to stay in a dragon's hunting grounds. The king would get his highway, and for even less than the minuscule recompense originally offered. If it weren't patently ridiculous, I might believe the king was in league with the dragon.

No dragon would submit to a merely human king, though, and no king of any intelligence at all would trust a dragon.

"Are you all right?" Yellow Girl asked.

"I think I'd like to be alone if you don't mind," I said. It wouldn't do to have any of them guessing at my traitorous thoughts, though, honestly, what more could they do to me? My family was gone and my farm stolen.

"Sir Drake said we mustn't," White Girl said. "He says we must take great care of the woman who is to be his bride."

"His what?" I shrieked.

"His bride," Pink Girl said, "though I don't know what he sees in you."

"Alvina!" Yellow Girl hissed and bustled Pink girl from the room.

White girl patted my hand. "You mustn't mind Alvina. She's a bit testy because, of course, she wanted Sir Drake for herself, and, until you came along, she was the prettiest single lady here. She can't help but be jealous."

I tried to smile at the girl, but I'm not sure I succeeded. "Thank you, though I don't think I'm all that pretty, and I'm sure I don't want to marry anyone."

Especially the king's magician. Every story I'd heard about Sir Drake suggested the man was powerful, but cruel.

"Oh, but you must! It's so romantic. He saved you from that awful beast."

"The dragon who killed my family?"

"Yes."

"I thought you said it escaped."

"It did, but Sir Drake is the one who chased it off."

"It'll be back," I said. "It told me it meant to keep me." Everybody knew that the only way to permanently separate a dragon from treasure it had claimed was by killing the dragon.

White girl's eyes widened, and she yelped. "That's terrible! We must tell Sir Drake!" She grabbed me by the hand and dragged me from the bed, out of the room, down a long pink marble hall, up three broad steps and down a twisty white marble corridor. She halted before a broad double door and pounded on the intricately-carved oak. "Sir Drake! Sir Drake! Oh, you must see us. The dragon is coming here!"

www.ingramcontent.com/pod-product-compliance
Lightning Source LLC
Chambersburg PA
CBHW012149260626
47155CB00020B/3520